754

D1165926

7/95

TOWN
ON
TRIAL

TOWN ON TRIAL

William Harrington

DONALD I. FINE, INC.
New York

To my cherished friend the late Judge Robert W. Murray, who would have tried this case with the skill, firmness, fairness, and patience that characterized his work as a judge.

Library of Congress Catalogue Card Number: 93-74480
ISBN: 1-55611-393-5

Manufactured in the United States of America

10 9 8 7 6 5 4 3 2 1

Designed by Irving Perkins Associates, Inc.

1

My favorite book, *Huckleberry Finn*, begins:

"You don't know about me without you have read a book by the name of *The Adventures of Tom Sawyer*; but that ain't no matter. That book was made by Mr. Mark Twain, and he told the truth, mainly. There was things which he stretched, but mainly he told the truth."

You don't know about me either, without you got interested in the Marietta Rheinlander trial. And I'm afraid you did. Everybody got interested in the Marietta Rheinlander trial. I was the judge. For a while I couldn't turn on a television set without seeing my own face, hearing my own voice. I couldn't read a newspaper, from anywhere, without seeing myself quoted. The news media told the truth, mainly, I suppose, with some "stretchers," as Mark Twain would have called them, and gave me fame I didn't want.

Well . . . Everyone protests he didn't want fame. A little of it was kind of fun.

I lived for sixty-two years in pleasant obscurity—never of course appreciating that obscurity was pleasant—and abruptly found my obscurity and privacy shattered. For a few weeks my name and face and voice were better known than those of the president of the United States.

But Mark Twain also wrote, "Fame is a vapor, popularity an accident; the only earthly certainty is oblivion," and he was right as usual. I could travel to, say, Columbus or Cleveland now and walk along the streets, and no one would recognize me.

The trial opened on Monday morning, October 19, 1992.

I open court at nine, break at noon for lunch, resume at one, and work till five—"the regime of a quaint, Middle-America, small-town court," the New York *Times* called it. I have always believed in being punctual, and Miss Rheinlander's out-of-town lawyers were warned by her local lawyer that when I said court would convene at nine, it would convene at nine.

So I left my office about ten to nine and walked over toward the courtroom. I should maybe explain that in our little courthouse we don't have a judge's "chambers." I have an office on the opposite side of the lobby from the courtroom. The most convenient way for me to get into the courtroom is through the clerk's office. I leave my robe in the jury room and go in there to put it on before I step out into the courtroom and take the bench.

That morning one of the women in the clerk's office, where I stopped to sign a couple of papers, told me Miss Rheinlander and her attorneys were in the jury room. They had been meeting in there the past quarter of an hour. I knocked on the door, then walked in. She was there, sitting at the jury table with her three lawyers. Margaret Vogt, a deputy sheriff, stood at the window staring down at the street. She'd got herself as far away from the others as she could, so as not to overhear what they were saying. Lying on the windowsill were the handcuffs and belly chain she had taken off Miss Rheinlander only after they were in the jury room. She was very careful about this prisoner, and for a time had made her wear leg irons, too, when she was brought from the jail to the courthouse. The woman was charged with three murders, and the state was asking for the death penalty. Besides, one day during the first week of her imprisonment she had lost her temper and shoved Margaret against a wall.

I should explain maybe that our county jail is about ten minutes' drive from the court. It used to be in the basement of the courthouse, but in the 1970s a low brick building that used to be a garage for county trucks was converted into a much more spacious and humane jail. The building also contains an apartment for one of the deputies and his wife. She cooks for the prisoners, and she and the deputy are the night guards. We have only two cells for women. If we ever had more, I don't know where we'd put them.

I first saw her on the day when her lawyers argued their motion that she be released on bond pending her trial. It was a motion I could not grant. She had been bound to the grand jury on three counts of aggravated murder, one with aggravating circumstances that carried the death penalty. Aggravated murder first is not a bailable offense. Actually, I did have discretion to grant the motion, and Kimball made a powerful argument that day—that Marietta Rheinlander was a public person who could not just disappear, that in any case she wanted to face trial and prove her innocence, and so on. But I really couldn't go for it. Three bodies, one of course the congressman. Three counts of murder. I suppose she had built up in her mind the kind of optimism people always build in such circumstances. Her lawyer's argument was so reasonable that surely I would make an exception for her.

I would have if I could. She had been in jail just a week at the time and clearly was devastated by it. Her face was bright pink that day, her eyes swollen and tearful. She was crushed by humiliation, too. She was well dressed, in a full white skirt and a pink blouse, but it was only one day since she had shoved Margaret Vogt off balance, and Margaret hadn't taken off her cuffs and leg irons for the hearing. I remember how she walked into the courtroom: in that odd, unnecessary, sideways, legs-apart gait people use the first time they have to walk with a chain between their ankles. I had issued an order keeping photographers out of the courthouse entirely. No pictures appeared of the pitiable spectacle she was that day.

When I said I could not grant the motion, she became so hysterical, screaming and thrashing around, that she demonstrated what good judgment Margaret had used in keeping restraints on her. Her lawyers renewed the motion twice, two weeks later and six weeks later, and each time I was similarly obliged to deny it. Miss Rheinlander remained grimly calm in the courtroom throughout those two hearings.

3

By October she had been in jail five months. Of course she hated it, but she was calm about it by then. One of the judge's duties is to conduct periodic inspections of the county jail. The last time I saw her before the trial date, she was sitting in her cell, working on a watercolor sketch. Her cot and the floor were littered with books and crossword puzzles. She had gained a little weight, from what she ate and lack of exercise. But she was not distraught. They had long since ceased to keep a suicide watch over her.

The deputies said she had become an easy person to talk to. She could even make weak little jokes about her situation. "I'll see you later," Margaret Vogt had said to her one day, and Miss Rheinlander had replied, "I'll be here."

How do I describe Marietta Rheinlander? Everyone knows what she looks like. She is not really blond, of course. Her hair is skillfully done, and it looks blond. A hairdresser from New York had flown and driven to Alexandria last week and had gone to the jail to do Miss Rheinlander's hair. Her hair is not yellow, the way some women's hair looks when they bleach it, and it is not coarse either. Her face is big and strong. It is not exceptionally beautiful, I suppose. The thing you first notice is that she has a wide mouth with evocative moist lips. But your glance moves next to her eyes, which are icy blue. *They* are exceptionally beautiful. The eyes and the mouth together are phenomenally expressive. Someone wrote of her that she has an *eloquent* face. That is true. Her face tells you what she has on her mind—maybe more than is good for her.

She was wearing a pink cashmere suit. She wore no rings or earrings, no watch, no bracelets. She did have a simple strand of pearls around her neck.

"Good morning, folks," I said. I took my robe off the coat tree. "Just a couple of minutes."

They all nodded and murmured good morning: Miss Rheinlander, Lloyd George Kimball, the senior of her two New York lawyers, Megan O'Reilly, his junior, and Bob Mitchell, her local lawyer.

"Your Honor," said Kimball, "can I have a word with you?"

I nodded. I couldn't talk to him about anything important when

4

the prosecuting attorney wasn't present, but he knew that, and I wasn't worried about an impropriety.

"I'm concerned," he said, "about the jury panel. Are you really confident we can pick a jury out of a panel of twenty-four?"

"I'm confident. We always do."

"But what if we can't?" Kimball persisted. He is a tall man, trim, well tailored, with a flushed face and white hair. He looks vaguely like Andy Griffith as Matlock, which doesn't hurt his credibility at all. "How do we get extra members for the panel?"

"It's never happened since I've been a judge," I told him, "but what we do if we have to is send the sheriff out on the street to look for veniremen. In half an hour or so he'll be back with six or seven men and women. And we can send him out a second time and a third time if necessary, till we get a jury."

"But— Will you recess for a day or two then?"

I shook my head. "No. No reason."

Kimball smiled: an odd little smile. I'm not sure if I saw condescension or didn't. "But I won't have time to check out those possible jurors, find out who they are."

"That's what *voir dire* is for," I said. *Voir dire* is the business of allowing the lawyers to question prospective jurors.

"I need to do our check, our investigation," he said.

I knew what he wanted. For two weeks a firm of private investigators had been set up in two rooms at the Holiday Inn. They'd been investigating the members of the jury panel, all twenty-four of them. They had given Kimball a fat report containing what they called profiles of all the prospective jurors. They had found out what churches, if any, the panelists attended, whether they owned or rented their houses, what their politics were, what newspapers they read, what magazines they subscribed to, what clubs they belonged to, and so on—all without ever approaching any of these people and asking them directly.

I believed at the time, and I believe now, that our big-city defense lawyer outsmarted himself with that. Private detectives are not well regarded in our town. Sneaky little paid snoops is what they're thought of as being. A lot of the jury panel resented being snooped on.

Anyway, Kimball wanted extra time, if the twenty-four panelists didn't fill the jury. "*Voir dire* is not enough," he said. "I need time to do the background checks on the prospective jurors."

"We'll make up a jury out of the two dozen we've got," I said. "If we have to send the sheriff out to waylay veniremen, you can make a motion for more time. If it happens, Mr. Kimball. If it happens . . ."

I rarely make up my mind about how I'll rule on a motion before the motion is made and argued, but Lloyd George Kimball was smart enough to know he had very little chance of getting a two-day continuance so his jury-investigation firm could do their background checks.

Margaret Vogt beckoned to Miss Rheinlander. It was time for her and her lawyers to enter the courtroom. The defendant stood. She glanced at me with a stricken look, as if I frightened her. She made me wish I could speak to her a moment alone and promise her I would do my best to see that she had a fair trial. I am sure she had no confidence about that.

I kept the door open after the defense group walked into the courtroom. A dozen strobe lights flashed: photographers taking pictures as the famous defendant and her lawyers entered and took their seats. Once I entered and convened the court, no more pictures could be taken, and they shot as many as they could while they could.

I glanced at my watch. I still had a couple of minutes before I walked into the courtroom, and I stood there, more than a little apprehensive. I could make a fool of myself in this trial. Very easily and in front of the whole nation. One wrong ruling from the bench—

In my youth I was as interested in fame and fortune as the next man, probably. To tell the truth, I was more anxious to win fame than to earn fortune. It dawned on me, though, that I had better concentrate on accumulating a little fortune because I was very unlikely ever to find fame.

I never did find fame. It was the other way around. Fame found me. I was just sitting in my office, doing my somewhat pedestrian job, and fame walked in and pushed a crown of laurels—thorns?—down on my head.

Enough, I will try not to wax literary hereafter. The prosaic facts are these:

My name is Bill McIntyre. I was born and reared in the Ohio River town of Alexandria. My father owned a butcher shop, in the days before the wire-cart supermarket when a man could earn a living cutting meat to the very specific requirements of a finicky clientele. I attended the public schools, then Alexandria College here in my home town, and went from there to Ohio State University College of Law, where I earned my LL.B. with no great distinction. I passed the bar examination and came home to Alexandria in 1955 to open my own office for the practice of law.

In that same year I married Linda Kintner, whom I had admired since my high school years, who'd experienced a misfortune in love—a marriage and a divorce—and was, I guess, pleased to settle down with a settle-down fellow like the town's youngest lawyer. I adopted her daughter, then she and I produced two sons.

I practiced law in Alexandria for thirty-three years. It did not make me wealthy, but my family was well provided for. We put the kids through college. We bought a little house on a hillside overlooking the Ohio River. We put up a dish antenna to pick up distant television broadcasts. I stretched a long antenna for my shortwave radio and can hear English-language broadcasts from cities as distant as Ulan Bator.

Doctors look back on the babies they delivered. I have written wills and lived to probate them. I have handled adoptions and watched the children grow up in new families, usually with good results. I have formed little business corporations and seen them prosper or fail. I have defended accused criminals. Some of them languish in the penitentiary to this day. Some have gone on to productive lives. Some have committed further crimes. I have done the documents for subdivisions and seen muddy land turn into tracts

7

of neat little houses. (Maybe "All made of ticky-tacky and all look alike," but pleasant homes just the same for a lot of people.) I have put families through bankruptcy. I have evicted tenants. I have defended tenants against eviction. I have put failing people into guardianship. I have gotten people just settlements out of felonious insurance companies. I have written a thousand deeds and a thousand leases.

On the other hand, I have never participated in a class-action suit. I have never prosecuted a malpractice suit, though I once threatened one and got a modest settlement. I have never appeared before the Supreme Court of the United States. I have never appeared before the tax court. I have never filed an SEC form for a stock offering. I have never defended a company against a hostile takeover. I have no idea how to write a Eurodollar bond agreement.

William D. McIntyre, attorney and counselor-at-law. In 1988 I was asked if I would consider becoming a candidate for judge of the court of common pleas. I was fifty-eight. I could serve two terms on the court and retire at the mandatory retirement age. I would have a reasonable, though not handsome, salary for twelve years, coupled with a nice retirement pension that would supplement my Social Security and IRA. I would be relieved of the necessity of keeping up our health insurance—which was increasingly burdensome—since my wife and I would be in the state system. Linda and I talked it over, then called the chairman of the Republican Party and said we'd accept.

Since January 1, 1989 I have been judge of the Court of Common Pleas of Alexandria County—which is how I came to be the "stern, dry-witted judge" who presided over the trial of Marietta Rheinlander.

Here is how the Associated Press correspondent described me:

> Judge McIntyre is a small man, no more than five feet seven. He combs his graying hair across his head in a futile effort to conceal the fact that he hasn't enough of it left to cover his baldness. His small face is thin, with enough lines to give it maturity and character. He

wears no glasses but has a pair of half-glasses for reading, and when he puts them on he stares over them with the owlish look half-glasses give everyone. He speaks with a flat Midwestern twang. A reporter accustomed to watching big-city judges preside over trials is surprised by how firmly this small-town judge controls his court. He intends to try this case this week, and it seems likely he will. It might have dragged out for three or four weeks in a city court, but it won't here.

I checked my watch. Nine o'clock, exactly. I nodded to my bailiff. He rapped the gavel.

"*All rise!* Hear ye! Hear ye! Hear ye! The Honorable Court of Common Pleas for the County of Alexandria, the State of Ohio is now in session pursuant to adjournment, the Honorable William D. McIntyre presiding! All persons having business before this honorable court will draw near and give attention!"

I walked across the front of the courtroom and mounted the bench. I took my seat, the bailiff rapped the gavel once again, and everyone sat down.

Our courthouse was built just before the Civil War. Its architecture is therefore simpler than that of the courthouses built in the gingerbread era. It is a brick building painted white and has something of the aspect of a New England Congregational church, except for the inevitable cannon on the lawn and the ornate benches where old men sit and talk and smoke. Four great oaks dominate the courthouse square and keep it comfortably shaded during the summer. The leaves were falling now of course, and I'd had the small pleasure of shuffling through their fragrance as I walked toward the entrance that morning.

The courtroom is like the courthouse itself: small but handsomely appointed with a dignified bench of carved oak, heavy tables, and solid chairs upholstered in black leather. Incandescent bulbs burn red inside white milk-glass globes, two on pillars to either side of the bench, others in sconces on the walls. We have resisted the installation of fluorescent lights, and some of the accounts of the trial referred to it as occurring in a "dimly lighted courtroom"—which it certainly wasn't when the lights I allowed the Court TV people to use were switched on. There is a jury box and a low platform for the clerk's desk, also a little enclosure for the court stenographer.

All and all, it is a proper courtroom: the right kind of room for doing justice. Or trying to.

This week, on each side, just behind the rail, a small television camera sat on its tripod, the cameraman standing behind it. The television lights hung from the ceiling. I wasn't entirely happy with this experiment in televised trial, but I'd received a telephone call from the administrator of the Supreme Court of Ohio, asking me to allow it. The cameras made me self-conscious. I should think they did the same to everyone.

I nodded at young Ken Simpson, the Alexandria County prosecuting attorney. He was the sole lawyer for the prosecution. I had offered to appoint someone to help him, but I think he felt that if he secured a conviction with the assistance of an older attorney the older attorney would get the credit. This was his chance to make a name for himself, and he meant to do it. He sat alone, except for a secretary who would take notes for him and hand him papers from his files.

"I begin with a word for the ladies and gentlemen of the news media," I said. "You are welcome here. We will extend to you appropriate cooperation in helping you to get your story. We do, however, expect you to abide by the rules we have set for this trial, which have been explained to you."

Twelve prospective jurors sat in the jury box. Twelve more sat on chairs just inside the bar. I knew about half of them, one way or another.

Behind the bar, the courtroom seats sixty-two people. Half of those seats had been allocated to reporters, and they had passes for them. Ten seats had been allocated to friends of Miss Marietta Rheinlander, who also had passes. The remaining seats were for the public on a first-come-first-served basis. There had been some unseemly jostling in the lobby: reporters who hadn't got passes contesting with locals for seats.

The sheriff had had to deputize eight new deputies to keep order in and around the courthouse. I had called on the state highway patrol to provide some help, and four of their men in Smokey hats were in the lobby or on the outside steps.

"On the trial docket this morning is the case of State of Ohio v. Marietta Rheinlander, case number 92–CR–58, the case of State of Ohio v. Marietta Rheinlander, number 92–CR–59, and the case of State of Ohio v. Marietta Rheinlander, number 92–CR–60. Let the record show that the defendant is present with her counsel. Mr. Kimball, are you ready to proceed?"

"We are, Your Honor."

"Mr. Simpson, are you ready to proceed?"

"I am, Your Honor."

"The clerk will read the indictments."

The clerk, a round old fellow named Harold McCluskey, stood at his desk, adjusted his gold-rimmed spectacles, and read the documents that looked like this—

THE STATE OF OHIO
ALEXANDRIA COUNTY^{ss}
IN THE COURT OF COMMON PLEAS

Of the term of September in the Year of Our Lord One Thousand Nine Hundred and Ninety-Two.

We, THE JURORS OF THE GRAND JURY of the said County, on our oaths and in the name and by the authority of the STATE OF OHIO, do find and present that:

MARIETTA R. RHEINLANDER, on or about the Ninth day of May in the Year of Our Lord One Thousand Nine Hundred and Ninety-Two, within the County of Alexandria aforesaid, did purposely and unlawfully and with prior calculation and design kill and destroy the life of and murder one Charles R. Bailey, while the said Charles R. Bailey was peaceably demeaning himself within the County of Alexandria aforesaid, by discharging a deadly weapon, to wit a .38 caliber Smith &

Wesson revolver, at the said Bailey, thereby causing fatal injury and the death of the said Bailey.

Contrary to the form of the statute in such case made and provided and against the peace and dignity of the STATE OF OHIO.

Signed: *Kenneth B. Simpson*   Signed: *Ford T. Baker*
    Prosecuting Attorney   Foreman

McCluskey then read the other two indictments, charging Marietta Rheinlander with the murder of Donald Finch and Elizabeth Erb.

The indictment in the case of Elizabeth Erb contained additional language:

The said Elizabeth Erb was a witness to one or more aggravated murders committed by the said Marietta Rheinlander and was purposely killed to prevent her testimony in any criminal proceeding.

That was heavy stuff. If the jury found that the defendant killed Miss Erb to silence her as a witness, the penalty could be death. It is what is called an aggravating circumstance.

That was the case against her. She was charged with shooting three people, killing all of them.

I spoke to the jury panel. "Ladies and gentlemen, you who've been called as possible jurors. I'm speaking to those in the jury box and those in the chairs here. Please stand up. The clerk will administer an oath."

"Raise your right hands," said McCluskey. They did. "Say 'I' and then your own name—" They did, a sort of mumbled jumble. "'—do solemnly swear that the answers I will give to the questions asked me as a prospective juror in the case at bar will be the truth, the whole truth, and nothing but the truth, so help me God.' Do you and each of you so solemnly swear?" All of them nodded or muttered. They sat down.

I spoke again. "I am going to ask you a few questions, ladies and gentlemen. If the answer to each question is no, you don't need to say anything. If it's yes, please raise your hand. The first question is, were any of you personally acquainted with Charles Bailey, Donald Finch, or Elizabeth Erb?"

All of them solemnly shook their heads.

"Are any of you personally acquainted with Marietta Rheinlander?"

They shook their heads.

"The prosecuting attorney for Alexandria County is Mr. Kenneth Simpson. Do any of you know him personally?"

Six hands went up. I had a seating chart of the jurors. I spoke first to Mrs. Grace Siegfried. I knew she was acquainted with Ken Simpson, and I knew how. "Mrs. Siegfried, in what regard do you know Mr. Simpson?"

She was a rail-thin, sharp-faced woman with hair dyed black. "I taught him geometry at Alexandria High School," she said. "*Tried* to teach him would be more accurate."

"Does your acquaintance with him make you any more or less inclined to take his word or sympathize with his position in this case?"

"No," she said firmly. "I have no reason to think he is anything but an honest young man, but I am more interested in the evidence we will hear than what he may say about it."

One prospective juror said she had dated Ken Simpson when they were in high school. One said he was a regular customer in his gas station. They assured me those facts would not influence their decision.

Then I came to Jim Burkholder. I knew what he had to say. "Mr. Simpson, he was the lawyer for my wife when she sued me for divorce."

"How do you feel about him?" I asked.

Burkholder, who was a big middle-aged man who did hard physical work in the oilfields around the county, grinned. "Tough little bastard," he said. "I'd have been better off if he'd been *my* lawyer."

Kimball was busy scratching his ballpoint pen across lines in his background reports. He knew about Mrs. Siegfried and Jim Burkholder, and I was covering points *he'd* meant to make.

One of the remaining two who said they knew Ken Simpson said he really knew Ken's father, not Ken particularly. The other said she had met him just once, when he'd come to her door and offered his card when he was running for the office of prosecuting attorney.

Maybe I should explain that in a county our size, the office of prosecuting attorney—which in many other states is called district attorney—is not a full-time job. The prosecuting attorney is typically one of the younger lawyers, serving as prosecutor of felony charges and counsel to the several departments of the county government: all of which does not take more than a third of his time.

Look at our case numbers. Miss Rheinlander's three indictments were the fifty-eighth, fifty-ninth, and sixtieth returned by our three grand juries of the year, in January, April, and September. Out of sixty indictments, probably forty of the defendants pleaded guilty. Of the remaining twenty, the majority were so simple that they were tried in half a day each—passing bad checks, most of them, occasionally a car theft, where the evidence was clear and uncomplicated. In my three and a half years on the bench, I had seen just one murder case before this one; and even that was a case where a farm wife shot her husband with a shotgun: open and shut, to use the cliché. Until the Rheinlander case I had never presided over a trial that took more than three days.

Ken Simpson was prosecuting attorney because it was a good way for a new young lawyer to get a start. He was paid $28,000 a year, plus an expense allowance that included half the salary of the secretary who sat beside him. He had a one-man staff: an investigator named Hudson Choate whom he had inherited from the last prosecuting attorney.

Ken is a nice-looking young fellow, with curly dark brown hair and a face that speaks sincerity. His Adam's apple bobs when he talks. He shouldn't wear hats on the street but does. This morning he was wearing a light brown suit and well-shined light brown shoes.

Lloyd George Kimball was a little apprehensive of Ken Simpson, I guessed. Kimball earned twenty times what Ken did, was far more experienced, and knew every trick; but Ken was the kind of naive, sincere young man a jury might like very well. I guessed that Kimball would be careful not to seem to overwhelm the young prosecutor.

Bob Mitchell was the local lawyer on the defense team. I asked the prospective jurors the same question about him. Eight of the jurors acknowledged that they knew Bob. He has practiced law here for twenty-five years. They ought to know him.

One venireman said that Bob had probated his father's estate. Another said Bob had been his attorney in forming a small business corporation. Others knew him in other contexts: as a customer, as a fellow member of the Masonic Lodge, and so on.

I asked if any of them knew Kimball or his assistant Miss O'Reilly. Of course, none of them did.

I asked if any of them had already made up his or her mind about the case. As I had expected, one woman said she had; she believed Miss Rheinlander was guilty. I recognized that for what it was: an attempt to get herself excused from jury duty.

"Mr. McCluskey," I said. "Please hand Mrs. Weinstock a list of the cases to be tried at this term." The clerk did, and I waited while she glanced over the list. Then I asked, "Do you see a single case on this list on which you have not made up your mind, Mrs. Weinstock?"

"I . . . I don't know what you mean."

"This," I said to her sternly, "is the third time in two weeks that you have told us you've already made up your mind about a case. Do you see a case on the fall docket where you *could* serve as a juror?"

"Well, I don't know," she said indignantly.

"Mrs. Weinstock," I said. "You are excused. You are excused permanently. You need not report anymore. Jury duty is a citizen's obligation, but obviously you have more pressing things to do and don't want to meet that obligation, so we won't demand it of you. You may go."

That got notice in the newspapers. NO-NONSENSE JUDGE IN RHEIN-LANDER TRIAL. JUDGE BANISHES RELUCTANT JUROR. I must confess I saved clippings.

Except for Mrs. Weinstock, I did not excuse jurors. I elicited

15

information the attorneys might use to challenge them for cause, but I would let them do it; I wouldn't do it for them.

Ken Simpson took only about ten minutes to question the panel. He discovered nothing he didn't already know.

Then Kimball went to work. Grace Siegfried was juror number one, sitting in the front row, at the right side of the jury box.

"Mrs. Siegfried," he said. "Have you read much about this case?"

"A good deal, yes," she said.

"In what publications?"

"The local newspaper, of course. The Columbus *Dispatch*. And I read the two stories about it in *Time*."

"Thinking back to the time before Miss Rheinlander was accused of these murders, had you ever heard her name before?"

"Yes. I subscribe to *People* magazine," said Mrs. Siegfried.

"Did you ever read anything about her in any other publication? I mean, before she was accused here."

Kimball had left his table and was standing in front of the jury box, in fact resting his hand on it—not directly in front of Mrs. Siegfried, at the opposite end. He played at looking comfortable and casual. He was wearing a dark gray suit with a white pinstripe, a white shirt, blue and red necktie, narrow stripes, and polished black loafers.

"I don't recall that I ever saw her name anywhere but in *People*," said Mrs. Siegfried.

"All right. What sort of impression did you have of her as a result of your reading? I mean before she was arrested here in Alexandria County."

"Well . . . I had a sort of impression that she was a wealthy person, what you might call a society person in New York. I understood she was an art collector . . . an art *dealer*, actually."

"Would you say your impression of her was favorable or unfavorable?"

Mrs. Siegfried shrugged. "Neither. I'm not a judgmental person."

He smiled. "You've said you never met Congressman Charles Bailey—"

"No, I didn't say that. I said I wasn't acquainted with him. I did meet him once, when he made a speech to the local chapter of the American Association of University Women. I shook his hand in the receiving line."

"Did you like his speech?"

"Yes."

"Did you, therefore, have a favorable impression of Congressman Bailey?"

"Yes. I thought he was a cut above most politicians."

"His death was a tragedy, wasn't it?"

"It certainly was."

"But that doesn't mean Miss Rheinlander killed him."

"No, it doesn't."

He was using *voir dire* to argue his case. I would let him get away with a little of that . . . but very little.

Kimball moved one step along the jury box, a little closer to Mrs. Siegfried. "You are retired, are you not?" he asked. She nodded, and he went on. "What do you do in your retirement?"

"Well, I'm active in my church. I am also active in the Order of the Eastern Star. I manage to keep myself occupied."

The lawyer drew a breath, held it for a long moment, then let it out. "Mrs. Siegfried," he said, "if the evidence in this case should indicate that Congressman Bailey and Miss Rheinlander had an intimate relationship—if in fact the evidence is that they were sharing a bedroom the night when he was killed—would that influence your judgment in any way?"

"If you are asking if I would be prejudiced against her because she was sleeping with him and wasn't married to him, the answer is no," said Mrs. Siegfried with schoolteacherish sharpness.

Kimball smiled broadly. "That is exactly what I was driving at," he said. "Thank you for your definite answer."

He got a very different answer about an hour later when he was questioning a truck farmer named Howard Mendenhall. He bore down on this point with Mendenhall, and I thought I knew why. The Mendenhall family are members of a Pentecostal church and take their Bible literally.

"Mr. Mendenhall, you've heard me ask the others if they would be prejudiced against Miss Rheinlander if the evidence indicated she and Congressman Bailey were sleeping together. Would you?"

"Is that what the evidence *is* going to show?" asked Mendenhall.

Kimball nodded. "Yes. That's what it's going to show."

"In biblical times, she'd of been stoned," said Mendenhall.

"Do you think she should be stoned today?" Kimball asked quietly.

"I don't say that. We don't live in biblical times."

Kimball turned and glanced at me. It was, I think, the first time he had taken his eyes off the jury since he began his *voir dire*. "Mr. Mendenhall," he said. "Miss Rheinlander has been married twice and divorced twice. How do you feel about that?"

"Too bad," said Mendenhall blandly. He is a man in his late thirties. He holds firm views and is not embarrassed by them. He raised his chin a little, turned down the corners of his mouth, and fixed a stare on Marietta Rheinlander.

It chilled her. She was afraid to be judged by this man.

"Would that fact prejudice you?" asked Kimball.

Mendenhall again turned down the corners of his mouth. "I'll vote fair," he said, obviously offended it should be suggested he would not.

Kimball turned to me. "Your Honor, the defense moves that Mr. Mendenhall be excused for cause."

Technically, he didn't have cause. Mendenhall had said nothing that demonstrated prejudice, as the word is defined in the law. I shared with Miss Rheinlander a strong disinclination to see her judged by Howard Mendenhall. He's a nice enough fellow, a good family man and a hard worker, but I am uncomfortable with the idea of his judging other people. I could not put him off the jury, even so. I had to leave that to one of the defense's peremptory challenges.

"The motion is overruled, Mr. Kimball," I said.

Now of course Kimball had to use a peremptory challenge against Mendenhall. He couldn't leave him on the jury after having moved he be put off.

At ten-thirty I recessed for fifteen minutes to let people go to the washrooms. In the clerk's office I was handed half a dozen papers to sign: judgment entries, rulings on written motions, and the like. *State* v. *Rheinlander* was not the only case pending in the court.

"Interesting-looking woman, isn't she?" said Pete Varner.

Pete is one of the twenty-five lawyers who practice in Alexandria. I should explain that any lawyer admitted to the practice is entitled to come inside the bar of the court and sit down to watch a trial, if he can find a seat, which he almost always can. Pete is my age, almost. He wears silver-rimmed eyeglasses and favors out-of-style fedoras in light colors. He is an unspectacular and capable lawyer who has made a good living at the bar. He had stepped out for a cigarette and come back in, encountering me standing at the desk in the clerk's office, signing.

"Yes," I agreed. "She sure is."

"Is it true she gets her meals brought in from the hotel?"

"Yeah, I ordered the sheriff to allow that. As long as she pays for them, it saves the county the expense of feeding her."

"With wine?" he asked.

"I haven't asked. I don't want to know."

"One of the papers says so."

"What's the difference?"

"She's got *style*," said Pete. "I had to go out to the jail to talk to Maggie Beech one day . . . August, I guess it was. Miss Rheinlander was in there, sitting on her cot painting a picture with watercolors. Had on a little pair of shorts and a New York Mets T-shirt. She looked like she was spending a day at a resort hotel."

I shook my head. "We kept a suicide watch on her the first two weeks she was in jail," I told Pete. "She hardly ever stopped crying."

"She's guilty as hell," he said.

"Well . . . I don't know."

Pete grinned. "Of course not. You're not supposed to know."

Kimball used the rest of the morning questioning the prospective jurors.

19

One of his questions was argumentative, but I let him get away with it. "Do you understand, Mrs. Lee, that the fact that Miss Rheinlander has been indicted by the grand jury is no evidence of guilt?" When the panelist said he or she understood that, Kimball would reinforce it. "Do you *accept* that principle of law, that the indictment is not evidence?"

I let him use this question, too—"Mrs. Lee, some of the testimony in this case will be from sheriff's deputies and other law-enforcement officers. Would you be more inclined to believe the testimony of a deputy or other officer than you would the testimony of another person?"

Mrs. Emily Lee had served on an automobile-accident jury about two weeks before. She was the wife of the superintendent of schools. She was a conscientious juror. During the other trial I'd had to ask her not to take notes. Some judges allow jurors to take notes, some even encourage it, as they do in British trials, but we've never allowed it in Alexandria County. The theory is that the juror with notes will have more influence in deliberations than the jurors without notes. I'm not sure I like the theory, but I haven't changed the rule my predecessors followed.

When we broke for lunch, Kimball seemed hours from completing his *voir dire.*

For Miss Rheinlander and Margaret Vogt, the quickest way to leave the courtroom without having to walk through a gauntlet of reporters and cameramen was through the jury room, into the clerk's office, and out a door into the parking lot behind the courthouse— where a sheriff's car was drawn up close to the door. I was still in the jury room, hanging up my robe, when the defendant and her lawyers, and the deputy, came in. Miss Rheinlander walked over to Margaret Vogt and submissively offered her hands to be cuffed. Margaret looped the chain around her waist, locked on the handcuffs, and led her out. The prisoner would have her lunch in her cell.

I watched from the window to see the two women hurry across the very short distance between door and car. A dozen cameramen elbowed each other, fighting for a shot of Marietta Rheinlander in handcuffs. That was an unfortunate element of the case. They were obsessed with getting film or tape of the woman wearing restraints. Even though Court TV televised the entire trial, the most often published and most often broadcast images of the proceeding were the pictures of Miss Rheinlander being led into the courthouse back when Margaret was still keeping leg irons on her.

"Your Honor," said Kimball as I stood staring down at the car. "I think we may be able after all to pick a jury from these two dozen."

"We always do," I said.

I was a little late for the Ad Club lunch, and I left a little early. I always did both on Mondays when court was in session. It was something of a joke.

After lunch Kimball went to work on a point I had been surprised he had not raised earlier. He returned to the first juror he had questioned, Grace Siegfried, and he asked, "Mrs. Siegfried, the prosecuting attorney will ask you, if you find Miss Rheinlander guilty, then in a separate proceeding to vote to have her executed in the electric chair. How do you feel about that?"

The question was difficult for Mrs. Siegfried. I could see that. She had been calm until now, her composure complete. "I, uh . . . I'd find that hard to do," she said. "If the evidence was really that—" She paused and looked thoughtfully at the defendant. "If the evidence were that she is a really evil person who could kill without regret, then I suppose I could vote for the death penalty."

"But you wouldn't like to?"

"Mr. Kimball, I don't think I'll *like* whatever vote I cast as a juror. Whichever way."

Kimball asked the same questions of the juror he had been questioning just before we broke for lunch. His name was Winston Pyle. He was an assistant professor of art at Alexandria College: a rosy-cheeked heavyset man with a brush haircut.

"I'll follow the law," he said earnestly. "I suppose the judge will tell us what the law is, and if the law says there are circumstances where she has to go to the chair, I'll vote accordingly."

"Let's suppose, Mr. Pyle, the jury has found her guilty. Then there's a separate part of the trial—which there will be—on the question of whether she should be put to death or spend the rest of her life in prison. Could you vote to have her put to death?"

"I guess the law is that if this is so and that is so, then we have to send her to the chair. If that's the way it is and this is so and that is so, then I'll vote to do it. I won't like it, but I'll do it."

He went on with this line of questioning, with other jurors.

Only once during the whole trial did I see Marietta Rheinlander close to breaking down, and that was it, on the first day. Imagine what she had to feel, sitting there listening to people calmly talking about whether she should spend the rest of her life in prison or die a horrible death. She held herself rigid. Her face was rigid. So was her body. Three or four times she shuddered.

Kimball waited until last to ask Howard Mendenhall. I am certain he got the answer he was looking for—

"'He that smiteth a man so that he die, shall surely be put to death,'" said Mendenhall with certainty born of simplicity.

I was a little surprised when Kimball said suddenly about two o'clock that he was finished with his *voir dire*.

We proceeded then to the peremptory challenges. Each side was entitled to excuse eight jurors, without stating a reason.

Ken Simpson grinned at Jim Burkholder and excused him. He was not certain that Jim did really forgive him for his aggressiveness in litigating Mrs. Burkholder's divorce.

Kimball excused Howard Mendenhall. That was understandable. The prosecutor used no more peremptory challenges.

Kimball used two more. I can only guess why, and my guesses would not be very good. He had seen something or suspected something, or his jury specialists had applied psychology and recommended he challenge those two.

Anyway, it was only two in the afternoon, and we had a jury.

Mrs. Grace Siegfried remained on the jury: the retired teacher of geometry. Mrs. Emily Lee, wife of the superintendent of schools, sat in the second row. Professor Winston Pyle sat beside her.

We also had two housewives, one in her twenties, one in her

forties; a retired brakeman from the B & O Railroad, a farmer, a bus driver, an insurance agent, a cost accountant from the Diamond Chemicals plant, a waitress, and a veterinarian. We took two alternates: a secretary from Alexandria Savings & Loan and the produce manager from the local Kroger Supermart.

McCluskey administered the jurors' oath. "You shall well and truly try and true deliverance make between the State of Ohio and the defendant Marietta Rheinlander. So help you God."

"Members of the jury," I said. "We are about to recess for half an hour to give the attorneys time to prepare their opening statements. During our recesses, including especially overnight recesses, you must not talk to anyone about the case, you must read nothing about the case, you must listen to nothing on the radio or on television about the case, and you must not discuss the case among yourselves."

Kimball was on his feet. "Your Honor," he said, his voice betraying a little excitement, "I had supposed we would have this evening to prepare opening statements and would give them in the morning."

"Mr. Kimball," I said, "each side will be given thirty minutes for an opening statement. Half an hour should be enough to prepare. After all, you *have* heard of the case before, and nothing has so far happened to change anything."

Kimball managed to smile. I suspect he had thought he'd prepare his opening speech overnight and use half the morning to deliver it. Or maybe he hadn't. Surely Bob Mitchell had warned him.

2

Prosecuting attorney Ken Simpson pushed back his chair, stood, and faced the jury. He pushed a yellow legal pad into the center of the table just ahead of himself, but I knew from experience that he would probably not glance at his notes even once as he made his opening statement to the jury.

"Ladies and gentlemen of the jury," he said. "The case that is before this court is almost certainly the most important thing that will ever happen to us in any of our lives. I know of course that other important things have happened to you: births, deaths ... all the things that happen to people. Never before and never again will any of us be asked to face as difficult a task as we are about to put before you. May I say I hope I never again have to prosecute a case as difficult as this one.

"Miss Marietta Rheinlander, the defendant, sits before you charged with three murders. Three aggravated murders. Let me read you the definition of aggravated murder." He reached for a book, and read, "'No person shall purposely, and with prior calculation and design, cause the death of another.'"

He laid the book aside and continued. "In the case of Elizabeth Erb, the only possible reason for the murder was to eliminate a witness to the other murders. Murdering a person for that reason invokes the death penalty. The state is asking for the death penalty. It is the first case in which I have ever asked for it. I hope I never have to ask for it again.

"I know I do not have to request of you that you give very careful attention to the evidence that is brought before you. That evidence, ladies and gentlemen, will prove the truth of the charges brought in the three indictments."

He is a good young lawyer. Lloyd George Kimball knew it, and if he didn't fully understand it before, he began to see it now. Ken Simpson, in the Rheinlander trial, exhibited just the right mix of small-town naiveté and innate shrewdness to win the attention and respect of the jury.

He had gone away to college, to Kenyon: a distinguished little Episcopal college in central Ohio, where a lot of the Ohio Valley had been washed off him by close association with boys from all over the East. From there he had gone on to law school at Western Reserve University in Cleveland. He did well there, making law journal and Order of the Coif. He could have joined a Cleveland firm, or one in Columbus or Cincinnati; but Ken Simpson thought he would like the simple life of the small town where he'd grown up. Besides, he loved his family and wanted to live near them.

Kimball knew every detail of this. His jury investigators had done profiles of Ken Simpson and of me, too.

"Ladies and gentlemen . . . As I am sure most of you know, but the evidence will tell you, on May 9 of this year Miss Marietta Rheinlander was a guest in a hilltop lodge owned by the late Congressman Charles Bailey. Mr. Bailey represented the district across the river in West Virginia. He kept a lodge here in Alexandria County, outside his district and outside his state, where he could entertain his friends in a location sufficiently remote and sufficiently confidential that his parties there would go unnoticed by most of the news media. He held parties there from time to time—what he called his 'cronies parties.'

"Miss Rheinlander arrived in Alexandria on Tuesday, May 5. She says she had asked Congressman Bailey to let her have the lodge for a week or two. She had been there before, to cronies parties and otherwise. She has distant relatives here. Her great-grandfather made a fortune here, in the oil business. It was a good place to come and relax, she said.

"The congressman was glad to let her have the lodge. In fact—she says he told her—he would come out and spend the week-end with her. And in fact he did arrive, on the morning of Saturday, May 9.

25

"We are not quite sure what passed between Miss Rheinlander and Congressman Bailey that day. Witnesses who might be able to tell us are dead. Witnesses who survived describe a quarrel between them, as you will hear.

"Congressman Bailey had brought three staff members with him, two from Washington, one from Huntington, West Virginia. Two of those three people are dead.

"The survivor of them is Mr. David Ogle, who will be an important witness. Mr. Ogle will testify that the congressman did not come to the lodge just to be company for Miss Rheinlander but to prepare an important speech he meant to deliver the following week to the Foreign Policy Association. Mr. Ogle will testify that the congressman became quite annoyed when Miss Rheinlander repeatedly interrupted his work. He will testify also that Miss Rheinlander became very angry when Congressman Bailey would not devote his entire attention to her.

"There is no question but that Congressman Bailey and Miss Marietta Rheinlander were engaged in a meretricious relationship. That is to say, they were sleeping together. In fact, their affair was described in gossip columns in Washington and New York newspapers with such words as 'flaming,' 'heated,' and 'notorious.' The evidence will show also that the congressman had become concerned that his affair with Miss Rheinlander was damaging his reputation and might damage his political career."

Ken Simpson walked away from his table. He took a position about four feet from the jury box and folded his arms.

"The three members of Congressman Bailey's staff went to bed about eleven-thirty. They had watched the news on television, then retired. Miss Rheinlander and the congressman had retired to their room much earlier, had in fact eaten dinner there. From time to time while the three staff members were at dinner, and again while they were watching the news, angry voices were heard from the room Congressman Bailey was sharing with Miss Rheinlander.

"David Ogle will testify that he had been in bed just long enough to drift off to sleep when he was wakened by the sound of a shot.

26

He scrambled out of bed and grabbed on some clothes. Then he heard more shots. When he arrived in the central living room of the lodge, he found Congressman Bailey, Donald Finch, and Elizabeth Erb lying on the floor, dead or dying. Miss Marietta Rheinlander stood with her back to the glass sliding doors, facing the three bodies.

"Miss Rheinlander held a .38 caliber Smith & Wesson revolver in her right hand. All six shots in its cylinder had been fired. Miss Rheinlander's fingerprints were found on the trigger and on other parts of the pistol. A paraffin test, taken on her right hand, proved that she had fired a revolver."

Ken turned around and walked back to the prosecutor's table. He leaned against it.

"When she saw David Ogle, Miss Rheinlander ran past him—in fact knocking him aside. She ran into the bedroom she had shared with the congressman and closed and locked the door.

"By this time, Mrs. Dorothy Merritt, the cook and housekeeper at the lodge, arrived in the living room, having run over from the wing of the house where she lived with her husband, Mr. Bernard Merritt. She had heard the shots and had already called the sheriff's office.

"When she entered the living room she found David Ogle kneeling over the bodies. At first she believed that *he* had killed the congressman and his two assistants. She ran from the room and returned to her living quarters, where by now her husband was up and dressed. She told him to load their shotgun and be prepared to defend them against David Ogle.

"Then they heard the sound of a car rushing down the driveway. They assumed it was Ogle, escaping. They returned to the living room, taking the precaution of carrying the shotgun. There they found David Ogle, talking on the telephone. He, too, had called the sheriff's office and was explaining to the deputy that medical assistance was also urgently needed.

"Miss Elizabeth Erb was still alive. She pointed toward the sliding glass doors, toward where Miss Rheinlander had been standing when David Ogle first saw her.

27

"It was not, of course, David Ogle who had sped away in the car. That was Miss Rheinlander, fleeing the scene. She did not get far. On County Road 6, within a mile of the lodge, she misjudged a turn and drove her rented Oldsmobile into Turkey Creek.

"The first assistance on the scene was an ambulance from Alexandria Hospital. By then Miss Erb had died. Congressman Bailey and Donald Finch had died earlier, probably within a minute after being shot. The first law officer to arrive was Sheriff Dan Phelps. He'd been wakened by the deputy on duty at his office and had hurried out to the lodge. On his way, on County Road 6, he'd noticed the Oldsmobile in the creek but had been on his way to the scene of a triple murder. He had radioed his deputies to investigate the accident.

"Arriving at the lodge, Sheriff Phelps learned that Miss Rheinlander had fled. He radioed then that the driver of the Oldsmobile was a possible suspect in the triple murder. Shortly after that, one of the deputies rushing to the lodge spotted Miss Marietta Rheinlander on the road and placed her under arrest. He took her back to the lodge, where she became hysterical and had to be restrained.

"You will hear the testimony of Deputy Margaret Vogt, who will tell you that on the way to jail Miss Rheinlander made statements that tend to support the clear evidence that she shot and killed Congressman Charles Bailey, Mr. Donald Finch, and Miss Elizabeth Erb."

Ken walked around the table and stood by his chair. "We will prove everything I have just told you, by evidence that will convince you beyond any reasonable doubt that the defendant Marietta Rheinlander is guilty on three counts of aggravated murder." He sat down.

I call our prosecuting attorney Ken. I did not come to know Lloyd George Kimball well enough to call him by his first name. I mean no prejudice against the man, but I cannot call him Lloyd.

In any event, he stood, wearing briefly a quizzical little smile, rubbed his hands together for a moment, as if he was gathering his thoughts, then began his opening statement.

"Ladies and gentlemen of the jury . . . Mr. Simpson will not be able to prove what he told you he will prove."

Kimball turned and smiled at Ken Simpson. It was definitely not a condescending smile. If a smile could communicate so complex a thought, he seemed to be saying, "The courtroom is a tough place for us lawyers, isn't it?" He looked down at the floor for a moment, his smile still in place.

Then he looked at the jury. "He will not be able to prove what he told you he will prove," he said. "And that is our case, and I could almost stop there. If the case against Miss Rheinlander were as simple as Mr. Simpson suggests, he wouldn't have much trouble gaining a conviction on all three counts. Unhappily for the prosecution, the case is not that simple. It is, to the contrary, rather complex. Something rather different from what Mr. Simpson has suggested, happened in Congressman Bailey's hillside lodge on the night of May 9."

Unlike Ken Simpson, Lloyd Kimball looked at his notes. I very much doubt he needed to look. They gave him chances to pause for effect—which effect he enhanced by pulling half-glasses from his breast pocket, settling them on his nose, and peering professorially at the paper—and he took advantage of those chances.

"To begin with, ladies and gentlemen—and this is a vital point— *no one saw Miss Rheinlander shoot and kill Congressman Bailey, Mr. Finch, or Miss Erb*. Oh yes, there is evidence that suggests she did, but please do not lose sight of the fact that no one saw her do it. Mr. Simpson has not promised to produce a witness that saw her do it. No one heard a cry like, 'Oh, please, Marietta, don't shoot!'

"The evidence is circumstantial. Her fingerprints were found on the pistol. The paraffin test proved she had fired a pistol. That evidence does not prove she shot these three people. There is another explanation, as we will show you. She tried to run away. *That* does not prove she committed murder . . . as we will show you. For every circumstance that seems to point to Marietta Rheinlander as the murderer there is another and logical—even more logical—explanation . . . as we will show you."

Many of us had wondered how the famous New York trial lawyer would perform. So far, this was pretty mild stuff. Any lawyer in town could have presented this opening statement so far. And I think that is what Kimball had in mind. The jurors knew he was an out-of-town trial lawyer. Probably they expected something flashy. They didn't get it. He was just as restrained as Ken Simpson.

"Let's look at some of the facts Mr. Simpson has mentioned," Kimball went on. "Miss Rheinlander was sleeping with Congressman Bailey. No one is going to deny that. Miss Rheinlander is divorced. The congressman was never married. Neither of them was breaking a marriage vow if they were intimate with each other. Mr. Mendenhall said people were stoned for such conduct in biblical times. My oh my, ladies and gentlemen. If in this day and age we stoned everybody who has an intimate relationship outside marriage, we'd be hard put to find stones; the earth would be denuded of them."

Some of the jurors laughed. And . . . "My oh my"? It sounded like hometown talk. Lloyd George Kimball was proving he could talk with anybody.

"Now. We are going to hear from testimony, I understand, that the congressman and Miss Rheinlander quarreled during the afternoon and evening of May 9. They raised their voices, so they could be heard through their bedroom door. Well . . . my wife and I have been married more than thirty years. Some evenings, if you were outside our bedroom door, you would hear some lively spats, sometimes with ugly words. And yet, my wife and I love each other. Isn't that within your experience, too, ladies and gentlemen?"

I interrupted, as gently as I could. "Points like that would be better made in final argument than in your preliminary statement, Mr. Kimball," I said.

He nodded at me, unruffled. "I will proceed to another point," he said.

There is a fine line between opening statement and argument. I just wanted him to know I understood it and would not let him argue his case at this point.

"The evidence will show, ladies and gentlemen," he went on, "that in spite of the fact that the congressman and Miss Rheinlander had argued and were continuing to argue, they did not take their dinner at the table with Congressman Bailey's staff members but had it brought to their room, so they could eat alone. Brought to their room also was a bottle of wine. They had, in other words, a romantic dinner in the confines of their bedroom."

He was back on the fine line again, but I let it go.

Kimball picked up his yellow legal pad and stared at it for a moment. "Certain facts remain unexplained," he said to the jury. "For example, where did that Smith & Wesson revolver come from? Miss Rheinlander flew from La Guardia Airport in New York to Wood County Airport at Parkersburg, West Virginia, then drove to the congressman's lodge. Obviously she was not carrying a pistol when she went through the security check at La Guardia. Neither was it in her luggage, since luggage is X-rayed, looking for bombs. Where did she get the pistol? What in fact is the origin of that pistol? Who owned it? Who bought it? And where?"

He tossed his legal pad back on the table. "Now, ladies and gentlemen . . . the evidence will show that Congressman Bailey, Mr. Finch, and Miss Erb were each killed with one shot. The evidence will show also that the shots were not fired at point-blank range, since no powder residue was found on the bodies or their clothes. The shots were fired in a room that was dimly lighted, perhaps even dark. Only Miss Erb was shot in the back. The other two victims faced the killer."

Kimball sighed audibly. "The dramatic scenario offered by the prosecution is that Miss Rheinlander shot Congressman Bailey because they were having a violent lovers' quarrel. Then she shot Mr. Finch and Miss Erb because they came running into the room as she was standing with the smoking gun in her hand, and they saw her, which made them witnesses.

"Now, ladies and gentlemen, the evidence will also show that Miss

Rheinlander never discharged a firearm before in her life. She lives in New York, where ownership of a pistol is strictly forbidden by law. You are asked to believe that she and the congressman quarreled violently in their bedroom, that she left the bedroom and went down the hall to the living room, carrying the pistol, that the congressman came after her, and that she turned and fired on him. You are asked to believe that the marksmanship of this woman who had never before fired a pistol was so good that she killed the congressman with one shot. You are then asked to believe that as Mr. Finch and Miss Erb came running out to see what had happened, she calmly dropped each of them with one well-placed shot."

Lloyd George Kimball stood shaking his head, smiling faintly, wryly. "Oh . . ." he said suddenly, as if he had forgotten something. "Maybe she didn't kill each with one shot. The revolver held six cartridges, so maybe she had two chances to kill each—or maybe she got the congressman with one shot, Mr. Finch with one, and had four shots left to fire at Miss Erb." He shook his head. "No. The evidence will show that there is not a single bullet hole anywhere in the house. Whoever fired at the three victims killed them with just three shots. Remarkable marksmanship for anybody, more than remarkable for a woman with no experience with firearms. Yes. And downright unbelievable, is it not, for a woman who has just shot her lover to remain so calm that she can kill two more people with amazingly accurate pistol fire?"

He had made a telling point.

"So what did happen, ladies and gentlemen? Miss Rheinlander explained what happened, to the sheriff and other investigators. She and Congressman Bailey were in bed. The congressman said he heard noises outside the house. He got up, pulled on a silk lounging jacket, saying he would go to the living room and look out through the sliding glass patio doors. He was gone for some time, maybe as long as ten minutes. Miss Rheinlander heard a shot. She was nude, so she grabbed a pair of panties and was struggling into them when she heard a second shot, then a third. She ran down the hall toward the living room and saw three people on the floor, dead or fatally wounded. The pistol lay on the floor. The glass sliding doors were open. She saw a figure retreating along the pool deck. She grabbed up the pistol and fired all the shots that remained in it in the direction of the fleeing figure. As she turned, David Ogle appeared and saw her standing there with the pistol in her hand."

Kimball paused again and stared at his yellow pad.

His scenario was weak. But he had an advantage. Ken Simpson had to prove his version beyond a reasonable doubt, and Kimball didn't have to prove anything.

"She was all but naked. She ran to her room to cover herself. While she was there she realized *she* was going to be accused of three murders. In terror and panic she ran to her car and drove away. Maybe I would have, too. Maybe you would have, too.

"Ladies and gentlemen, as His Honor will charge you, we of the defense don't have to prove Miss Rheinlander didn't kill three people. The prosecution has to prove she did . . . and that beyond reasonable doubt. I firmly believe, ladies and gentlemen, that when you have heard all the evidence you will not be convinced that Marietta Rheinlander killed Congressman Bailey, Donald Finch, and Elizabeth Erb—or any one of them. Indeed, I believe you will be convinced she didn't."

Now it was my turn. At the end of the trial I would charge the jury about the law. Now I would charge them about their duties as jurors and about the probative value of evidence.

"Ladies and gentlemen of the jury, from this point on you will be sequestered. That is to say, you will not go home overnight but will stay at the Mariott Inn. The radios and television sets have been removed from your rooms, so you cannot see news accounts of this trial. A big color set has been placed in a conference room so you can watch entertainment-type shows, but the bailiff who will be with you will turn it off if anything comes on about this case or this trial. Newspapers will be brought to you, but everything about the trial will be cut out. You may talk to your families on the telephone, but a bailiff will be listening and will cut you off if anyone begins to talk about the trial. Similarly, family members can visit you, but only in the presence of a bailiff. You were asked to bring along clothes and toiletries this morning. If you need more, tell a bailiff, and we will arrange to have more brought to you from home.

"Until the trial is over, you must not talk to anyone about the case—and that includes your fellow jurors. Just don't talk about it at all. Wait until you have heard all the evidence. Then you will have plenty of opportunity to talk about it.

"Please remember this. You must not decide this case on the basis of any information except what you see or hear in the courtroom. When you listen to a witness, you are entitled to make up your minds as to whether or not you want to believe that witness—but you must make up your minds strictly on the basis of what you hear the witness say, plus his or her appearance and demeanor on the witness stand. If you think you know something about the witness, something you learned before, you must not take that into consideration.

"The comments and arguments of the lawyers are not evidence. They are entitled to try to persuade you that some testimony is more important than other testimony, but their arguments are arguments, not evidence. Remember, too, that the lawyers are not on trial here. You may decide you like a particular lawyer, or dislike one. That is not evidence either. You must not be influenced by your feelings toward any of the lawyers.

"Miss Rheinlander has been indicted by the grand jury. That is not evidence of guilt. It is not true that another jury has already found her guilty. All the indictments mean is that the grand jury saw enough evidence to make them think the defendant should be tried on these charges. The defense lawyers did not appear before the grand jury, only the prosecutor. The indictments are not evidence.

"It is your duty to hear the evidence and decide what facts are true. You are not concerned with the law. That is my business. The law is not what you think it is or think it *should* be. The law is what I tell you it is. When you have heard the evidence I will charge you about the law. I will define the crimes exactly for you and tell you what you must find is true in order to convict. I will give you that in writing, so you may have it in the jury room with you.

"You have already heard the statement that the prosecution must prove guilt beyond a reasonable doubt. I will charge you later as to what reasonable doubt is. But do not sit waiting for the defense to prove the defendant innocent. The defense doesn't have to do that. The prosecution has to prove guilt. That is a basic element of our Anglo-American system of law and a basic right of every American.

"Finally, I will ask you to keep an open mind throughout the trial. Do not make up your minds until you have heard everything, including the lawyers' final arguments and my charge. When you retire to deliberate on your verdict, only then should you make up your minds, and not before."

I recessed for the day, even though it was early. We could begin to hear evidence in the morning.

After I hung up my robe, I glanced out into the courtroom. Marietta Rheinlander and her counsel were still at the defense table, so none of the reporters and cameramen had left. I couldn't understand why they did not hurry out. Then I saw and understood. The defendant's mother and father were inside the bar of the court, huddled with her and talking earnestly with her.

My chief bailiff—in fact, my only bailiff ordinarily; I'd had to appoint three temporary ones to help with the sequestration of this jury—is Gene Hockenberry. I beckoned Gene into the jury room and told him to invite Miss Rheinlander and her family in there for their conference. I slipped out before they came in.

It is my intention to present this story of a trial just as the jury saw and heard it, without much additional information. I am going to outline the family history of the Rheinlanders, though. I imagine most of the jurors knew it anyway.

Marietta Rheinlander's great-grandfather came to Ohio in the 1890s, in the oil boom. He made a fortune in oil, then left for New York. Two of his daughters had married into local families and so stayed here. Their descendants are distant cousins of Marietta Rheinlander. The family has kept in touch casually over the years. That is Miss Rheinlander's connection to our town and county.

The great-grandfather was nearly wiped out in the crash of 1929, but his son, Marietta's grandfather, invested the remnants of the fortune shrewdly and actually managed to build it back to as much as it had been before 1929. Seeing what could happen to a family if members invested recklessly, the grandfather funded trusts for each of his grandchildren. From her birth, Marietta Rheinlander was assured she would never be in want. Besides that, she inherited a share of her grandfather's estate when he died in the early 1980s. She is not *immensely* wealthy, but she is certainly well off.

I had noticed Mr. Jason and Mrs. Rose Rheinlander, Marietta's parents, sitting in the courtroom during the day. I had seen both of them before, and I felt sorry for them. Mr. Rheinlander was a fragile man at sixty-five, in precarious health. Mrs. Rheinlander—her name is Rose—had flown out here to see her daughter almost every week since Marietta had been in jail. Ordinarily Friday is visiting day for the jail, but I had told the sheriff to let Mrs. Rheinlander see her daughter any day that she came. She is a small woman, her hair and clothes always perfectly attended to. Like an Englishwoman, she never fails to wear a hat.

Back in my office, I phoned Linda and asked her if she'd like to go out to dinner. Of course she would. I'd entertained no doubt about that. I told her I'd meet her in the bar at the hotel at six-thirty. Then I called the hotel and reserved a table. Good thing I did, too. The newshawks had just about filled the place up.

There is always plenty to do when you're a judge. I sat at my desk and studied a separation agreement offered by the lawyers for a couple seeking a divorce. Oh, yes. We have no special domestic relations court. I'm it. Common Pleas gets everything but probate, for which a special judge is elected.

So what was I doing reading a separation agreement? Well, I'm supposed to see to it that the children of a marriage are properly provided for. That's the first thing. This was what I'd call a yuppie couple, and they didn't have any children. He was a real estate salesman, and she was a dental technician. They'd been married two years, lived in a rented apartment, and each owned a car. The separation agreement committed the young husband to paying his ex-wife $250 a month for the rest of his life. Why? She had her own career and her own income. She hadn't given up a career to help him build his. Why in the world had he committed himself to alimony? I knew why. He had a stupid lawyer. I won't of course mention the name. I laid the decree aside. I wouldn't sign it as long as it incorporated a separation agreement I considered unfair.

My predecessor would sign any decree, so long as the parties had agreed. A lot of the lawyers were annoyed that I stuck my nib in and wouldn't sign what I didn't think fair.

So Linda and I met at the Alexandria House, in the bar. Someone once said that if a bomb went off in the Alexandria House bar at six-thirty or seven, it would wipe out half the lawyers and all the doctors in the county. And that was about right. That evening it was very convenient. We regulars took almost all the seats, leaving only three or four for the members of the news media who were thirsty for "color" and for something from the vats as well.

A columnist for *Newsday* wrote this of us:

> At the end of a day in Alexandria, Ohio, the judges and lawyers, the physicians and surgeons, and assorted accountants, realtors, insurance agents, and merchants assemble in the quiet, cozy bar at the Alexandria House to sip the juice of the grape and schmooze about everything but business. It is as much like Rumpole's Thames-side pub as anything to be found this side of the Atlantic, and one half expects to hear Judge Bill McIntyre call out for a bottle of "Chateau Thames Embankment."
>
> The judge does not order wine, actually. Like Franklin D. Roosevelt, he favors two martinis at the end of the working day. If one were a traveling salesman instead of a pushy reporter, he'd likely invite you to pull up a stool. He was even willing to talk to this pushy reporter, though he confined the conversation to a disquisition on the beauty of the autumn leaves this year and some talk about how the Ohio

River had been so well cleaned up you could fish for bass and perch in it again. He said he couldn't talk about the Rheinlander case because he didn't know anything about it. "I'm not supposed to know anything about it until I hear the evidence," he said. "Right?"

His wife, sitting beside him, laughed. "He used to talk like a lawyer," she said. "It's only recently he's started talking like a judge." Mrs. McIntyre is a handsome, graying woman, a little taller than her husband. Her Ohio Valley accent is more noticeable than his.

Marietta Rheinlander is apprehensive about being tried before the jury picked this morning and before this small-town judge. She might be less apprehensive if she saw him in the bar at the Alexandria House. Judge McIntyre impressed me at the bar as he did today in court—a very human jurist with a perspective about life and the law that big-city judges would do well to emulate.

Isn't that nice? I wouldn't have quoted it of course if it weren't so complimentary. That's one of the clippings someone sent us, since we don't get *Newsday*. Linda keeps a scrapbook.

There were no surgeons at the bar that night, as I recall. The doctor who'd been sitting with Linda when I came in was Forrest Allen, a gynecologist who's been the butt of every gynecologist joke anyone ever heard of or could invent—while still keeping his good humor about it. ("After all," he laughs, "it's nothing but jealousy that makes them talk like that.")

When we'd had our two drinks, Linda and I went into the dining room. It's a pleasant room, furnished with heavy maple tables and chairs. They use red and white checkered tablecloths, and in the evening they light the room mostly with candles burning inside lamps on all the tables. The walls are decorated with oil paintings. I suppose it's bad art, but the pictures are supposed to represent the early days of the town. When this town was settled, there were still hostile Indians loose in the woods. The settlers built a stockade and two or three times fled inside it.

My family came here about 1805. Linda's came in the 1830s. I suppose the place has pretty thoroughly rubbed off on us.

We had been at our table only a few minutes when Mr. and Mrs.

Rheinlander came in and were taken to a table. The reporters had the decency to leave them alone. Looking around, the Rheinlanders soon spotted me. They turned their eyes away.

I first saw them on the day when their daughter's attorneys moved to allow her to go free on bond pending the trial. When their daughter became hysterical after I denied their motion, both parents wept.

I was sorry, but I could not release her, no matter how high the bond. She was charged with three murders. She had tried to run away. I simply couldn't do it.

Even so, I imagine she had convinced herself that her request was so eminently reasonable that I could not refuse it. Even knowing, as she must have been told, that aggravated murder is not a bailable offense, I imagine she had persuaded herself that she was the exception and that I would let her out pending trial. If she thought that, she was being wholly unrealistic. But it isn't unusual. I have seen, for example, a veteran car thief sit in the courtroom and listen to evidence that condemns him with categorical certainty—and show genuine befuddlement and disappointment when the jury comes back with a conviction.

I suppose her parents thought I was a cold, unfeeling man. I wish they hadn't felt that way. That evening when I saw them at dinner in the Alexandria House, I think they were afraid of me, too. I understand why, but I wish it had not been so.

3

I don't want to give the impression that I sat on the bench taking shorthand notes of the Rheinlander trial. No. When I decided to write a book about it, I had the court reporter type up the transcript. It cost me half of what I got for an advance for this book, and only time will tell if it was a good investment.

When we convened on Tuesday morning, the order of business was the case for the prosecution. We had a jury, opening statements had been heard, a preliminary charge had been given, and now it was time for the prosecution to begin offering evidence.

The New York *Post* commented:

> In a Manhattan courtroom the first witness might not take the stand during the first week of an important trial. In the Alexandria, Ohio, courtroom where Marietta Rheinlander is on trial for her life, the first witness was heard as soon as court opened on the second day—and the judge seemed to think the trial was already off schedule, taking too much time.

That was wrong. I did not think the trial was off schedule.

The *Post* also described Miss Rheinlander's appearance and demeanor on the second day of the trial:

> Marietta Rheinlander is not at her best in this setting and these circumstances. She shows the strain inherent in her situation and also the effects of having spent five months locked in a small jail cell. Even her celebrated chic seems to have abandoned her. She wore a conspicuously expensive pink cashmere suit yesterday, and today a handsome white linen dress, but she does not wear her clothes with

40

the flair that is characteristic of her. For the time being at least, and maybe forever, the glamor has gone out of her life.

Several options were available to Ken Simpson. He might have elected to start with the sheriff, go on to the medical examiner, and so on—in other words, establish the deaths and the brutality with which they had been caused, then go back to who had caused them. He chose instead to go first with his chief witness.

"The State of Ohio calls David W. Ogle."

The witness, who had been waiting in the clerk's office, came into the courtroom the same way I came: through the jury room. He was a handsome man of more than average height. He had, as the jury was soon to see, a taut, jerky personality, coupled with a tendency to smile inappropriately. His hair was dark brown and curly, and a wisp of it usually fell over his forehead. He wore a dark blue three-piece suit. He did not swagger into the courtroom but walked to the witness stand with conspicuous self-confidence.

McKluskey walked over. "Raise your right hand. Do you solemnly swear that the testimony you are about to give in the case at bar will be the truth, the whole truth, and nothing but the truth, so help you God?"

"I do."

Ogle sat down. He crossed his legs and pulled the microphone closer to himself, as if this were something he did every day.

Simpson did not stand up. "State your full name, please."

"David William Ogle."

"Your place of residence?"

"I live at 4410 Thoreau Drive, Bethesda, Maryland."

"How old are you, Mr. Ogle?"

"I am thirty-seven."

"You are, I believe, a lawyer."

"Yes, sir. I graduated from the College of Law, University of West Virginia, in 1973. I am admitted before the courts of West Virginia and the several federal courts."

"Did you practice law for a time?"

41

"Yes, sir. I practiced in Huntington, West Virginia from 1973 until 1984, with the firm of Wilcoxen, Branch & Bailey."

"What happened in 1984?"

"After Mr. Bailey was elected to Congress that year, I resigned from the firm and went with him to Washington. I helped him set up and staff his congressional office, then stayed with him as counsel and chief of staff."

"Were those still your titles at the time of the congressman's death?"

"Yes, they were."

Ken Simpson sat with his chair a little back from his table, his legs crossed, relaxed. These were the easy questions. "Were you and Congressman Bailey close personal friends?"

"Yes, sir. The congressman was only seven years older than I am, and I had known him from the time I joined his law firm. I had worked hard on his first campaign, and we came to know each other quite well."

"Was that on a personal and social basis as well as a business basis?"

"Yes, sir. The congressman was not married. Neither was I. We often ate dinner together in Washington restaurants. We played golf together."

"Did Congressman Bailey confide in you?"

"I'm going to object to that question, Your Honor," said Lloyd Kimball quietly, as if reluctantly. "That calls for a conclusion."

"The objection is sustained," I said, even though I understood that Kimball had raised it only to see if Ken Simpson could be rattled.

The rule here is that a witness cannot testify as to his opinion or conclusion drawn from facts. Ken could have asked Ogle to recite facts that would lead the jury to conclude that the congressman confided in him. But it must be the jury that reaches the conclusion, not the witness. It was a minor point and a technicality, but the law is the law. I hoped the trial would not be one objection after another.

"To your knowledge," asked Ken, "did the congressman tell you things about his personal life that he did not tell other members of his staff?"

Kimball shook his head. "Again, Your Honor, that's asking for a conclusion."

"Mr. Simpson," I said, "I'm going to give you a chance to ask the question a different way."

Ken Simpson frowned, glanced at me, frowned at Kimball, then asked—"Mr. Ogle, did Congressman Bailey ever say to you words to this effect, 'I'm going to tell you something personal that I am not telling anyone else on the staff'?"

Ogle glanced at Kimball, expecting another objection. Kimball sat poker-faced. "Yes," said Ogle. "On a number of occasions."

The jury was of course confused and curious. They could see no difference in getting the answer this way and getting it the original way. They could not guess what Kimball had been driving at. I have often wondered if a lawyer makes points that way. It can make the jury think he's too contentious. On the other hand, since I sustained the objections, some jurors may have thought the big-town lawyer had just given the small-town lawyer a little lesson in the law. You never know what they think.

Kimball had rattled Ken. He wasn't as comfortable now.

"Mr. Ogle," said Ken with a sort of hard-pressed new precision in his words, "did Congressman Bailey ever use words like that— words to the effect that he was telling you something he wasn't telling other members of his staff—to preface a statement about Miss Marietta Rheinlander?"

"Yes."

Ken began to pump his hands, parallel before him. "Did the congressman ever say to you any words to the following effect—'I am going to confide to you something about Marietta Rheinlander'?"

"Yes."

"What did he then tell you?"

"Congressman Bailey told me she had become an impossible burden on him and that he was going to have to break off his relationship with her."

"Did he elaborate as to what the burden was?"

"He told me he could not run for the United States Senate unless he broke off his relationship with Marietta Rheinlander."

Miss Rheinlander sat rigid in her chair, staring hard at David Ogle. No one who looked at her could have any doubt that she hated the man. By her adamantine glare, and by that alone, she spoke eloquently to the jury, telling them not to believe a word this man said.

"Did he say anything further in that regard?" Ken asked.

"He said her demands on him were impossible for him to meet."

"Did he say specifically what her demands were?"

"No, but I knew what he meant. He—"

Ken interrupted him. "You surmised or guessed what he meant, and you can't testify to that."

"No."

Ken looked a little more comfortable. He flipped a sheet on his yellow legal pad. "When did you first meet Miss Marietta Rheinlander?" he asked.

"I think it was in March of 1989. I can't be sure. About that time."

"In what context did you meet her?"

David Ogle had not been in the least fazed by the objections. He was a paradigm of the confident witness with facts to tell and nothing to conceal. He recrossed his legs to make himself more comfortable and again tugged on the microphone. Some witnesses bob their heads toward the mike whenever they speak. He never did. He spoke to the prosecutor or to the jury, as if the microphone were not there.

"I had become aware that there was some kind of close relationship between Congressman Bailey and Miss Rheinlander," he said. "She called the office and left messages for him to call her. I knew he went out of his way to answer. I became interested and decided to find out who she was. I—"

"Objection," said Kimball, again quietly. "If the witness is about to tell us that he read articles about the defendant or inquired of other people about her, he will be giving us hearsay."

"Well, we won't know if this is true or not until we find out what he was going to say," I ruled. "You may continue, Mr. Ogle."

44

Now Ogle was a little flustered. I don't know why. If he was any kind of lawyer, he should have known he couldn't testify about what he read in newspaper articles. "I, uh . . . I did read several articles about her."

"I renew my objection," said Kimball.

"Mr. Ogle," I said, "since you are a lawyer yourself, you know you can't testify about what you read in newspapers, only about facts within your personal knowledge."

Ken Simpson rose to his feet. "Your Honor, I ask that the reporter read the last question I asked Mr. Ogle."

I nodded to the reporter, and she read: " 'In what context did you meet her?' "

"That is the question I would like to have answered, Your Honor," said Ken.

"Please do answer that question, Mr. Ogle," I said.

Ogle licked his lips. "Congressman Bailey introduced her to me as 'my friend.' "

"Where and when?"

"At Duke Zeibert's," said Ogle.

"That is a Washington restaurant, is it not?" asked Ken. "Was that at noon or in the evening, and is that restaurant expensive?"

"It was at dinner, and the restaurant is expensive."

"What did you observe then and later about the personal relationship between Congressman Bailey and Miss Marietta Rheinlander?"

"That it was an intimate relationship. It had been before I met her. It remained so afterward."

"What did you observe that causes you to use the word 'intimate'?"

Ogle sighed and glanced around the courtroom. "When Miss Rheinlander was in Washington, she stayed in the congressman's apartment. When he was in New York, he stayed in hers."

"How do you know that?"

"She would answer his telephone. If something important came up when he was in New York, I could reach him at her apartment."

"Would it be correct, then, to say that the relationship between them was public and notorious?"

"Objection," Kimball muttered. "Another conclusion."

"Sustained."

Ken Simpson closed his eyes for a moment. "Within your observation, did Congressman Bailey make any effort to conceal the fact that Miss Rheinlander stayed in his apartment and he stayed in hers?"

"Objection."

"Sustained."

"If you know from personal observation, did other members of the congressman's staff know he stayed in Miss Rheinlander's apartment and she stayed in his?"

That was the question he should have asked in the first place, and Ogle answered yes.

"If you know from personal observation, was this *generally known* to the congressman's staff?"

"Yes. I don't suppose every secretary knew it, but everyone who needed to reach him evenings and weekends knew it."

"If you know from personal observation, were the same facts known to any members of the news media?"

"Yes. Virginia Clark of the Washington *Post* knew about it. Other reporters knew it. They wrote about it."

"If you know from personal observation of facts, was the relationship between Congressman Charles Bailey and Miss Marietta Rheinlander widely known, even to the public?"

"It was very widely known," said Ogle somberly.

"What facts lead you to that conclusion?"

"I have seen at least a dozen newspaper articles saying the two of them had an intimate relationship."

Kimball let all this colloquy pass without objection. Ken was asking his questions the right way.

"What, if you know facts about it, was the nature of the intimacy between the congressman and Miss Rheinlander?"

"I only know that they often shared the same apartment, sometimes the same room. They held hands. They kissed. That sort of thing."

"Did the congressman ever tell you he and Miss Rheinlander had sexual intercourse?"

"No."

"Did he ever tell you he was in love with her?"

"No."

"Did he ever tell you she was in love with him?"

"Yes, he said she was."

Every eye turned now to Marietta Rheinlander. She looked stricken. If it was an act, it was damned well done.

"Your Honor . . ."

"Yes, Mr. Kimball. Ladies and gentlemen of the jury, notice that Mr. Ogle has testified that the congressman *said* Miss Rheinlander was in love with him. That is evidence of what the congressman said, not evidence as to whether or not she *was* in love with him."

"Thank you, Your Honor," said Kimball.

Once again, this was a small point, but it could be an essential one. That Congressman Bailey said Miss Rheinlander was in love with him did not prove she was. We might hear more on the point, and the jury should understand the question was open.

"Did the congressman ever speak to you of marrying Miss Rheinlander?"

"No."

Ken turned to the next sheet on his pad. "Now," he said, "I would like to turn to the events of May 9 of this year. When did you first learn that the congressman would be going to Ohio and would want you to accompany him?"

"On the preceding Wednesday. He told me he wanted to spend the weekend at the lodge. He was going to deliver a speech on Thursday, May 14, to the Foreign Policy Association, and he said he wanted to write that speech over the weekend."

"When did he plan to return to Washington?"

"Not until Tuesday. He planned to spend Monday in Huntington, doing a little campaigning for his 1992 reelection."

"Why did Donald Finch accompany you to Ohio?"

"He had done most of the research for the speech. He brought a considerable volume of material with him."

"Who, incidentally, was Donald Finch?"

"Don was a graduate student at Georgetown. He came with us last year as a staff researcher, part time."

"And who was Elizabeth Erb, and why was she at the lodge on the night of May 9?"

"Miss Erb was a secretary in the congressman's Huntington office. She could type. None of the rest of us could. She brought a laptop computer with printer and would have typed the speech drafts."

"How did each of you travel, and when did you arrive?"

"The three of us from Washington flew into Parkersburg airport, picked up a rental car, and drove to Alexandria and out to the lodge. We arrived at about two in the afternoon. Miss Erb drove up from Huntington. She was there when we arrived."

"Was Miss Rheinlander there when you arrived?"

"Yes. There is a heated swimming pool behind the lodge. She was in the pool." The witness paused and smiled faintly: a curious little smile, I thought. "So was Miss Erb."

"Then what happened?"

"Miss Rheinlander came out of the water and kissed Congressman Bailey. She urged him to come in swimming with her. He said he had work to do. She said he could spare half an hour. So he did. He changed his clothes and went in the pool with her. In fact, we hadn't eaten lunch, and Mrs. Merritt brought out sandwiches and beer."

"Explain to the jury who Mrs. Merritt is."

"Mrs. Merritt is the housekeeper and cook at the lodge. She and her husband, who works on the grounds and so on, live in a suite in a wing of the house."

At this point, Ken Simpson turned to Hudson Choate, his investigator, who sat in a chair just behind the prosecutor's table, and said something we could not hear. Hudson, a sober, dutiful young man with dark hair that falls in a cowlick, rose and carried forward a tripod, which he set up facing the bench and the jury. Then he carried to it a diagram drawn on a big piece of poster board.

This was the diagram:

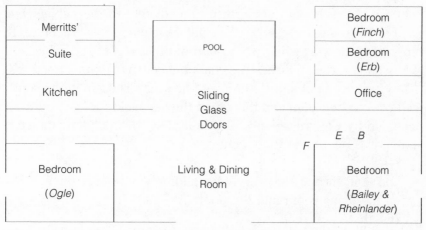

Lloyd Kimball rose from his chair and stepped to the front of the courtroom, to where he could see the chart.

"We have a copy for you, Mr. Kimball," said Ken Simpson, and Hudson carried a small version of the chart to the defense attorney.

"Now, Mr. Ogle," said Ken, "I will ask you to look at this chart and tell the jury if it fairly represents the outline of the house, showing the location of rooms. You will of course notice that bathrooms are not shown. Each bedroom had a bathroom, did it not?"

Ogle studied the chart for the better part of a minute, then said, "That is how the rooms at the lodge are laid out."

"Please notice the letters *F*, *E*, and *B* in the northwest corner of the living-dining room. Do those letters accurately represent the location of the bodies of Donald Finch, Elizabeth Erb, and Congressman Bailey as you observed them?"

"Your Honor," said Kimball with an air of patience. "Let's first establish that Mr. Ogle did see the bodies, and when, and then let him testify as to whether or not the letters show where he saw them."

That was in fact a lesson for Ken Simpson. "I think that would be an appropriate sequence, Mr. Simpson," I said.

Ken nodded. He did not return immediately to the subject but went on to something else. "Do the names in parentheses accurately represent who was using what bedroom that night?" he asked.

Ken had moved up beside the chart and began to point at features. "The chart does not show windows," he said. "The gap in the south wall of your bedroom and the gap in the north side of the bedroom occupied by Congressman Bailey and Miss Rheinlander represent sliding glass doors. Is that accurate?"

"Yes."

"And is it correct that very wide sliding glass doors opened between the living room and the pool?"

"Yes, that is correct."

"Mr. Ogle, I direct your attention to the north wing, containing an office and two bedrooms. How could a person in one of those rooms enter the main house?"

"Only by going outdoors and walking along a brick walk beside the pool to the big sliding doors into the living room," said Ogle.

"How could the Merritts get into the main house?"

"The same way," said Ogle. "Of course, anyone could go in through the kitchen, or they could walk around the house to the front door."

"The house was designed, was it not, to give the people in each of the bedrooms a great deal of privacy? In other words, you could leave any of the bedrooms and go to your car and drive away without coming through the living-dining area."

Kimball shook his head. "Sometime, Your Honor, we are going to have to ask the prosecutor to stop leading his witnesses."

"I withdraw the question," said Ken Simpson abruptly, without waiting for me to rule.

Once again, the point Kimball was making was not major. Ken should have asked this question—"Was the layout of the house such that an occupant of any bedroom could leave the house without going through the living room?" The way he asked the question told the witness what answer he wanted. And under the law that is not the correct way to ask the question. You can do it on cross-examination but not on direct examination of your own witness. On direct examination a witness is supposed to tell facts he knows, without prompting from the lawyer as to what point the lawyer is trying to make.

With his objections, Kimball was putting Ken Simpson on notice that he would require him to adhere strictly to the rules—which would compel Ken to think about the rule each time he asked a question, diverting some of his attention from what he wanted to ask.

Of course, Ken withdrew the question. The jury had heard his point. He may have welcomed an objection, knowing I would sustain. That would only lay emphasis on the point he'd already gotten to the jury by the way he phrased the question.

Ken sat down again. "When we left the congressman and Miss Rheinlander, they were in the pool," he said. "How long did they remain there?"

"The better part of an hour," said Ogle.

"Then what happened?"

"Then Congressman Bailey told Miss Rheinlander he had work to do. She protested that he was a stick-in-the-mud, or words like that; but he left the pool and dressed, and we went into the office to work on his speech."

" 'We'?"

"The congressman, Don Finch, Miss Erb, and myself."

"How long did you work on the speech?"

"Until sometime between seven-thirty and eight. That speech was very important to the congressman."

"Then what happened?"

"We came out of the office. Mrs. Merritt had set up a bar and a big tray of hors d'oeuvres in the living room. Miss Rheinlander was already there, having a drink. We all gathered and shared drinks and snacks."

51

"What, if you can describe it from observed facts without drawing a conclusion, was the mood of the party?"

Kimball chuckled. "A good try, Your Honor, but let's allow Mr. Ogle to testify as to whatever he observed that might give the jury a chance to judge the mood of the party."

"Mr. Ogle," Ken interjected before I could get a word in, "tell us what you saw or overheard during the party."

I guess Ogle was primed for this question—anxious to address it. "We talked about Ross Perot," he said. "We talked about Governor Clinton. There was a good deal of laughing. Miss Rheinlander held the congressman by the arm all the while and whispered in his ear. I could not overhear what she said, but I did see Congressman Bailey frown and shake his head a couple of times. She became more emphatic. I mean her whispering became more shrill, more nearly audible. Even so, I could not overhear what she was saying. A little later he bent over her and whispered something to her. She grinned and nodded. The congressman reached around her back and squeezed her breast, and she laughed."

"How long did the cocktail party last?"

"I would guess about an hour and a half."

"What if anything did you observe about the congressman and Miss Rheinlander during that time?"

"There was a very definite tension between them."

"Objection. What facts did he observe that led to the conclusion there was tension?"

"Sustained. Please confine yourself to observed facts, Mr. Ogle."

"What facts did you observe that might have caused you to suspect there was tension?" asked Ken Simpson.

"They were brittle toward each other," said Ogle.

Kimball smiled and shook his head, but he let it go.

"What facts did you observe that lead you to use the word 'brittle'?" Ken asked.

"She told him to go to hell," said Ogle.

"Anything else?"

"He told her she was drinking too much."

"Anything else?"

"Not that I heard or saw."

"All right. What happened next?"

"Dinner was served. It was served on a table along the south wall of the living-dining room."

"Was served to whom?"

"Served only to Miss Erb, Don Finch, and myself. Mrs. Merritt carried the congressman's dinner and Miss Rheinlander's to their bedroom suite."

"How long were you at the dinner table?"

"That was probably another hour and a half."

"At what time did you finish dinner?"

"Shortly before eleven. We switched on the television to watch the eleven o'clock news."

"During the time you were at the table and during the time when you were watching the television news, did you hear voices from the bedroom shared by the congressman and Miss Rheinlander?"

"Yes, I did."

"Tell the jury what you heard."

"Well, the house is well built; the walls are thick. We couldn't hear exactly what was being said, but we heard angry voices."

"If the court please," said Kimball, rising for the first time. "Mr. Ogle says 'we' heard. Who is 'we' and what evidence do we have that anyone but Mr. Ogle heard anything?"

Ken Simpson shrugged. "Mr. Ogle," he said, "did Mr. Finch or Miss Erb indicate in any way that they heard the voices of the congressman and Miss Rheinlander?"

"Yes, they did. By facial expressions. By pointing. By shrugging."

"Tell the jury what you heard."

"We heard Miss Rheinlander's voice using the word 'bastard.' We heard the congressman's voice using the word 'bitch.' These words were used in the middle of angry yelling."

Ken flipped another sheet on his pad. He stood again, and this time he came around his table and stood in front of it, resting his backside on the table. He stared at his pad for a long moment, as if

53

he were collecting his thoughts. It was a forensic pause. He knew very well what he was going to ask next.

"When did you go to bed, Mr. Ogle?"

"A little before eleven-thirty. The news broadcast by then was dealing with sports and the local weather, and we weren't much interested in that."

"Did you and Mr. Finch and Miss Erb go to bed at the same time?"

"Don turned off the television set. He and Miss Erb went out through the sliding glass doors toward the pool and along the walk to the north wing. I went into the hallway and into my bedroom."

"Did you go to bed immediately?"

"I did. It had been a long day for me: the flight from Washington, the drive, the work on the speech, and so on. I was in the bathroom a few minutes, then went to bed."

"Did you go to sleep?"

"Yes. Within ten minutes, I would guess."

"What were you next aware of?"

"I heard a shot. I woke up instantly. But you know how it is when you are asleep. I couldn't be sure the shot was real or something from a dream. I remember I first had the impression someone had fired a shot at *me* and that I should hide before another shot was fired. Then I heard two more shots. I was awake then and knew it was real. I heard a scream. Someone was screaming."

"What did you do?"

"Well, I . . . I sleep in the nude, so I wasn't wearing anything at all. And I hadn't brought a robe. I got up and pulled on my trousers. I should explain that I was doing this before I heard the last shots. As soon as I had my pants on, I hurried out of my bedroom and back to the living room. I saw the three people on the floor."

Ogle's voice had become low and throaty. He nodded rhythmically and stared across the courtroom as if his eyes were not focused, rather as if they were focused on his memory.

Ken paused for a moment, then asked, "Did you see the defendant Marietta Rheinlander?"

"Yes, I did," Ogle said in a hoarse whisper. He cleared his throat and repeated, "Yes, I did. She was standing beside the sliding glass doors. She had a pistol in her right hand. She looked at me, and for a moment I thought she was going to shoot me."

"Tell us about the people on the floor."

"Congressman Bailey was lying in the little hallway that runs north and south across the lodge, not far from his bedroom door. Just outside the little hallway, at the point where the hall ends and the living room begins, Miss Erb lay on her back. Very close to her, but in the living room, lay Don Finch. At first I wasn't sure who they were."

"Were all of them dead?"

"I could see that Miss Erb was not," said Ogle. "The others—" He shook his head. "They didn't move."

The courtroom was dead silent. Everyone's eyes were fixed unmoving on the witness. Except Marietta Rheinlander's, and she stared at her hands clasped before her on the table. Her parents' eyes turned from Ogle to their daughter. They knew the details of the charge, but they had not heard testimony about it before.

"Do the letters on the chart fairly represent the position of the three people as you saw them?"

"Yes, they do."

"Does the *E* accurately represent the position of Miss Erb?"

"Yes, and the *F* and *B* show where the congressman and Don Finch were."

"What did you do then?"

"I ran across the room and dropped down beside Miss Erb, who was still alive."

"What did Miss Rheinlander do?"

Ogle drew a breath, then fixed a stare on the defendant. "She dropped the pistol on the floor and ran past the bodies and into the bedroom. She bumped me as she ran by."

"Did she say anything?"

"No."

"What happened then?"

"I took Miss Erb's hand and said to her I would call for help. About that time, Mrs. Merritt came in through the sliding glass doors. She took a quick look and ran back out. I was holding Miss Erb's right hand, and she raised her left and pointed toward where Miss Rheinlander had been standing."

"Did Miss Erb speak?"

"No. She never spoke. She was dying. I got up and went to the telephone. I tried dialing 911, but that doesn't work in rural Alexandria County, and an operator came on the line. I told her I had a terrible emergency, and she rang the sheriff's office. The man who came on the line told me he'd already had a call about shots fired at Congressman Bailey's lodge. I told him three people had been shot, and he said he'd send an ambulance."

"Then what happened?"

"Mrs. Merritt returned. Her husband was with her. He was carrying a shotgun. They told me later they supposed I had killed those people. We stood there trying to sort things out, and suddenly we heard the shriek of tires. I ran to the front door and looked out just in time to see a car speed by. I didn't recognize the car. I didn't know who was in it. I was told later it was a car Miss Rheinlander had rented."

His last sentence was hearsay, to which Kimball could have objected; but Kimball wisely thought it better at this point not to interrupt a dramatic statement. It was better, tactically, to let the statement go on and not interrupt it with nit-picking over technicalities in the law of evidence.

"When did you next see Miss Rheinlander?"

"When a deputy brought her back to the lodge."

"Please identify the person you have referred to in your testimony as Marietta Rheinlander. Is she present in the courtroom?"

"She is," said David Ogle soberly. "That is she, sitting there."

"Thank you, Mr. Ogle," said Ken Simpson.

"The court will recess for fifteen minutes," I said.

Again, the procedures in a small-town courtroom in rural Ohio had startled Lloyd George Kimball. He had expected the testimony of the state's chief witness to take the entire day—at least the entire morning. He had a computer system at work. The transcript of each witness's testimony was put in the computer and arranged by a program called Folio Views so he could recover from computer memory at any time exactly what any witness had said on any subject. It was a technological marvel, but it could not be used until the testimony was transcribed from the reporter's stenotype tapes or from the audio taping system Kimball had attached to our courtroom sound system. He was now faced with the necessity of cross-examining David Ogle without the assistance of this computer.

He knew there was no point in asking me to recess until he could get the Ogle testimony into his computer. He was going to have to go at it with his own brains, without the help of his electronic brain.

4

"Hey, Bill. Got your tickets for the ox roast here."

Bob Millken stopped me as I came out of my office on the way to the courtroom. He was the secretary of the local Masonic Lodge, which was sponsoring its annual ox roast on the following Saturday. He handed me two ten-dollar tickets.

"Gotta get in the men's room before I open court again," I said to Bob. "C'mon in there, and I'll give you the money."

Bob was retired. He had owned and operated a jewelry store in Alexandria for more than forty years. The great thing in his life, though, was the Masonic Lodge, to which he had devoted much of his life. Besides being a Past Master of Alexandria Lodge, he was a Knight of the York Cross of Honor—meaning he had made his way through all the subordinate offices and had been elected presiding officer of every York Rite Masonic body, including Knights Templars. He was also a 32° Mason in the Scottish Rite and besides that had three times served as Worthy Patron of the Order of the Eastern Star. He had rarely had a free evening for the past thirty years.

He happily handed over my tickets and accepted my twenty dollars. Buying your ox-roast tickets was something you did annually in Alexandria, if you were a professional of any kind or if you held a political office. Also, you would *go* to the ox roast. Even a good many Catholics would be there, as Bob Millken would buy his tickets and be present for the annual spaghetti dinner of the Knights of Columbus.

I have never confided this to more than a few people before, but of the two affairs I have always been partial to the K. of C. dinner. With their fine spaghetti and meatballs, they serve red wine from jugs—while the Masons' parties are always dry. I am a

Mason, of course, 32°, but I do enjoy a drop of wine with my beef or pasta.

Immediately on returning to the courtroom, I noticed something that troubled me. Marietta Rheinlander was upset. Her face was flushed and gleamed with perspiration. I guessed why. I guessed that Lloyd George Kimball had been unable to cloak his discomposure during the recess and had probably complained within her hearing that the trial was moving too fast.

That he had been deprived of an entire evening in which to review the testimony of David Ogle was undoubtedly a disadvantage to him. But he should have been prepared for it, because Bob Mitchell, his local co-counsel, had undoubtedly briefed him on how a trial would proceed in Alexandria County, Ohio.

I noticed something else. David Ogle, now back on the witness stand, sat with his legs crossed, the picture of serene self-confidence. I hoped the jury reacted to that as I did: that having this woman's life in our hands in this trial was no time for chutzpah. (Oh yes, we know these words in Ohio. I'm no schlemiel.) I was beginning to dislike this young man. I'm a judge, not a juror, and I can dislike a witness if I want to.

Lloyd George Kimball did not rise but sat at the defense table and addressed the witness. "Mr. Ogle, let's get something straight from the outset. You did not see Marietta Rheinlander shoot anyone. Isn't that right?"

"I saw her standing with a gun in her hand and—"

"That's not what I asked you," Kimball interrupted curtly. "This shouldn't be so difficult, Mr. Ogle. You've already testified to it. You did not see the defendant shoot anyone. Isn't that right? I believe I am not imposing on you if I ask you to answer yes or no."

Ogle drew a breath, hesitated for a moment, and said, "No."

"No. That's right. No. Furthermore, you did not see her discharge the revolver at all. Isn't that right?"

"That's right."

"That's a rather important point, isn't it?"

"Objection," snapped Ken Simpson. "Whether or not the witness thinks it's important is irrelevant."

Kimball nodded and spoke before I could rule. "I withdraw the question, Your Honor. Mr. Simpson is entirely right. What the witness *thinks* of the importance of the fact that he saw no shots fired is really not relevant."

I hope Ken Simpson realized he had fallen into a little trap. The little drama of objection and withdrawal of the question gave Kimball the chance to repeat that this was an important point. Also, the little drama fixed the point more firmly in the minds of at least some of the jurors. Jurors *will* believe that if something is objected to it must be important.

"Now, Mr. Ogle, Congressman Bailey did not speak to you when you arrived in the living-dining room and found him lying on the floor. Is that not correct?"

"I think he was dead, or nearly so."

"Yes. He did not, therefore, speak to you and tell you Miss Rheinlander had shot him. Nor did he point to her. Isn't that correct?"

Ogle had begun to understand what this cross-examination was going to amount to, and his self-confidence had already begun to fade. "That is correct," he said, and he would have been a more effective witness if he had not spoken sullenly.

"Did Donald Finch speak to you or point to Miss Rheinlander?"

"No."

"On the other hand, you testified that Miss Erb raised her hand and pointed. Did you not?"

"I did."

"And you said she pointed at where Miss Rheinlander had been standing."

"Yes."

"Mr. Ogle, I am going to ask you to look once again at the excellent floor plan of the Bailey property that was prepared by the prosecution. And—unless of course Mr. Simpson objects to your making a mark on his chart—I will ask you to take this marker pen and make an *X* at the point where Miss Rheinlander was standing when you entered the living-dining room."

Ogle stepped down from the witness stand and marked the chart:

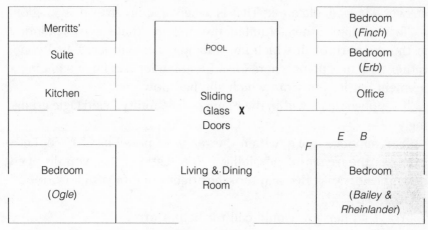

NORTH ————>

"Thank you, sir," said Kimball. "Now, how many feet was it from where you have placed your *X* to the point where Donald Finch lay?"

"Uh . . . about five feet, maybe six."

"From your *X* to Miss Erb?"

"Ten or twelve feet."

"To the congressman?"

"Twelve or fifteen feet."

"Now. At the time when Miss Erb lifted her hand and feebly pointed, where was Miss Rheinlander?"

"In the bedroom. She had run into the bedroom."

"Miss Erb did not point in the direction of the bedroom, did she? You so testified."

Ogle raised his chin and stared at the chart. "No."

"She pointed at the sliding glass doors, did she not?"

Ogle nodded. "Yes."

I should maybe explain that all these, "Isn't that correct?"s and "Didn't she?"s and "Did you not?"s are blatant examples of what is called leading the witness, to which Kimball had strenuously objected when Ken was questioning Ogle on direct examination. Ken did not object. The reason is that the law prohibits leading a witness on direct examination but allows it on cross. Questions so phrased suggest the answer—indeed, dictate it. That is acceptable on cross-examination.

"Is it not likely, then," Kimball pressed on, "that she was pointing at the doors through which her attacker, her murderer, had gone, rather than at a point where Miss Rheinlander had been standing a moment earlier but from which she had now fled?"

"I suppose that's within the realm of possibility," said Ogle grudgingly.

"You suppose that's 'within the realm of possibility.' I see. Let's examine the 'realm of possibility.' You testified that you dropped down beside Miss Erb and took her right hand in yours. Correct?"

"Correct."

"You told her you would call for help. Correct?"

"Correct."

"And you testified that at that moment someone entered the room through the sliding glass doors. Who was that, once more?"

"Mrs. Merritt."

"Mrs. Dorothy Merritt, the housekeeper," said Kimball. "You testified that Mrs. Merritt took one look and then ran. Is that not correct?"

"Yes."

"Now, Mr. Ogle, let's get our time sequence straight. You heard shots. You dressed and ran from your bedroom into the living-dining room. You saw three people lying on the floor and Miss Rheinlander standing with a pistol in her hand. Miss Rheinlander dropped the pistol and ran into the bedroom she had shared with Congressman Bailey. You knelt over Miss Erb and took her hand. At this point, Mrs. Merritt appeared at the sliding glass doors. You testified that Mrs. Merritt *came in* through the sliding glass doors. Were those doors open?"

"Yes, they were open."

"So Mrs. Merritt stepped inside. But immediately she turned and ran. Correct?"

"Correct."

"And then, only then, Miss Erb raised her left hand and pointed toward the sliding glass doors. Isn't that the sequence of events?"

Ogle paused for a long moment. "Yes . . . that is the sequence of events."

"Is it not then possible that Miss Erb, who might have been pointing just at the doors, to show you where the murderer had gone, might also possibly have been pointing toward the fleeing Mrs. Merritt?"

"Are you suggesting Mrs. Merritt killed those people?" asked Ogle, raising his voice.

"No, are you?"

Ogle flushed. "No, of course not."

"Maybe Miss Erb was pointing at Mrs. Merritt, trying to say, 'There's a woman who can help me. *She* knows how to call the sheriff.' Is that not possible?"

Ogle shrugged. "Many things are possible."

"Or—though of course we sincerely doubt it—maybe she was pointing at Mrs. Merritt to accuse her. Or maybe she didn't at that point recognize Mrs. Merritt but was just calling your attention to someone who had appeared in the door through which she had seen the murderer flee."

"You can make up any story you want, Mr. Kimball," said Ogle.

"As can you, Mr. Ogle," said Kimball. "As can you."

Ogle had allowed his temper to boil and had made a serious mistake.

Lloyd George Kimball was a smart lawyer. He had made his point, Ogle had strongly reinforced it with his sarcasm, and Kimball glanced at his watch and at the courtroom clock and said, "Your Honor, may I suggest we take the lunch break now? I've come to a logical break point in my cross-examination. If I went on for another ten or fifteen minutes, we'd have to break at an awkward point."

I accepted his suggestion, and we broke until one o'clock.

*   *   *

By mid-October it is usually not yet cold in the Ohio Valley. But it is damp. Often the river water is warmer than the air, and shrouds of fog hang over the green river and the still-green valley, settling down early in the morning as a heavy dew. Then the trees drip, and the falling leaves are wet and heavy and impossible to rake until they dry. Alexandria is a transplanted New England town, populated originally by families from Connecticut and Massachusetts because Revolutionary War veterans had been given land grants in the "Ohio country" in lieu of the accumulated pay that was owed them. The town never looks so New Englandish as it does on autumn mornings when the leaves are falling through a wet fog.

I wore my raincoat and a gray tweed hat as I walked from the courthouse to the Alexandria House for lunch. As I passed the doors of the First National Bank Building, Dick Winter happened to be coming out, and he fell in step beside me. He had been in the courtroom for half an hour or so and had watched some of the cross-examination. He had a comment—

"Ken Simpson's outclassed, between you and me. He's got an awful problem. That man Kimball is one hell of a lawyer."

Dick Winter ought to know. He is our town's most successful trial lawyer. He's made his son a partner, and they practice as Winter & Winter. Dick is no taller than I am—and you remember I am only five feet seven. He is four years older than I am and about twenty pounds heavier, which makes him rotund. He is also bald. He has dark brown eyes and a ready smile; and he is a shrewd and convincing advocate, effective even before juries who are inclined to believe that a client who has hired the town's most expensive trial lawyer must surely be in the wrong. He wears a champagne-colored Stetson and somehow manages not to look ridiculous in it, and as he walked along with me he was wearing a raincoat just like mine.

"I feel sorry for Ken. I know he wants to do well in this case."

What Dick was saying, I think, was that Ken Simpson should have asked him to help him. If he had, Dick would have conducted the prosecution. That is why Ken didn't ask him.

"I feel sorry for the woman, too," Dick went on. "Imagine being what *she* is and being locked up in our county jail all this time."

"I can think of a reason for feeling even sorrier for her," I said.

"Oh, yeah? What you have in mind?"

"Off the record, Dick," I said. "Like you said, imagine being what she is: rich, educated, sophisticated . . . with what Bush and Quayle persist in calling different values. Imagine being Marietta Rheinlander and knowing you are going to be judged by a retired geometry teacher, the wife of a small-town superintendent of schools, a couple of housewives, a farmer, a waitress, and so on. Good, honest people, all of them, but they're as different from her as twelve Patagonians."

Dick chuckled. "So's her judge."

"Yes, and it must terrify her."

"You think she feels she's better than we are?"

"Probably. Wouldn't *you* if you were Marietta Rheinlander? And she's got to be worried that that's the impression she gives. How's she gonna talk to us? How's she gonna make herself come across as just folks? She can't, any more than one of us could circulate in a Park Avenue cocktail party without looking like a plowhorse among the racehorses."

"Do you think's she's gonna take the stand and testify?"

I shrugged. "Good question."

"Anyway, you think any of those jurors will hold it against her that she's the rich and famous Marietta Rheinlander?"

"No, I don't think so. What I'm saying is that *she* must wonder about it."

Dick laughed. "'You shall well and truly try and true deliverance make between the state of Ohio and the defendant Marietta Rheinlander. So help you God.'"

In the Alexandria House dining room at noon, three tables are pushed together to make one long table, and always six or eight of the town's lawyers and assorted businessmen sit down together for a drink and lunch. It's not a club. Anyone can sit down . . . Well, not anyone, come to think of it. But any one of a group of maybe twenty or twenty-five men. It's nice, because you know you will always find someone there to have lunch with. If you have brought along a client and need to talk business, you sit somewhere else. If you've brought your wife, you sit at another table. There are no rules. It's just an understanding.

Dick Winter and I sat down. Dick ordered a beer. When I am trying a case, I do not have a drink at lunch.

No such scruple troubled Glen Myers. He had a martini before him and would probably have two more before he ate his lunch—which would have no discernible influence on him. Only we who sat with him at this table and watched him drink them would know how much he'd had to drink. Back in his office in the afternoon, or even in the courtroom if he came there to try a case, he would be just as incisive as if he had drunk nothing but ice water.

Glenwood is his name, actually. Glenwood Brittigan Myers. He is in his late forties, and in some ways he is the best lawyer in town. He specializes in things like arranging imaginative financing for new businesses. If you want to start a business and don't have enough credit, you go to Myers. He also does a lot of tax work and a lot of probate. He's a somewhat unusual lawyer for a small town. He won't, for example, handle a divorce. He won't defend a criminal case. Many of us think he'd make more money if he practiced more kinds of law. But maybe not. Lawyers in other small towns refer clients to him, when they face problems that come within his specialties.

Glen is a small fellow: short, slight, prematurely gray, and nearly bald. He wears none but dark blue three-button suits with narrow lapels. He wears white shirts and dark-blue-white-polka-dot bow ties that he ties himself, no clip-on ties, ever.

Pete Varner was there, and Dick Winter asked him, "Say, Pete, how do you like that Lexus by now?"

"Finest car I ever drove," said Pete.

"Lot of money, wasn't it?"

"Well, I decided to indulge myself. You ought to look at one. You might decide not to drive those Cadillacs anymore."

Dick grinned. "I have clients that *expect* me to drive a Cadillac, wouldn't think they had as good a lawyer if I drove anything else."

"Or wore a different hat," I said, which drew a general laugh around the table.

Glen was sitting at my left, and he said quietly to me, "I had a very nice note from Marietta Rheinlander. I don't think I told you before."

"No, you didn't. What'd she have to say?"

"She thanked me for the books I sent to her. Said they were a comfort to her."

"What'd you send her, Glen? A Bible?" asked Pete Varner.

Glen is capable of dropping the most disdainful glances. To anyone not used to Glen, they are withering. He dropped one now, on Pete, who was not abashed or offended. "I sent her the new Boorstin book, *The Creators*, and the McCullough biography of Harry Truman," he said.

"Those are expensive books," said one of the men at the far end of the table. "You must—"

"Well, of course, I *lent* them to her," said Glen. "Her thank-you note was in the Boorstin when I picked the books up at the sheriff's office. It was written on the back of a little watercolor she'd done."

"What did she paint?" I asked.

"The view from her cell," he said. "Through the bars. The painted brick wall, the radiator, then the window, with the trees showing outside."

"Talent?" Dick asked.

"If I'm any judge, which I'm not. You know . . . all gray, cell bars, wall, window bars—but then the green of the trees and some blue sky. That little painting is damned touching, if you want to know the truth."

"You've sent her more books, I understand," I said to him.

"Yes. Fat books. Long reads. She spends a lot of long, boring hours in that cell."

"You'd like to see her acquitted, I suppose," said Dick.

"Absolutely," said Glen. "Even if she did kill him. I never met her, but I did know Bailey, rather well, in fact."

"Before you prejudice the judge, I'm going to change the subject," said Dick Winter. "Has anybody got this damned Perot figured out?"

Miss Rheinlander's hands were still chained to her waist when I entered the jury room to don my robe. She stood at the window, looking out at the falling leaves. Margaret Vogt stood beside her. She was taller than Margaret and of course taller than I am.

"I had lunch with Glen Myers," I told her. "He says you are a talented watercolorist."

She turned toward me and smiled. "I'm not," she said. "It kills time." Her hands hung slack in the cuffs, her fingers loosely interlaced. She spoke affably, showing no sign I could see that she felt abashed. "Mr. Myers has been very kind. Learning that I'd read everything I had available, he's been sending me books."

"He's having your painting framed. He's going to bring it to me to see."

"I've done several of the same little scene," she said. "At different times of day, with different light. That's the best one, I think."

The defense lawyers came in through the door from the courtroom, and Margaret unlocked the handcuffs and pulled the chain from around Miss Rheinlander's waist.

"A prominent local lawyer complimented your cross-examination this morning," I said to Kimball.

"Really. I hope when the trial is over Your Honor will be able to compliment it."

"Let's hope the jury likes it," said Bob Mitchell.

"Mr. Ogle, when you observed the bodies of Mr. Finch and Miss Erb lying on the floor of the living-dining room, how was the room lighted?"

"Uh . . . reasonably well lighted. We'd left a lamp on."

"You testified that at first you didn't know who the three bodies were. Was that because the light on them was not sufficient?"

"It was because I couldn't believe those three people were dead."

"No, Mr. Ogle. You testified you didn't know at first who they were. It was too dark to tell at first, right?"

"I ran to them. I saw who they were pretty quick."

"But not at first. All right. How were they dressed?"

"Don Finch was wearing a light blue terry-cloth bathrobe. His feet and legs were bare. I understand he was wearing nothing under the robe. Miss Erb was wearing a white cotton nightgown with little pink flowers on it."

"And Congressman Bailey?"

"He was wearing a sort of bed jacket: Japanese type of thing. It was black, with a Japanese character in a white circle on the back. Silk, I think. Frankly it didn't cover him. He was exposed."

"And what was Miss Rheinlander wearing?"

"A pair of panties."

"What color?"

"White. Bikini style."

"Now, Mr. Ogle, the reporter has been kind enough during the lunch break to go back with me and locate a bit of your testimony from this morning. I am going to ask her to read it to you."

The court reporter is Alice Tutweiler. She is the only stenotype-trained person in the county, and she takes all the depositions, makes all the transcripts. She had marked the place on her stenotype tape, and she seated her half-glasses on her nose and read:

Question, Mr. Simpson: Did you go to sleep?

Answer, Mr. Ogle: Yes. Within ten minutes, I would guess.

Question, Mr. Simpson: What were you next aware of?

Answer, Mr. Ogle: I heard a shot. I woke up instantly, but you know how it is when you are asleep, I couldn't be sure the shot was real or something from a dream. I remember I first had the impression someone had fired a shot at me and that I should hide before another

69

shot was fired. Then I heard two more shots. I was awake then and knew it was real. I heard a scream. Someone was screaming.

"Thank you very much, Mrs. Tutweiler," said Kimball. "Now, Mr. Ogle, you testified, 'I heard a shot . . . then I heard two more shots.' It is your testimony that you heard three shots. Do you know how many shots were actually fired from that revolver?"

"Yes. I was told. But if I testify to that, it will be hearsay, won't it?"

"Yes, it will be. But suppose you let Mr. Simpson and me worry about that. We will have plenty of evidence later as to how many shots were fired. Mr. Simpson, do you want to object?"

"No," said Ken. As Kimball had said, there was plenty of evidence as to how many shots were fired, and Ogle's testimony on the point was not crucial.

"How many, Mr. Ogle?"

"Six."

"Correct. But you heard three. Have you any explanation as to why you heard only three of the six?"

"I can only assume it was because I was sound asleep."

"You'd had a few drinks in the hours before you went to bed."

"Yes."

"So three shots were fired before you woke up?"

"I suppose so."

"You suppose so? It's a fact, isn't it?"

"Yes."

"Do you know how many bullets struck each of the victims?"

"I was told that one struck each of them."

"Your testimony is that you heard one shot, which woke you, and then you heard two more. Let's talk about the two more. How much time elapsed between those last two shots?"

"I don't know, exactly."

"Of course not, exactly. But your best guess. Mr. and Mrs. Merritt will testify as to their recollection on that point. What is your best guess?"

"A second. Maybe two."

"Maybe even less?"

"I don't know."

"In rapid succession, in any event?"

"I suppose you could call it that."

"How much time elapsed between the first shot you heard and the last two?"

"A little more. Maybe the two seconds."

"In other words, the final three shots were fired within a maximum of four seconds?"

"I guess so."

I saw what he was driving at. Each victim was killed with one shot. If all three shots were fired within four seconds—each one a fatal shot, striking a vital organ—it was a remarkable feat of marksmanship. It assumed, among other things, that all three stood stark still and allowed themselves to be targets. As Kimball well knew, evidence we would hear later showed that Elizabeth Erb was shot in the back, suggesting that she was trying to flee.

Kimball went on. "Mr. Ogle, how long after you heard the first shot was it before you came out of your bedroom and witnessed the grisly scene?"

"I don't know."

"Well, let's see. You testified that you were nude and had to pull on your pants before you could run out and see what was going on. How long would that take? Ten seconds? Fifteen?"

"More like ten, I suppose."

"All right. Let us conjecture that Congressman Bailey was shot first. Hearing that shot, you jumped out of bed and pulled on your pants. Maybe Mr. Finch jumped out of bed and pulled on his robe, because he heard the same shot. And Miss Erb, already dressed in her nightgown, jumped out of bed and ran to the living-dining room. But none of them could have reached there within four seconds, could they, Mr. Ogle?"

"I have to object," said Ken Simpson. "That's a lot of conjecture. The question is argument."

I ruled. "Mr. Kimball, I think you can state your question better than that."

Kimball smiled smoothly and nodded. "Mr. Ogle, you have testified that the maximum time between the first shot you heard and the last was four seconds. Could Miss Erb or Mr. Finch have jumped out of bed, opened their bedroom doors, and run along the swimming pool and through the sliding glass doors into the living-dining room in four seconds?"

"I have no idea, Mr. Kimball."

"Very well. Thank you, Mr. Ogle. We'll go on to something else."

Ogle was being stupid. One of Kimball's points was to make him out an uncooperative and hostile witness. The answer to the question was obvious: they could not have jumped out of bed and run into the living room in four seconds. Ogle should have answered no.

Lloyd George Kimball got up and stood in front of the defense table, leaning back against it. "You testified that Congressman Bailey was 'exposed' by his black Japanese-type night jacket. Didn't you?"

"Yes," said Ogle.

"By that do you mean his genitals were exposed?"

"Yes."

"And his buttocks?"

"Yes."

"Was this jacket closed or open?"

"Closed."

"How?"

"It was tied with a loose silk belt."

"Why, do you suppose, Congressman Bailey was in the living-dining room dressed in a bed jacket that didn't reach down far enough to cover his private parts?"

Ogle shrugged. "My idea was that she threatened him with a pistol, so he ran out of the bedroom."

"Taking time to pull on a bed jacket and knot the belt?"

"Maybe he had it on in the bedroom."

"Why would he be wearing something that covered his shoulders and chest but not his bottom?"

Ogle shook his head. "I really don't know, Mr. Kimball."

This was not the best cross-examination I ever heard. I don't know what Kimball thought he might elicit, but whatever it was, he didn't get it. On the other hand, who knows what a juror may think? What the prosecution hoped would be seen as a straightforward case of triple murder could be confused by questions like this.

"Who served dinner, Mr. Ogle? Was it Mrs. Merritt?"

"Yes, Mrs. Merritt."

"And she served dinner to the congressman and Miss Rheinlander in their bedroom?"

"Yes."

"You testified that during the cocktail hour the congressman told Miss Rheinlander she was drinking too much. Except for Mr. Finch and Miss Erb, who can't testify, did anyone else hear that?"

"No, I suppose not."

"You testified that she told him to go to hell. Can anyone besides you testify to that?"

"No."

"You testified that you heard angry yelling in the bedroom. Can anyone but you testify to that?"

"I don't suppose so. But I know what I heard."

"Did Mrs. Merritt or anyone else go to the bedroom to collect the dirty dishes?"

"Not to my knowledge."

"At the time when you retired to your room, the congressman and Miss Rheinlander had been alone in their bedroom for an hour and a half. Right?"

"Right."

"They did not come out?"

"No."

* * *

Lloyd George Kimball sat down again behind the defense table.
"How long did you know Congressman Bailey?"

"Nineteen years. I met him in 1973."

"How old was the congressman at the time of his death?"

"He was forty-eight."

"Can you briefly outline his *curriculum vitae*?"

"He graduated from Yale in 1965, then from the law school at the
University of West Virginia in 1969. He was from Huntington and
went back there to practice law. He was elected to Congress in
1984."

"Did he ever serve in the armed forces?"

"Yes. He was a member of the West Virginia national guard from
1969 until 1975."

"In what capacity did he serve in the national guard, do you
know?"

"He was a staff aide to the West Virginia adjutant general, with
the rank of first lieutenant."

"Now, Mr. Ogle," said Kimball. "Congressman Bailey joined the
firm of—" He put on his half-glasses and peered at his note. "—
Wilcoxen, Branch & Bailey in 1969. Was the firm then just Wilcoxen &
Branch?"

"Yes."

"And when you came along it was already Wilcoxen, Branch &
Bailey. How long after young Mr. Bailey joined it was his name added
to the firm?"

"I believe within the first year," said Ogle.

"With his name on the firm, I suppose Mr. Bailey was a partner."
"Isn't that unusual, for a young man to come to a firm directly out
of law school and be made immediately a partner?"

"Mr. Kimball, Huntington is a town of some sixty-five thousand
people. We do things a little differently from what you are accustomed to in New York."

"I see," said Kimball, gazing at Ogle over the tops of his reading glasses. "I believe you said you were with the firm for eleven years, until you went to Washington with Congressman Bailey. Did *you* make partner?"

"Yes, sir."

"When?"

"In 1978."

"After five years. Did other young lawyers join the firm, and did *they* make partner, and how long did it take?"

"If Your Honor please," said Ken Simpson, rising to his feet. "I object on the grounds of relevancy."

"Mr. Kimball," I asked, "is this line of question leading somewhere? If so, when will you reach your point?"

"Very quickly, Your Honor," said Kimball. "And I do have a point."

"Let's try to be a little more brisk about it, sir," I said. "You may answer, Mr. Ogle."

"Two others joined and were made partners after about five years."

"So why did Mr. Bailey make it so much sooner?"

"For the obvious reasons," said Ogle.

Another mistake by the witness. Again, Kimball had a secondary purpose in this cross-examination: to show that David Ogle, the chief witness for the prosecution, was hostile to the defense. If Ogle wanted to see Marietta Rheinlander convicted, he should have been a bland witness, just testifying to the facts as he had seen them. Even if he bested Lloyd George Kimball in some game of wit, it would only hurt his credibility.

Kimball took every advantage. "Yes, Mr. Ogle. It is obvious to you and me. But the members of the jury may not be as familiar as we are of the means and standards by which young lawyers rise to the rank of partners in law firms. Why don't you just explain why Mr. Bailey was promoted to partner in his first year and others took five years."

Ogle glanced around the courtroom with a fixed little smile that suggested, whether that was what he meant to suggest or not, that he doubted anyone was so naive as not to understand so elementary

75

a point. "The Bailey family are prominent people in West Virginia," he said. "With extensive connections. Well thought of. Prosperous. They were in a position to direct business toward the firm, and they did."

"Was Congressman Bailey wealthy?" asked Kimball.

"I would say he was prosperous . . . well off," said Ogle. "He had family money, and he made money as a lawyer for fifteen years before he went to Congress."

Lloyd George Kimball leaned back in his chair and clasped his hands behind his head. "Congressman Bailey never married, did he?"

"No."

"But he . . . let's use the old-fashioned term 'dated' a number of women over the years, did he not?"

"Yes."

"In the nineteen years that you knew the congressman was there ever a time when he was not dating a woman?"

"No, I don't think so. He was always seeing someone."

"Is it not true, Mr. Ogle, that the women he dated were almost always prominent? I mean, they were women whose names got in the newspapers from time to time. In Huntington, the leaders of charity drives, or the daughters of leaders of charity drives, or women prominent in country-club circles, and so on. Am I right?"

"Relevance, Your Honor?" grumbled Ken Simpson.

"Continue, Mr. Kimball," I said. "But let's get to it."

Kimball continued as if he hadn't heard either one of us. "Am I right, Mr. Ogle?"

"I believe most of the women he dated were . . . prominent."

"And the same in Washington, only on a somewhat larger stage?"

"I suppose you could say that, too."

"Is it not true, Mr. Ogle, that one could make several voluminous scrapbooks of the newspaper mentions of Congressman Bailey's relationships with newsworthy women?"

"I wouldn't know."

"Well, Mr. Ogle, we ran a check on a computerized news-story retrieval service called NEXIS. In the past eight years, The Washington *Post* alone mentioned Congressman Bailey in more than a hundred fifty news stories in which he was described as squiring this woman and that to various social events."

David Ogle shrugged.

"You don't deny that?"

"I neither confirm nor deny it. I don't know."

"Did the congressman ever tell you he had sexual relationships with any of those women?"

"Yes. He said he did. With several of them. Most of them, I suppose."

Kimball spoke to me. "I won't belabor the point further for the present, Your Honor. We may have to return to it." He spoke to the witness. "When did Congressman Bailey acquire the lodge where he died?"

"I believe it was in 1986," said Ogle.

"How many times have you been there, Mr. Ogle?"

"I don't know. I never counted."

"Well . . . Twice? Twenty times? Two hundred times?"

Ogle considered for a moment. "I would say more than fifty times."

"Why did the congressman buy and maintain the lodge?"

"For privacy. It was a place where he could get away, be with friends, relax."

"Did he ever go there alone? If you know."

"Yes. Sometimes."

"Were there times when you and he went together, with no one else?"

"I . . . guess there were occasions, yes."

"Did Congressman Bailey often take the women he was dating to the lodge?"

"No. Usually he didn't."

"To your knowledge and recollection, did he ever take any woman other than Marietta Rheinlander to the lodge as his date?"

Ogle shook his head. "I don't remember."

"Does that mean you don't remember if he did or not, or that you don't remember he ever did?"

"I'm not sure."

"Well, of course, the Merritts can probably help us out with this point. I was just wondering what you could contribute. Can you remember an instance when the congressman brought a woman to the lodge as his date—except of course Miss Rheinlander?"

Ogle shook his head. "No."

"How about you? Did you ever bring a woman friend with you to the lodge?"

"No."

"Incidentally, you are not married, are you?"

"No, I'm not."

"Have you ever been married?"

"No."

"What about Donald Finch? Was he married?"

"No."

"Did Congressman Bailey tell you he was engaged to marry Miss Marietta Rheinlander?"

"He most assuredly did not!"

"Thank you, Mr. Ogle. That will be all."

5

I think Lloyd George Kimball was astonished at having finished his cross-examination of the state's chief witness by mid-afternoon of the second day of the trial. He may have been surprised, too, that Ken Simpson did not open a redirect. We were finished with the state's chief witness.

If Kimball was surprised, many of us were mystified. We could not believe Kimball would pursue any course of questions without purpose, but we could not imagine what he had been driving at during the last half hour of his cross-examination. I myself had, in fact, begun to develop a dark suspicion. I kept the idea to myself, even when Linda asked me that evening what Kimball had been driving at.

At the desk in the clerk's office, where I stood during the recess reviewing two motions filed by attorneys in civil cases pending before my court, Pete Varner came up to me. He had sat in the courtroom most of the afternoon, on one of the chairs inside the bar of the court where as a lawyer he was entitled to sit. "What the hell was all that about?" he asked.

"Damn 'f I know. Big-city lawyer making his case."

I was not entirely truthful.

Ken Simpson called his next witness, Mrs. Dorothy Merritt, housekeeper at the Bailey lodge.

Mrs. Merritt was a solid, muscular woman in her early sixties: the archetypal housekeeper and cook for a country establishment. She was dressed in clothes she had obviously purchased for her appearance as a witness: a gray tweed jacket and matching slacks, a pleated white blouse. She testified that Congressman Bailey had acquired the property in 1985 and had substantially remodeled it. She and her husband had lived there six years before, under the former owner, and they had admired the way the congressman had renewed it and brought new life to it. She and her husband had been fascinated by the way Congressman Bailey brought prominent people to the lodge. They had asked for some autographs.

Knowing that Mrs. Merritt was just a little hard of hearing, Ken moved to a point on the floor halfway between his table and the witness stand. "Mrs. Merritt, we now have to talk about the events of the first full week of May. When did you first learn that the lodge was to be opened to receive guests that week?"

"Mr. Donald Finch called from Washington to say the congressman would be coming out on the weekend. He also said that Miss Rheinlander would be coming earlier and would stay in the lodge most of the week."

"When did Miss Rheinlander in fact arrive?"

"It was on Tuesday. Tuesday afternoon."

"How did she arrive?"

"In a car she said she'd rented."

"What kind of car was it, if you recall?"

"An Oldsmobile Cutlass. Bright red."

"When did Congressman Bailey arrive?"

"That was Saturday morning."

"What did Miss Rheinlander do from Tuesday till Saturday?"

"Nothing much, that I could see. She wasn't around much. I guess she had dinner at the lodge on Thursday night. Just one night. Never there for lunch. Had coffee in the morning. Drove off in the morning and came back at night."

"Was this the first time that Miss Rheinlander had been a guest at the Bailey lodge?"

"No, she'd been there several times before."

"Mrs. Merritt, I don't want to ask an embarrassing question, but do you know what the sleeping arrangements were when the congressman and Miss Rheinlander stayed at the lodge at the same time?"

Mrs. Merritt frowned at Ken, then smiled. "Nothin' embarrassing about it," she said. "They were grown-up people, and they slept together."

"And did they share a bedroom on Saturday night?"

"Yes."

"Describe the events of that evening, prior to the time when you heard shots."

"It was the usual thing. I was always expected to lay out a tray of hors d'oeuvres, plenty for whatever number of guests we had, plus have the bar stocked with plenty to drink. When there were lots of guests, we set up a buffet then. But that night it was dinner at the table."

"Did the congressman and Miss Rheinlander sit down at that table?"

"No. I wheeled a serving cart into their bedroom. They had dinner alone in there."

"What happened after you served dinner?"

"I sat down to my own dinner, with my husband, in our rooms. About eleven I went back to the living room to see if the folks had finished. They'd moved over and were watching the TV news. I carried a tray of dishes to the kitchen. Then I came back and got another tray. I ran some garbage down the disposal and loaded the dishwasher. I'd saved some coffee in a carafe, and I took that and some cookies in our rooms and sat down with my husband. We checked *Saturday Night Live* and didn't much care for what they were doing, so we started watching a movie. After a while we heard the shots."

"At what time was that, Mrs. Merritt?"

"It was pretty close to twelve o'clock, give or take a few minutes one way or the other."

"How many shots did you hear?"

"Six. I think it was six. I didn't count. Lots of 'em."

"Were the shots all together, or in groups?"

"In groups. I heard some shots. Three, probably. Then there was . . . what you'd call a pause. Then some more."

"How much time elapsed between the first and third shots, as best you can recall?"

"I don't know. They were bang, bang, bang. Pretty quick, maybe a second or so between."

"How long was the pause?"

"A lot more time. Maybe fifteen seconds. Then bang, bang, bang again, quicker than the first three."

"Did you hear anyone shout or scream?"

"Yes. In the pause time. Then while the last shots were being fired."

"What did you do?"

"I grabbed for the telephone and called the sheriff. My husband, he ran in the bedroom to get our shotgun. I told the sheriff's office what we'd heard; then I went out and walked along between the house and the pool. The doors were open, and I could see Mr. Ogle on his knees beside a person stretched out on the floor. I was scared. It looked like *he'd* shot somebody. I ran back to our rooms. By that time my husband was halfway across the pool deck, with the shotgun. I told him to be sure it was loaded, 'cause somebody had killed somebody. He said he had it loaded, both barrels, so we started kind of edging back toward the main part of the house. And that was when we heard the car."

"Tell us about that."

"We just heard this car. You could hear its tires spinning, throwing up gravel. Then we heard it go down the hill. Then we didn't hear it anymore."

"Then what happened?"

"By the time we got to the doors again, Mr. Ogle was up and was on the phone. I was surprised to see him, 'cause I'd figured he was the one driving away in such a big hurry. Then I looked at the bodies, and I knew Congressman Bailey was dead, and so was Mr. Finch and Miss Erb. I won't kid ya. I pert near threw up. I couldn't believe what had happened . . ."

Mrs. Merritt's voice failed, and she pulled a white handkerchief from her pocket and covered her eyes for a moment. She trembled. Her face was red, and she wiped away tears.

Ken waited for a full minute—whether out of sympathy or from a sense of the dramatic, I don't know. Then he asked, "Can you go on?"

She nodded.

"Just go on with the story. What happened next?"

"I saw the gun lying on the floor. I listened to Mr. Ogle on the phone and understood he was trying to get help. When he hung up, he said the sheriff and an ambulance were on their way. That's when my husband shook his head and said it wouldn't make no difference, they were all dead."

"Did you turn on any lights when you entered the living room, Mrs. Merritt?"

"No."

"Were any lights on?"

"A lamp, I think."

"Was there enought light for you to recognize Mr. Ogle and identify the three victims?"

"Yes, I could tell who they all were."

Kimball, too, moved closer to the witness as he cross-examined. He stood about where Ken had stood.

"Mrs. Merritt, what can you tell us about the relationship between Congressman Bailey and Miss Rheinlander?"

"I'm not sure what you mean."

"Well, you saw them together quite a few times, didn't you? Were they friendly, affectionate . . . ?"

"Yes. I'd have to say they were sort of lovey."

"What did you see them do that caused you to think so?"

"Well . . . I saw them kiss several times. They held hands sometimes. And he'd slap her on the backside."

"'Slap her . . .' What do you mean?"

Mrs. Merritt shrugged. "He'd slap her backside. You know, a little playful pat on the fanny."

"What about the last day, that is, Saturday, May 9? Were they affectionate then?"

"I didn't see any difference. She was out beside the pool in her bikini, and he gave her a pat on the rear. I saw that."

"When you wheeled their dinner into the bedroom, did you notice anything about the congressman and Miss Rheinlander?"

"Like what?"

"Did you see any sign of tension or hostility between them?"

Mrs. Merritt shook her head. "No," she said quietly.

"Did they seem to have been involved in an argument?"

"Objection," said Ken Simpson. "The question calls for a conclusion."

"Rephrase the question, please, Mr. Kimball," I said.

"Mrs. Merritt, did you observe anything about the appearance or demeanor of the congressman or Miss Rheinlander that gave you the impression they had been arguing?"

"No."

"Did you at any time on Saturday, May 9 overhear any argument or hard words between Congressman Bailey and Miss Rheinlander?"

"No."

I was pleased with the jury. Their attention was fixed on the trial. They were not distracted by the television lights or cameras. I could see them react when Mrs. Merritt's description of the interplay between an amiable couple was so distinctly at variance with Ogle's description of tension and argument. The jury had changed its seating arrangement, and Prof. Winston Pyle now sat in the front row beside Mrs. Grace Siegfried. Occasionally one of them whispered something to the other.

I think those two had begun to suspect what I did: the surprising course the defense was going to take.

Lloyd George Kimball returned to that course with his next line of questions.

"Mrs. Merritt, did Congressman Bailey ever explain to you why he bought a lodge on a hilltop on the Ohio side of the river, outside his district and outside his state, a hundred miles from his home town?"

"Objection, that calls for hearsay."

"If the Court please," said Kimball with mock patience, "I want to know how the congressman *explained* his purchase of the lodge, not what the truth was."

"The objection is overruled. Ladies and gentlemen of the jury, please notice the distinction. The witness's answer will be evidence of how Congressman Bailey explained why he bought the lodge, not evidence of why he really bought it—which might be something entirely different."

"He just said he wanted a lot of privacy," said Mrs. Merritt.

"Did anything that occurred during his ownership of the lodge explain why he wanted privacy?"

Mrs. Merritt hesitated for half a minute. "I don't know . . . I— I guess he might not have wanted everybody to see how much his friends drank."

"What about women, Mrs. Merritt? Did the congressman bring women to the lodge?"

"You mean . . . women to entertain?"

"Let's start with that."

"A coupla times, I think, there were women at his parties that weren't what you'd call pure."

"If you know, and not as a guess, did the congressman himself associate with those women?"

"I don't know, sir."

"He did not, within your observation. Is that correct?"

"Right."

Ken Simpson stood. "Your Honor, I keep wondering what is the relevance of this line of questioning."

I ruled. "In the defense of a case of this nature, we will allow counsel for the defense a good deal of latitude."

Lloyd George Kimball continued as if he had not heard the objection or ruling. "Miss Marietta Rheinlander came here with Congress-

85

man Bailey and slept with him, did she not? Within your observation, did any other women come here and sleep in the same room with the congressman?"

Mrs. Merritt shook her head. "Could have done. Could have done, that I didn't know about."

"Did the congressman *bring* any other women here?"

Mrs. Merritt rubbed her hands together. "Well . . . there was another woman came once or twice. She had her own room."

"Was it only Miss Rheinlander that had no separate room?"

"So far as I saw, she was the only woman who came here that seemed to have any kind of special relationship with Congressman Bailey."

"How many times was Miss Rheinlander at the lodge?"

"I didn't count. I'd say four or five times."

"How often did the congressman use the lodge?"

"Oh, I'd say he was here one weekend a month, on average."

"How often did he have what were called 'cronies parties'?"

"Those were once a year."

"How often did he have smaller parties, with, say, ten or more people at the lodge?"

"Two or three times a year."

"How many times a year did he come alone?"

"I don't remember he ever came alone."

"Mr. Ogle testified that he was at the lodge maybe fifty times. Does that match your recollection?"

"I wouldn't argue the point."

"What about Mr. Finch? Was he a frequent visitor?"

"Yes. Was during the last year."

"What about Miss Erb?"

"Two or three times, is all I remember."

"Were you able to identify everyone who came to the lodge? I don't mean at the parties, when large groups were there; I mean on ordinary weekends when only a few came. Can you name all the people who came on those weekends?"

Mrs. Merritt shook her head gravely. "No, sir," she said. "Congressman Bailey never made it a point to introduce me to everybody. After all, I was just the housekeeper."

"Well, what kind of people were they?"

Ken Simpson stood and shook his head. "Your Honor, is this going anywhere at all?"

"Is it, Mr. Kimball?" I asked.

"I assure you it is, Your Honor," said Kimball.

"Well, do try to reach your point more efficiently," I said.

"Mrs. Merritt," said Kimball, "I will be straightforward about this. These guests that came on what we may call private weekends. Were they women? Were they possibly prostitutes?"

"No, sir. No women. They were all men."

Kimball rubbed his hands together in front of his chin. "What sort of things did they do? How did they spend their weekends?"

"In summer they used the pool. In cold weather they played cards a lot."

"From your observation, to the best of your knowledge, did they seem to have a good time?"

"Your Honor! This is totally irrelevant!"

"I'm going to sustain this time, Mr. Kimball."

Kimball was smooth. "Thank you for your tolerance to this point, Your Honor. The relevancy will become clear later. For now, I have on the record all I need."

Ken Simpson moved closer to Mrs. Merritt for redirect examination. "Just one point, Mrs. Merritt," he said. "You testified that when you went into the bedroom to serve dinner for Congressman Bailey and Miss Rheinlander you observed no tension between them, no sign of an argument. When you wheeled their dinner in there, where was the congressman?"

"He was standing in front of the bedroom television, looking at something on the screen."

"And where was Miss Rheinlander?"

"In the bathroom."

"They were not together?"

"No."

"If there had been tension between them, if they were angry at each other, you couldn't have seen it?"

"Couldn't have, no."

"Thank you."

Kimball, to my surprise, chose to recross. "When you went in the bedroom to bring dinner, what was the congressman wearing?"

"That Japanese coat he had on when he was killed. Also the black pants that went with it."

"Silk pants?"

"I guess so. Shiny."

"Could you see Miss Rheinlander in the bathroom?"

"Yeah. You see, the way that room is arranged, the toilet and the tub are in a little room to one side, but the two basins and the big mirror are in a room that's just a kind of alcove off the bedroom. I could see her."

"What was *she* wearing?"

"Nothing."

The next witness for the prosecution was Bernard Merritt, handyman and gardener for the Bailey lodge. His testimony was almost identical to his wife's. He'd heard three shots fired, then a long pause, then another shot, then two more. He'd loaded his shotgun and gone to see what was happening. He saw what his wife had seen.

Kimball did not cross-examine Bernard Merritt.

I recessed for the day.

Linda had sat in the courtroom during the afternoon, and we took an hour to stop by the Alexandria House for a single drink before we drove home.

Glen Myers was there, showing in early evening the delayed effect of his daylong consumption of gin. He was still erect and witty, but we could all hope he would sit down over a steak soon and not order another martini. He asked me if I would consent to his going out to the jail and visiting Marietta Rheinlander. I said I didn't think it was a good idea during the trial, since she would probably be spending all her evening hours with her lawyers. On the other hand, I said, I would tell the sheriff to let him visit if she was willing to see him.

At home we switched on a television set and tuned to one of our cable channels, Court TV. There I was in all my glory. What had been broadcast live all day was now being repeated on tape. There is no way a person is going to turn away from his own image on television, even when it compels him to see again what he has seen all day.

For some odd reason, the director seemed to find me more interesting than either of the lawyers. When the picture was not of the witness, it was of me, more often than of the lawyers. Naturally, more tape broadcast time was given to the cross-examination of David Ogle than to the testimony of Mr. and Mrs. Merritt. The camera was often focused on my face as the testimony developed, and I hope the jury did not see the skepticism the camera saw and broadcast to the nation.

The screen was often filled with the face of Marietta Rheinlander, sometimes with her hands. The zoom lenses brought the television viewers much closer to the woman than any of us in the courtroom were, except maybe the lawyers sitting beside her, and viewers saw strain that we in the courtroom did not see. I imagine television viewers had a more sympathetic view of her than her jurors had.

The television commentators were either naive or pretended they did not see the defense strategy. If I saw it, one of the experienced trial attorneys who commented on the trial must have seen what was developing.

I had imposed certain restrictions on the television cameramen. One was that they were not to broadcast pictures of the jury—a restriction I would relax when the jury returned with a verdict. Another was that they were not to turn their cameras around and focus on Miss Rheinlander's parents sitting behind the bar, or for that matter on anyone else in the courtroom.

That meant that Court TV missed a touching drama I had forbidden them to broadcast.

I hoped that none of the jurors had read the profile of Marietta Rheinlander published in the October, 1991, issue of Vanity Fair— an article dated seven months before the murders at the Bailey lodge.

I had known a little of her history, from local legends and from blurbs in People Magazine, but Glen Myers lent me that back issue of Vanity Fair, which outlined the whole story in detail and in terms I could not be sure were entirely accurate but that made sense and were probably true.

According to the magazine, Marietta Rheinlander was born in 1952, which of course made her forty years old when she was on trial for three murders.

Her great-grandfather, Adolf Rheinlander, had come to Alexandria, Ohio, in 1898. Our town had a flourishing German community, and Adolf had found it appealing, welcoming. He had immigrated from Münster, bringing with him a little money from the family fortune, and in Ohio he had gone into the oil business. He arrived during the great southern-Ohio oil boom, invested shrewdly, and in the course of six or eight years made himself a wealthy man.

In 1927 Adolf Rheinlander left Alexandria and moved to New York. Two of his children had married in the town and elected to stay. They are Marietta Rheinlander's distant cousins. In New York, Adolf threw his fortune into the stock market and lost nearly all of it in the crash of 1929.

Adolf Rheinlander's eldest son was Frederick Rheinlander, usually called Fritz. Seeing the way his father had lost so much in the 1929 crash, Fritz Rheinlander reached the somewhat eccentric conclusion that the best way to survive and prosper in the American business world was to buy and sell stocks, not just on your own account but for others. He entered a brokerage firm and by 1934 held a seat on the New York Stock Exchange. He invested the remnant of his father's estate in stocks unrealistically depressed by the crash, and by 1937, when Adolf died, the Rheinlander fortune was twice what it had been ten years earlier.

Fritz was Marietta's grandfather. Her father, Jason Rheinlander, followed his own father into the brokerage business. He became an arbitrageur. He retired in 1990, aged sixty-five, having evaded prosecution during the Levine-Boesky-Siegel-Miliken scandals by giving a sworn statement thousands of pages in length, divesting himself of certain stocks at a loss, and retiring from the brokerage business. The sacrifice did not bankrupt him. The parent who sat tearfully watching his daughter's trial for murder was worth at least twenty million dollars.

These were things I hoped the jury did not know. If Ken Simpson had tried to introduce evidence of any of it, Kimball would have objected strenuously, and I would have sustained him.

Fritz Rheinlander had never been confident that his son Jason would not risk all on some wild scheme and bankrupt himself. Against that possibility he created a group of trust funds. Marietta Rheinlander was the beneficiary of one of them. However badly her father managed the family fortune—and in the event he had not done at all badly—Marietta and her brother and cousins would have enough to live comfortably.

Fritz died in 1981. Marietta Rheinlander inherited a share of his estate.

In the photos published in Vanity Fair, great-grandfather Adolf appeared as a stolid patriarch in white muttonchop whiskers. His son Frederick—Fritz—appeared as a ponderous, probably righteous businessman: bald, with huge gray-white eyebrows, staring defiantly at the camera. Jason Rheinlander appeared as a younger version of the man I saw in the courtroom: now a strong man challenged to the limit of his strength.

Other pictures were of the young Marietta. The girl she had been was embraced in the woman she was; every image from that half-dozen photographs had been assimilated into the face and body of the woman I had stared at from the bench today.

She had played tennis. One of the pictures is of a sixteen-year-old Marietta, gripping a racket and grinning in bright sunlight: dressed in tennis whites and showing tanned muscular legs below a short skirt. A taller older brother, tolerating little sister, smiles down on her.

She was educated at Smith College, and another photograph is of Marietta Rheinlander in an antiwar demonstration (or, as the magazine acknowledged, it may have been a civil-rights demonstration; no matter since the girl demonstrated for both causes) in Northhampton: screaming vehemently, fist clenched in the air, dressed in jeans and a college sweatshirt, her hair tied back, wearing owlish round horn-rimmed eyeglasses and no makeup. The shrill emotions of the protester were not entirely subdued in the woman in the courtroom, I thought.

Still another picture was taken, one guesses, by a street photographer, and it shows a grinning Marietta standing beside a young man on the place du Tertre in Montmartre. The young man was her first husband, whom she married within a month after her graduation. In the Marietta Rheinlander on trial for murder I could see distinct traces of the well-dressed, conspicuously self-assured young woman enjoying a romantic honeymoon. Not a hint of the protester is seen in the honeymooner, though. Maybe that's only a coincidence of the moment when the picture was taken.

Her first marriage lasted only three years. Her husband, Timothy Gibbons, was eight years older than she was: a tall, handsome, ambitious, aggressive, and reportedly humorless young lawyer in the firm of Milbank, Tweed, Hadley & McCloy. The Vanity Fair reporter wrote that Marietta had been pushed into the marriage by her parents, who had been anxious to see their somewhat wayward daughter (the demonstrator) safely married to the scion of a prominent and secure family. She was quoted as saying at the time that it was "awfully glamorous" to come to the firm's offices to meet Tim and sit and wait for him in a reception room with a broad-window view of the Statue of Liberty. Apparently that, and the honeymoon in France, were all that was "awfully glamorous" about the marriage. The couple were not compatible, and neither, the magazine speculated, was entirely committed to the marriage.

Marietta Rheinlander did not remarry for five years. During those five years she established her reputation as an astute judge of contemporary art and became an art broker. She became a connoisseur with a following of collectors. Identified with what was at the time called the New Realism, she herself collected and encouraged others to collect the explicit male and female nudes of such artists as Steve Hawley, Philip Pearlstein, and John DeAndrea, also the colorful Western scenes of artists like Don Nice and Willard Midgette, and literal still-lifes by James Valerio and Audrey Flack among others. I myself could not identify any of these artists, and thank heaven Vanity Fair chose to illustrate the kind of art identified with her by reproducing two or three paintings.

She invested much of her time and some of her money in a gallery on Park Avenue. In her apartment on Park Avenue, Marietta Rheinlander maintained a minigallery, where "cunningly contrived lighting dramatized the stunning works of her personal collection— every item of which is for sale." She became known for cocktail parties, where the milling wealthy guests "acquire an interest, then form an attachment to one or another painting, print, or sculpture, and before the end of the evening write a check for it."

One of the photographs accompanying the article showed her in her long, narrow living and dining room, uncarpeted and spare of furniture, where paintings hung in "incandescences from ceiling spots" and life-size, oil-painted polyvinyl sculptures stood or sat, looking as though they were unembarrassed stark-naked guests who might at any moment ask for a drink—or such was my impression. Marietta Rheinlander stood in the middle of the room, posing for the magazine photographer. It was a season when miniskirts were in fashion, and her handsome legs were on display below the skirt of her black knit dress. She stood with a hand resting on the shoulder of a polyvinyl man, and you had to stare hard at the picture to see that the woman was real and the man was not.

That was a contemporary picture, taken in 1991 when she was all but universally acknowledged as a discriminating collector and dealer, a major figure in the New York art world, and a celebrity of perhaps a second rank—that is, not nearly as famous as Jacqueline Kennedy Onassis or Ivana Trump but a person worth a comprehensive profile in Vanity Fair.

She had remarried in 1981, to a French art dealer named Alain Boulanger: again, a man five years her senior, handsome and charming, an established success in the business of collecting and selling art. According to Vanity Fair he was loftily condescending about her New Realism and offered to make her an expert on the kind of art *he* admired, knew, and dealt in—Medieval triptychs, crucifix panels, reliquary panels, ivory reliefs, and polychrome statues, also illuminated manuscripts, breviaries, psalters, and bestiaries, and incunabula. (I had to look up that last one. An incunabulum is a document printed with moveable type, before 1501.) He dealt in an international market, in works that rarely changed hands for less than a million French francs. Whereas Marietta Rheinlander sold ten or twelve works a month, Alain Boulanger sold one or two—and made more money than she did.

He forbade her to offer any of her contemporary realists to his clientele. Instead, he set her up in a sideline specialty of his Paris gallery: erotica, but only erotica that had been produced by artists better known for other achievements, no photographs, and nothing dating later than 1930. As the centerpiece of the room where Boulanger offered his erotica hung a priceless etching by Rembrandt, graphically showing a couple copulating in a four-poster bed. It was meant to set the tone for the offerings, to demonstrate that erotic art had august ancestry. In Galerie Boulanger when Marietta was there, she presided over his collection of paintings by Boucher, Courbet, and David, watercolors by Grosz and Rowlandson, and sketches by Rodin and Picasso. In her Park Avenue apartment gallery—in leather portfolios that she opened only for selected friends and clients—a collection of salacious drawings, etchings, and watercolors, most of them by artists known only to *cognoscenti* for ever having produced such works. In New York she broke her husband's rule that nothing produced since 1930 would be offered and included works by Claes Oldenburg, Salvador Dali, and Andy Warhol.

This was another of the elements of her history that had just as soon not be known to the jury.

The marriage to Boulanger was of short duration: four years. The reason for the divorce, according to the magazine, was that Alain Boulanger was anything but monogamous—while expecting his wife to be absolutely so. During her month-long sojourns in Paris—she spent about half her time there during the marriage, and half in New York—she discovered that her husband kept a mistress in a flat in the Fifth arrondissement, dallied with at least one other woman, and had an intimate relationship with a young man as well. If, said the magazine, she had no other reason for terminating the marriage, the fear of AIDS was motive enough.

Marietta Rheinlander herself, the writer insisted, was resolutely monogamous. She had lovers when she was single. She had even broken off with one lover to move to another. But she had never had more than one at a time, and she expected a corollary commitment from any man she slept with.

She was one of New York's most esteemed hostesses. People were flattered by her invitations, even if they did have to suspect a part of her reason for inviting them to dinner was the possibility they might purchase something from her gallery. She was also a sought-after guest. As people who were her guests knew her art was for sale, she knew that when she was a guest she might be asked to offer an informal judgment of some work of art her hosts had just bought or inherited.

"Well, it's a good representative of its genre," she was quoted as saying over and over. "Personally, I wouldn't buy it, but I certainly wouldn't hide it away."

The full-page photo that introduced the article showed Marietta

Rheinlander alighting from a Mercedes limousine at the opening of an opera at Lincoln Center. She was the guest of a man whose name I did not recognize but who was described as wealthy and prominent. Her ankle-length gown, tailored of some glittering fabric, clung to her. The skirt was slit to her knees on both sides. The décolletage was interesting. She wore a diamond and emerald necklace. She was smiling, greeting someone behind the photographer apparently. If there is an image anywhere of glamour and sophistication, that is it—at least in the innocent judgment of this small-town lawyer.

And this small-town lawyer was the man who might have to send her to prison for the rest of her life, if not to the electric chair. If ever I was sorry I took this judgeship, I was sorry about it that night.

Court TV was not the only channel that covered the Marietta Rheinlander trial that night. The contrast in coverage was interesting.

A Pittsburgh station we get on cable, using a CBS feed from New York, reported this way:

> The murder charges against Park Avenue art-dealer-socialite Marietta Rheinlander continued to fall apart in the courtroom today as her counsel, Manhattan trial lawyer Lloyd George Kimball, scored point after point as he cross-examined the prosecution's chief witness, Congressional aide David Ogle. Ogle made it abundantly clear that he personally believes Miss Rheinlander killed his boss and friend, Congressman Charles Bailey. Unfortunately for the prosecution, Ogle's conspicuous resentment of the defense has made him a less-than-effective witness.

A Huntington station, which had its own reporter in the courtroom, saw the trial differently:

> In spite of the efforts of a New York lawyer to undermine the prosecution's case against New York playgirl Marietta Rheinlander, charged in the murder of Congressman Charles Bailey and two of his

staff, nothing brought out by the defense so far has in the least overcome the most damaging evidence against Miss Rheinlander—that she was found with the murder weapon in her hand, that it bore her fingerprints and no one else's, and that she attempted to flee. All day today, the jury listened intently to the cross-examination of the chief witness for the prosecution, Congressional aide and Huntington attorney David Ogle, without hearing any point of his testimony-in-chief effectively challenged. Calm on the witness stand, testifying only to the facts, David Ogle was not broken by the ordeal of cross-examination.

I was glad the jury did not hear either of those analyses. I didn't find the case as simple as either report made it.

6

Wednesday morning is Rotary Club breakfast day in Alexandria. The club meets in the back room of the Bon Ton Restaurant.

Meetings begin with the singing of "America," then a prayer, then the singing of the Rotary song:

> R-O-T-A-R-Y
> That spells Rotary!
> R-O-T-A-R-Y
> Is known on land and sea!
> (And in the air!)
> From north to south,
> From east to west,
> He profits most who serves the best.
> R-O-T-A-R-Y
> That spells Rotary!

Seated next to me at the breakfast table that morning was Woody Schramm, one of the town's two or three leading insurance agents—since deceased, unfortunately. George Babbitt redux.

Whether or not it had anything to do with his demise at seventy-three, I wouldn't want to testify, but Woody was always a lusty trencherman, who filled two plates at our breakfast buffets with a stack of pancakes, a dollop of scrambled eggs, and ham, sausage, and bacon. ("All comes for the same price," he would say.) He would be back in the Bon Ton for lunch, where his favorite meal was fried Ohio River catfish and home-fried potatoes. Some say such victuals would have killed anyone.

Anyway, Woody was heavy. The lower rims of his spectacles

rested comfortably on his fleshy pink cheeks, relieving the bridge of his nose.

"What's that New York lawyer tryin' to do, make out that woman didn't kill those people?" he asked me.

"That's his job," I said.

"Well . . . I wouldn't want his job. That woman is a pretty sorry example of the human race."

"How do you mean?"

"What I read, she'd sleep with any man that asked her. And a good many asked her, too. What's more, she's a parasite. Lived off what her family had, never worked for a living. It's no wonder she could shoot somebody without a second thought. Work and responsibility is what gives a person the right kind of character and principles. You remember how Ida worked right alongside me in the agency as long as she lived, and had our children too, and was the highest kind of woman that ever was. Nothin' like this Rheinlander woman. I guess you have to have a trial, but she's guilty all right. That kind . . ."

A couple of my Rotary brethren chimed in and agreed with Woody. Then a couple of others disagreed, and so an argument started; and I had to end it by saying it was unseemly to talk so much about the case in front of the judge who had to try it.

"Well, I read somewhere that she was a dealer in dirty pictures," still another member said, "and I sure hope that gets out and is understood by the jury."

Ken Simpson opened the third day of the trial by calling Sheriff Dan Phelps.

I should say of Dan that he is about fifty years old, a trim man except for a bit of a paunch. He wears the prescribed gray uniform of an Ohio sheriff, with a revolver hanging from his belt, always. Dan tends to bustle, and when he does he walks with his backside sort of extended behind him, and he pumps his arms. He is in his fifth term as sheriff and is quite well thought of.

After identifying Dan, Ken asked him, "Did you, on the night of May 9 of this year, receive a telephone call about a shooting at the Bailey lodge?"

"Yes, I did," said Dan briskly. It came out "Yesuhdid."

"Who called you?"

"Deputy Doug Eddy. He was on night duty that night."

"At what time did Deputy Doug Eddy call you?"

Dan looked at a little notepad he had brought to the witness stand. He was of course an experienced witness and knew he was entitled to look at his notes. "That was 12:28 A.M.," he said.

"What did you do?"

"Well, I had to get up and dress, go out and start the car. I expect it was twelve-thirty-two or -three by the time I was on the road."

"Did you drive directly to the Bailey lodge?"

"Yesuhdid."

"By what route did you go, and how long did it take you to get there?"

"Well, I went up State Highway 26 and turned off on County Road 8, then used County Road 12. The Bailey lodge is right off County Road 12, up a private drive about a hundred yards or so."

"As you were driving, did you see anything unusual?"

"Yesuhdid. I see a red Oldsmobile off the road and sorta nosed into the crick down there. That's Turkey Crick. Ordinarily, I'd of stopped, but I was on my way to look into a triple murder, so all I did was radio for a car to come see. I suspicioned that car had something to do with the murder, but I figured my first duty was to get to the lodge and see if anybody could be helped."

"When you reached the lodge, what did you see?"

"Well, the congressman was dead all right, and so was the two younger people. A ambulance had got there ahead of me, but it didn't make no difference; them people was dead, and there wasn't nothing we could do about it."

"What did you do?"

"Well, Mr. Merritt, he told me a woman had run off as fast as she could in a red Oldsmobile, so I put out a radio call, telling my fellas to figure the red Oldsmobile in Turkey Crick was prob'ly driven by a suspect in these murders. I said she was maybe a woman, so Deputy Martha Vogt should be woke up and asked to get out there."

"When was the first time you saw Miss Marietta Rheinlander?"

"When my deputy, Bob Johnson, brought her to the lodge."

"Is Marietta Rheinlander in the courtroom now?"

"Sure. That's her, sittin' over there."

The defendant apparently meant to alternate between two outfits to be seen by the jury. Having worn her white linen dress and white sweater yesterday, today she was again dressed in the pink cashmere suit she had worn on Monday.

"Did you perform a paraffin test on the woman you have identified as Marietta Rheinlander?"

"Well, I did half the test. I put the stuff on her hands. The Ohio Crime Laboratory examined the paraffin to see if—"

"Please explain to the jury what the Ohio Crime Laboratory is."

"Well, a county our size can't afford to have all the scientific instruments and the trained people you need to do a lot of things like fingerprint work and handwritin' analysis and lie detector and like all that. The crime lab is not just a place; it's also a bunch of vans that come to the smaller counties when you need 'em. I'd had my office put in a call for a crime-lab van when I was woke in bed and told we had a triple murder."

"All right. And what is a paraffin test?"

"A paraffin test"—Dan Phelps pronounces it "parafeen"—"is a test that tells whether or not a person has fired a gun recently. My part of the test was to press warm paraffin onto her hands, then save that paraffin for the crime lab to test it. I done that and saved the paraffin."

"And the technician from the crime lab will be able to testify as to the results of that test, right?"

"Yes, sir."

"When you entered the lodge, did you see a pistol lying on the floor?"

"Yesuhdid."

"It was layin' on the floor. I guess it was closest to Miss Erb's body."

"I now hand you a .38 caliber Smith & Wesson revolver and ask you if it is the revolver you saw lying on the floor that night."

The revolver had a tag on it, and Dan looked it over for a moment, then nodded, and said, "This is the gun."

Ken handed it to Kimball to examine and said, "I ask the revolver be received in evidence as a state's exhibit."

"It will be received," I said, and Kimball handed it back to Ken, who passed it to Mrs. Tutweiler to be tagged as an exhibit.

"Where has Marietta Rheinlander been the past five months?" Ken asked.

"In the county jail."

"In your custody?"

"Officially, she's in my custody."

"During the time she has been in your custody, has she been a cooperative prisoner?"

"Objection!" said Kimball sharply.

"Ask it differently," I said dryly to Ken.

"During the time she has been in your custody, what facts have you observed that suggest she has been a cooperative or uncooperative prisoner?"

Kimball rose, shaking his head. "Apart from the fact that the question calls for hearsay, the answer, even if it is not hearsay, is one hundred per cent irrelevant, Your Honor."

"Counsel will approach the bench," I said. I raised a hand toward Mrs. Tutweiler and said, "Off the record."

We held a short bench conference out of the hearing of the jury.

"What do you have in mind?" I asked Ken Simpson.

"I mean to show a predilection for violence."

"By doing what?" I asked.

"She gave Margaret Vogt a shove that knocked her off balance. She has a hot temper."

"Did the sheriff see this shove?" Kimball asked.

"He— Well, I guess he didn't *see* it. He knows about it."

"Because she told him," I said. "Which is hearsay. I am going to sustain the objection. I'll rule on relevancy if you ask a similar question of Margaret Vogt."

Back on the record, Ken asked another question that drew an objection:

"During her confinement in the county jail, has Miss Rheinlander asked for or received any special privileges not ordinarily afforded other prisoners?"

"I object! That is immaterial and prejudicial."

I shook my head. "Sustained."

"The State of Ohio has no further questions for the witness, Your Honor," said Ken a little sullenly.

"I have only two or three questions for the sheriff, Your Honor," said Kimball. "Sheriff Phelps . . . when you examined the Bailey lodge, did you find any bullet holes in the walls, doors, windows, furniture . . . anywhere, in anything?"

"No, sir."

"Did you look?"

"Yes, sir."

"I believe the evidence yet to be introduced will show there was only one bullet in each body, yet six were fired. Do you have any explanation as to where the other three shots went?"

"Out the slidin' glass doors, into the night," said Dan.

"Were the bodies lying in front of those doors?"

"No, sir."

"Where *were* the bodies?"

"In the living room and hall."

"Sheriff Phelps, I hand you now a key attached to a tag. Can you identify that key?"

"Well, keys look pretty much alike, but the tag says this is a key I took from the pocket of a pair of pants in the congressman's suitcase."

"I ask that the key be received as Defense Exhibit A. Your Honor, in order to save time and the expense of flying a locksmith back and forth between Alexandria and New York, the prosecuting attorney has kindly agreed to stipulate that this is a key to Miss Marietta Rheinlander's apartment on Park Avenue in New York City."

Ken nodded to me that he had in fact agreed, and I said, "The evidence will be received as stipulated."

"Thank you, Sheriff," said Kimball. I have no further questions."

Lloyd George Kimball was correct in not cross-examining Dan Phelps any further—even though I think Dan was disappointed. The fact was, his testimony on direct examination had established nothing. He hadn't seen anything. His testimony served to fix the time of the murders a little more closely, by his telling when he was wakened by a call; and his having seen the Oldsmobile in the creek explained how Deputy Bob Johnson happened to come along when he did and arrest Marietta Rheinlander. By dismissing him without asking him any questions, Kimball denied the sheriff any opportunity to add anything to his testimony and showed the jury that he didn't think the sheriff's testimony was important—which it wasn't.

The testimony of Deputy Bob Johnson was a little more important.

Bob Johnson is a big man, a big powerful man. He was a star football player for Alexandria High School, not good enough for a football scholarship—which may have been just as well, since he has never been academically oriented. He plays industrial-league softball today, and catchers think twice or more about blocking the plate when he charges from third. He is light-haired and florid.

Bob was the subject of controversy around here three or four years ago. He stopped a stolen car, in daylight. The driver jumped out and ran, pulling a pistol from his belt. Bob yelled at him to stop, and when the driver did not stop Bob leveled his service revolver with both hands and shot him dead. The pistol drawn by the driver turned out to be a cap gun. He was sixteen years old.

The community is divided yet, between those who believe Bob

did what he had to do, never guessing the driver was a boy with a cap gun, and those who believe he used extremely bad judgment. Bad judgment and carelessness are the worst charges made. No one suggests he wantonly or vengefully killed a teenage boy. Still, there remain some who think he should not be a deputy anymore.

"Where were you when you got a radio call about an automobile in Turkey Creek?"

"I'd stopped at the Gem Diner on Route 7 to have a cup of coffee. I heard the call on my walkie-talkie."

"At what time was that?"

"I'd say about ten to one."

"How long after that was it when you reached the car in the creek?"

"About ten minutes. Maybe fifteen."

"So it was about one o'clock when you found the Oldsmobile?"

"Yes, sir."

"Describe what you saw."

"Well . . . this bright red Oldsmobile Cutlass—it had West Virginia plates—was sitting with its front in Turkey Creek and its wheels back up the bank. It wasn't damaged much; it looked like it had just run off the road and bumped down the creek bank till it nosed into the mud and water. You couldn't have backed it out, for sure. But it wasn't what you'd call wrecked."

"What did you do?"

"I walked down and looked at it, to be sure there wasn't anybody in it. Then I went back to the car and radioed in, telling I'd found the Oldsmobile and looked it over, and saying I'd look around for the driver."

"Did you find the driver?"

"Yes. I drove along slow, using my spotlight on both sides of the road, and I saw a woman standing off the road in some brush."

"Is the woman you saw standing in the brush in the courtroom at this moment?"

"Yes, sir. That's her over there. Miss Rheinlander."

"Then what did you do?"

"I got out of the car and went up to her and asked her if she was hurt."

"What did she tell you?"

"She said she wasn't. She said she was all right. So I asked to see her driver's license, and she showed it to me. I told her she'd have to go back to the Bailey lodge with me till we got a problem up there straightened out."

"Did she ask you what the problem was?"

"No, sir. She just picked up her suitcase—she had a suitcase— and walked up to my car."

"Did you tell her she was under arrest?"

"No. She wasn't."

"How far was this from the lodge?"

"Three-quarters of a mile, something like that."

"Did she tell you how she ran the car off the road?"

"She said she misjudged a curve and skidded on the gravel. It's a gravel road."

"Can you describe her demeanor while she was in the car?"

"It looked to me like she was just sad."

"What happened when you got to the lodge?"

"I pulled up in front. When I came around and opened the door on her side, she said she didn't want to go in. I told her she wasn't under arrest, but I'd have to put her under arrest if she wouldn't cooperate. She said she didn't want to go in anyway. She was pretty huffy about it."

You may wonder why all this "she said" testimony was not subject to objection for hearsay.

It was not, and the distinction is this: If the issue is whether or not a patient was given an injection, a doctor cannot testify that he ordered a nurse to give it and she later told him she did give it. If the issue is whether or not the doctor *believed* the injection was given, he can testify that the nurse told him she gave it. In the first example, the party who knows the facts—the nurse—is not a witness, is not under oath, and cannot be cross-examined about whether or not the injection was actually given. *She* must testify to that fact, assuming she is alive and can be called to testify. In the second example, the doctor does personally know the fact we are looking for—what the nurse told him—and he is under oath and can be cross-examined.

Bob Johnson's testimony about what Marietta Rheinlander told him about how the car skidded off the road was not evidence of how the car got in the creek. It was evidence of how *she explained* how the car got in the creek.

Of course, there was no problem about Johnson's testifying that Marietta Rheinlander told him she didn't want to go back inside the lodge. That was a simple fact—that she didn't want to go—and her saying so was not hearsay.

Juries must often wonder how we make these distinctions. I can offer a simple explanation—simple but not complete. Through experience over centuries, trial courts have observed that gossip testimony is not reliable. For that reason, we demand that facts be proved from what witnesses saw, not from what someone told them *they* saw.

"Then what happened?"

"The sheriff came out of the house and asked me what was going on."

"Then what happened?"

"I told him. So, he said, 'Arrest her.' I told her she was under arrest, read her her rights, and told her now she had to go in the house. Then she started to yell and scream and said she wouldn't go in. So we grabbed her, handcuffed her hands behind her back, and took her by both arms and took her in the house."

"Then what happened?"

"She kept yelling and jerking and trying to get away and not look at the bodies. They were covered by sheets, but she didn't want to see."

Bob Johnson is usually a well-spoken witness, better than the sheriff, but he says "dit'n" for "didn't."

"Then what happened?"

107

"Well . . . to tell you the truth, I didn't see any reason why she had to stand there and look at the bodies, so I took her back out to the car and put her in the back, behind the screen, and locked her in."

"Thank you," said Ken Simpson. "Your witness, Mr. Kimball."

Lloyd George Kimball rose behind the defense table. Before he spoke, he glanced down at his client, who was flushed and tense. He gave her a reassuring smile.

"Deputy Johnson . . ." he said. "Did you participate in the investigation of the three murders? You have testified that you found Miss Rheinlander and brought her to the lodge, but after that did you take an active part in examining the premises?"

"Yes, I did."

"Did you look for bullet holes in the walls, the windows and doors, the furniture and so on?"

"Yes, sir."

"Did you find any?"

"No, sir."

"We know six shots were fired. There will be evidence that each victim had been shot only once. Where did the other three bullets go?"

"They had to go outside somewheres, like out the doors that opened on the swimming pool."

"Were the bodies lying in front of the sliding glass doors?"

"No, sir."

"Did you take the photographs of the crime scene, make the diagrams, and so on?"

"Yes, sir."

"Did you make the diagram of the lodge that now stands there on the easel?"

"I made the sketch, with the measurements on, to show where everything was. I made the measurements that show where the bodies were before they were taken away. I made the rest of the measurements, to show the layout of the house, several days later. Mr. Simpson had a commercial artist make it like you see it."

"Is the diagram an accurate representation of what you witnessed?"

"Yes, sir."

"In particular, does it accurately represent the location of the three bodies?"

"Yes, sir."

"Please observe the X that has been put on the chart by the witness Mr. Ogle, who testified that was where Miss Rheinlander was standing when he first saw her after he heard the shooting. How far is it from that spot to where you saw the body of Donald Finch?"

"I would call that six feet, about."

"How far from the X to where you saw the body of Elizabeth Finch?"

"About ten or eleven feet."

"How far to the body of the congressman?"

"Twelve to fifteen feet."

"How long were you in the house that night?"

"About four hours."

"And you never spotted any bullet holes."

"I never found any. I looked for bullet holes, but I didn't find any."

"You did, on the other hand, find a bullet, I believe. Tell us about that."

"Yes, sir. There was a bullet lying on the floor about two feet behind the body of Congressman Bailey. It was a deformed bullet, all bloody."

"Will you point out on the chart where that bullet was lying?"

Bob Johnson pointed to a spot near the wall between the hall and the office.

"What did you do about that bullet?"

"We left it where it was until Dr. Chamblas got there and could see it and where it was."

"All right. Thank you. Now, when you encountered Miss Rheinlander on the road—County Road 12, I believe it was—was she *beyond* where she had skidded off the road . . . or back toward the lodge?"

"Back . . . she was closer to the lodge."

"Deputy Johnson, in your experience as an officer of the law in this county, has there ever been an instance where a woman alone after midnight on a remote rural road was *molested*?"

"Mr. Kimball, I don't remember that any woman has ever been molested on a county road," said Bob Johnson solemnly. He understood the import of the question and did not mean to put Kimball down, but he believed he was being honest.

"Well, Deputy Johnson . . . do you mind if I call you *Mr.* Johnson?"

"You can call me Bob. Everybody does."

"Thank you. I don't mean to be disrespectful, but it is a little awkward, isn't it? So if you don't mind . . . Bob . . . do you remember the case of Melissa Whiting?"

"Well, yeah, as a matter of fact—"

Ken Simpson objected. "Is there any relevancy—"

"I see the relevancy, Mr. Simpson," I said. (A commentator on Court TV said I cut off improper objections before the lawyer even got them out of his mouth.) "Overruled."

"Yeah, I remember the Melissa Whiting case," said Bob Johnson, frowning and a bit uncertain.

"Tell us what happened," said Kimball.

"Well . . . she was walking on the road. And . . . and she was raped."

"So it can happen," said Kimball. "Can't it? Now put yourself in the position of a New York woman with a car in a creek after midnight on a remote country road, in a wooded area. And look at it this way, Bob. If you found yourself alone on a deserted street in the Bronx— Well, these hills might seem friendly to you, and a New York street might seem friendly to a New Yorker. Let's put you in the Bronx and Miss Rheinlander on County Road 12. You see the lights of a car coming. You might duck back and wait to see what car that was and who was in it, before you stepped out and raised your hand and asked for help. Mightn't you?"

"Is that a question or a speech?" Ken Simpson asked—which was another mistake, since Kimball had made his point and an objection only served to underline it.

"You may answer the question," I said to Johnson.

"I was a woman walking on a county road at night, I'd wait to see who was coming along before I jumped out and yelled for help," said Bob Johnson solemnly.

"That's very honest of you, Bob, and I appreciate it," said Kimball. It was a very shrewd ploy on Kimball's part, and I feel sure it had its effect on the jury—the big-town lawyer thanking the little-town deputy. Ken Simpson had no ground for objection, even if it was inadmissibly argumentative.

"Did you judge that Miss Rheinlander was intoxicated at that time?"

"Yes, sir. I thought she was. If we hadn't arrested her later in the murder cases, I'd probably have cited her for operating under the influence."

Kimball walked out from behind the table and stood in front of it. Today he was wearing a dark blue suit. I admired his tailoring. Besides, the dark blue contrasted dramatically with his white hair and even with his flushed face. "Bob," he said, "have you ever had occasion before to require a woman to enter a room where a murder had been committed, where a body lay on the floor? Whether she was a suspect or a witness."

"Yes, sir."

"Objection on the ground of relevance," said Ken Simpson. Ken was for some reason more nervous this morning. He had to know that when a defendant is on trial on a serious criminal charge, a judge will allow the defense a great deal of latitude about relevancy—more than he can allow the prosecution. Relevancy is not a very strong objection at best. "I cannot see how this is relevant," Ken went on.

"Overruled," I said and nodded to Bob Johnson. "You may answer."

"The way it was this one time, this man and woman, who were living together but weren't married, had a big fight, 'cause the man

111

had hit the woman's eighteen-year-old daughter so hard he'd busted her jaw. The woman shot the man finally, and killed him. The daughter was upstairs when we got there, and I had to make her come downstairs and get in the ambulance to go to the hospital, 'cause she was bleeding from the mouth and so on. So she had to walk through the living room where the man was on the floor dead."

"And how did she react?"

"Oh, she didn't want to go through there. She didn't want to see him. I told her the body was covered, but she held her hands over her eyes, and I had to lead her through the room."

"And this was the man who had broken her jaw?"

"Yes, sir."

I was a little surprised at Lloyd George Kimball. I don't think he knew about the incident Bob Johnson had just described. I knew what question he was going to ask next, and I don't think he knew the answer. It is a general rule of cross-examination that you don't ask a question unless you know what the answer has to be—and that the answer will be favorable to your case. Kimball was fishing here, as lawyers put it, and he might have gotten an answer he didn't want.

"In your experience, Bob, do women generally try to avoid seeing the bodies of murder victims?"

"Objection! How do we know he has enough experience to make a judgment."

"You may inquire on redirect," I said.

"My experience is that nobody likes to see the bodies of murder victims," said Bob Johnson solemnly.

"And will shrink from them, try hard to avoid seeing them?"

"Yes, sir."

"So there was nothing unusual in Miss Rheinlander vehemently refusing to go in the house and confront the bodies?"

"No. I didn't think it was unusual."

"And the fact that she didn't want to see three dead bodies in no way suggests that she was responsible for their deaths, wouldn't you say?"

"Objection!"

I smiled at Kimball. "Sustained. You can make your argument later, Mr. Kimball."

Kimball too smiled. "I have no further questions of this witness, Your Honor."

The next witness for the prosecution was Deena DeFelice, a technician for the Ohio Crime Laboratory. Mrs. DeFelice had testified in my court several times before, and it was always something of a pleasure to hear her testify. She was a professional witness. That was in fact what the state paid her to be. She testified only about subjects on which she was qualified. She spoke concisely and calmly, setting forth the facts she had learned by her technological expertise, never offering anything more, and never giving a jury any hint of what judgment she had formed of the guilt or innocence of the accused.

What was more, I think I am not being sexist when I say she was a pleasure to look at. A slight young woman in her late twenties, she was— well, there is no other way to put it: she was *beautiful*. She was of Italian descent. Born Dina, she had changed her name to Deena, because she did not want to hear the pronunciation Dinah. Her dark brown eyes focused in the most extraordinary way: soft yet concentrated. She wore her dark hair in a youthful style, neither short nor long but in supple curls around her ears. She wore a white blouse with a blue scarf at her throat and a knee-length dark blue skirt.

Ken Simpson asked her the questions that identified her. She was from Cleveland, was a graduate of Ohio State University, where she had studied biology and chemistry. She had done graduate study in criminology and held certificates in various technical specialties: polygraph, fingerprint analysis, ballistics, and so on.

"Mrs. DeFelice, will you please explain to the jury what a paraffin test is?"

"When a pistol is discharged, either a revolver or an automatic, the explosion of the gunpowder propels hot gases from the body of the pistol with great force. They escape through any crack or seam between the machined parts of the pistol and strike the skin of the person firing the weapon. Sometimes this causes pain, a burning sensation. Usually it does not. The escaping gas carries with it tiny particles of solid residues of the gunpowder. These particles become imbedded shallowly in the skin. They may sometimes cause irritation, but usually the person is not aware of them. Washing the hands does not eliminate them. In time they disappear, but washing the hands, no matter how thoroughly, does not remove them. If warm paraffin is applied to the hands within the first two or three hours after a person fires a pistol, the paraffin will penetrate into the pores and tiny crevices in the skin, and some of these particles will attach to the paraffin. We can then perform tests on the paraffin to determine if any of the gunpowder residue is present."

"On May 10 of this year," asked Ken Simpson, "did you receive a sample of paraffin from Sheriff Dan Phelps?"

"I did."

"How was the sample identified?"

"As paraffin applied to the hands of one Marietta Rheinlander."

"Did you test that paraffin for the presence of gunpowder residue?"

"I did."

"And what did you find?"

"The paraffin from the sample identified as Marietta Rheinlander, right hand, contained distinct traces of gunpowder residue."

"Leading to what conclusion?"

"That the subject person had fired a pistol not long before the paraffin was applied."

"Thank you, Mrs. DeFelice. Now I hand you a .38 caliber Smith & Wesson revolver that has been marked as State's Exhibit A. It carries a tag put on it by our court reporter and another tag. Can you tell the jury what the other tag is?"

Mrs. DeFelice looked at the pistol and the tag. "This is a crime lab tag I put on this revolver."

"Did you perform certain tests on that revolver, Miss DeFelice? If so, what?"

"I checked it for fingerprints, and I also performed a ballistics test on it," she said.

Ken Simpson turned to Lloyd George Kimball. "Mr. Kimball," he said, "will the defense stipulate that no two people in the world have identical fingerprints?"

"The defense will so stipulate," said Kimball dryly.

I have seen trials—not in my own court—where the fingerprint expert is required to testify for ten minutes to establish the proposition that every person's fingerprints are unique. This little exchange between the prosecution and defense saved us ten minutes.

"What fingerprints did you find on this revolver, Mrs. DeFelice?"

"I found the fingerprints of the defendant Marietta Rheinlander," said Mrs. DeFelice with calm precision. "Besides those, there were some smudges, but there were no other identifiable fingerprints."

"What additional tests did you perform?"

"I fired the pistol into a box filled with cotton wadding, to obtain spent slugs for comparison with certain other slugs that were given me."

"In your expert opinion, were the bullets you were given for comparison fired from the same pistol as the bullets you fired into the box?"

"The three slugs given me for comparison purposes were fired from the pistol I fired into the box."

"I now hand you three bullets. Are these the ones that were given you for comparison purposes?"

"Yes, they are."

"How do you know?"

"I marked them by scratching an identification number into the soft metal of the slugs."

Ken handed the slugs to Kimball and asked that they be received as state's exhibits. Kimball offered no objection, and they were so received.

"In summary, Mrs. DeFelice, is it correct that the three bullets received as exhibits were fired from the pistol that bore the finger-prints of the defendant?"

"Yes."

"Thank you. I have no further questions."

Lloyd George Kimball knew how to deal with this kind of witness. She was qualified to testify on the subjects about which she testified, and any effort to undermine her testimony on the ground of competency could only have a negative impact—assuming, that is, he found no hole in her qualifications. She testified concisely and professionally. He would cross-examine the same way.

"Mrs. DeFelice, did the .38 caliber Smith & Wesson revolver you tested bear its serial number intact?"

"Yes, it did. 94225."

"No attempt had been made to file it off, or anything like that?"

"No. It was undamaged."

"Did the Ohio Crime Laboratory check that serial number against the various files, FBI and so on, in an effort to learn who owned or had owned that pistol?"

"Yes, sir, and we learned nothing. The pistol was manufactured in 1953. There is no further record of it."

"Well then, Mrs. DeFelice, I would like to review with you for just a moment the results of your paraffin test."

"Yes, sir," she said calmly. She had not seen Kimball before, but she had been cross-examined by some immoderately aggressive lawyers, and she was apprehensive about this New York lawyer.

"To what extent, Mrs. DeFelice, does the paraffin test *quantify* the gunpowder residue taken from a subject's skin?"

"Could you be more specific?" she asked cautiously.

"Yes, of course," he said disarmingly. "Let me put it this way. The purpose of a paraffin test is to learn whether or not the subject has fired a pistol within the preceding few hours. Is that not right?"

"Yes," she said, nodding. "That's right."

"The test is really not used to determine how many *rounds* the subject has fired. Is that right?"

"No, it's not used that way."

"Right. Now. If the subject had fired twenty or fifty rounds, I suppose the amount of powder residue in the paraffin would be noticeable. Is that right?"

"That's right. I suppose so. I've never examined a sample where the subject was supposed to have fired that many rounds."

"All right. Now. If the subject fires one round, that should produce a trace of residue that you can detect. Right?"

"Right."

"But you really couldn't tell from the paraffin test if the subject had fired *two* rounds—one or two. Right?"

"That's right."

"And similarly you couldn't tell if the subject had fired three or six. Isn't that right?"

Deena DeFelice, as I had observed her in other trials, did not think of herself as a crusader for convictions. I imagine she was responsible for many criminal convictions, but I sensed of her in this trial and others that she would not prostitute herself or her expertise to bolster a weak case for the prosecution. She testified to facts. If the facts convicted the accused, fine. If they didn't, they didn't. I think juries sensed that too, even though they saw her only once. I admired her.

"No," she said. "I could not tell how many shots Miss Rheinlander fired."

"Are you aware that she has admitted firing three?"

"I heard that."

"Your paraffin test does not suggest she fired any more?"

Deena DeFelice shook her head. "It doesn't suggest that."

"Well, thank you, Mrs. DeFelice. Now . . . you have testified that you found Miss Rheinlander's fingerprints on the pistol. And you testified you found smudges also but no other identifiable finger-prints. Is that correct?"

117

"Correct."

"When you examined the pistol, had the empty shell casings been expelled from it, or were they still in it?"

"There were six empty shell casings in the chambers."

Kimball was not fishing here. He had interviewed this witness and knew the answers. "Did you examine *them* for fingerprints?"

"Yes. And I didn't find any."

"In your experience, Mrs. DeFelice, does not a person who loads a pistol ordinarily leave fingerprints on the cartridges as well as on the pistol?"

"Yes, I would think so."

"But these shell casings had no fingerprints on them. I would like to go a little further, Mrs. DeFelice. On what *parts* of the revolver did you find Miss Rheinlander's fingerprints?"

"On the grip and trigger."

"On the parts needed to fire it, in other words."

"Right."

"But none on the parts needed to load it?"

"Well . . . there were none on the cylinder."

"Is that not an unusual circumstance?" Kimball asked. "Indeed, how could a person load a revolver without leaving fingerprints on the cylinder and shell casings?"

"I'm not sure, Mr. Kimball."

"With gloves, Mrs. DeFelice?"

"That's possible."

"The person wearing gloves could, then, have also fired the revolver without leaving fingerprints on the grip and trigger. Right?"

"That is right."

"Mrs. DeFelice, I would like to turn to some tests I believe you performed, which the prosecuting attorney has not seen fit to inquire about. Did you examine the clothing taken from the bodies of the three victims?"

"Yes, I did."

"What tests did you perform on those items of clothing?"

"Well, first we took samples of the blood from various areas on

118

each item, to perform a blood typing test. That was to see if any of
the bloodstains were from the blood of anyone but the victim."

"With what result?"

"Bloodstains on the lower part of Miss Erb's nightgown were of
the congressman's blood type, not hers."

"How is that explained, Mrs. DeFelice?"

"The congressman's blood had run across the floor. You can see
that in the photographs of the scene."

I should explain that it had been agreed in meetings before the
trial began that the sickening color photographs taken by Bob Johnson would not be introduced in evidence and would not be seen by
the jury. Kimball objected to them on the ground that they proved
nothing but that the three people had been brutally murdered, said
nothing about who had done it, and could only serve to inflame the
minds of the jurors. Ken Simpson did not insist they be shown,
suspecting, I imagine, that I would have ruled to exclude them. I
would have so ruled.

"What other tests did you perform on those items of clothing?"

"We checked them for gunpowder residue."

"Why did you do that?"

"If the bullets had been fired into the victims at close range—say,
less than three feet—that would have left gunpowder residue in the
area where the bullet passed through the fabric."

"What did you find?"

"No gunpowder residue."

"Meaning?"

"Meaning that the shots were fired from a greater distance."

"Thank you very much, Mrs. DeFelice. I have no further questions."

At this point we took the break for lunch.

7

I ate lunch in my office in the courthouse. Linda brought it to me—a ham sandwich with lettuce, tomato, and mayonnaise, my favorite, with an apple and a Diet Coke—and she sat and chatted for a few minutes before she went on about her business. The defense team had asked that they and their client be permitted to lunch in the jury room, rather than Miss Rheinlander being taken back to jail for an hour, and I had ordered the sheriff's office to comply with that request.

Someone asked me later why no one had put a "lie detector" test into evidence—neither the prosecution nor the defense. The answer is that almost no court anywhere will allow polygraph tests—the correct name—to be put in evidence. The reason is that the so-called lie detector is a fantasy; there is no such thing as a machine that can tell whether a person is telling the truth or lying.

In the first place, the machine produces nothing but lines of squiggles on a moving paper. An "expert" must read those squiggles, and two "experts" may read the same squiggles differently. In the second place, personalities react differently. A person who murdered his grandmother may have no measurable emotional reaction to being asked if he murdered his grandmother, while another person will produce bouncy squiggles when asked what time it is.

A polygraph can sometimes be useful. For example, you can ask a subject attached to a polygraph where he hid a body. "Did you hide it at place A? place B? place C?" When you mention the place where he did hide it, he will generate bouncy squiggles. Maybe. Maybe he will and maybe he won't, depending on a number of factors. But to imagine that the machine can "detect" a lie is pure foolishness. The law cannot allow a gadget to replace trial by jury.

Our system of justice may not be perfect, but it is immeasurably superior to the so-called lie detector.

While I ate my lunch and read the New York *Times*, which had been delivered to my office during the morning, Court TV commentators were talking about how fast the trial was going. (I saw them on tape, that evening.) I didn't think it was going particularly fast. The prosecution was getting in its evidence. The defense was cross-examining. The case was not in fact immensely complicated.

The *Times* covered the trial. The Wednesday story was about the testimony of David Ogle and Kimball's cross-examination. Accompanying it was a profile of Lloyd George Kimball.

I was glad to read it. He was not exactly the man I had thought he was. Not a native New Yorker, he was a New Hampshireman. He was a veteran of the Korean War, in which he served as a Marine corporal and was wounded at Inchon. His service had interrupted his education, and he returned to graduate from Dartmouth, followed by law school at the University of Virginia. He was given a clerkship under a judge of the United States Circuit Court for the First Circuit: a distinct honor, recognizing ability in a young lawyer. Two years later he was recruited by a Boston firm. He remained with that firm for eight years, was made a partner, but left it because of dissatisfaction with the rigidity of its hierarchy—according to the New York *Times* reporter. Having married a young woman from New York City, he succumbed to her desire to return to Manhattan life. He moved to the city, passed the New York bar examination, and opened his own small office in Lower Manhattan.

Obviously there was money in the background. His wife's family had made the move possible. It was the last time anyone else's money helped Lloyd George Kimball. In 1971 he won the multimillion-dollar verdict in *Johnson* v. *Pan Pacific Airways*. It made his fortune and reputation. In 1973 he won acquittal for Dr. Virgil Kreinbihl. In 1974 he won the hundred-million-dollar class-action verdict in the Glamour Home Permanent case. And so on. His firm, soon established uptown in Manhattan, has never been Kimball and Somebody. It is Kimball and Associates.

He is, in an overused word, a workaholic. His eldest daughter is a concert violinist. His son is a lawyer in his firm. His younger daughter is married to an architect but is in her own right an artist whose welded sculptures bring very respectable prices. His wife, after rearing the children, went back to school and is a psychologist specializing in the emotional problems of the children of workaholic parents.

Kimball owns a sloop that he sails on Long Island Sound. The family gathers on the boat on summer weekends. He enjoys hockey and has season tickets for Rangers games.

The *Times* had apparently been quite impressed with Lloyd George Kimball, and the article was a little too laudatory to be called entirely objective. He won his cases, the article said, not by gimmicks, forensics, or by showing juries an appealing personality. He won because he was always thoroughly prepared.

It is true that hard work is the secret of a trial lawyer's success. That is why statistically trial lawyers have a shorter life expectancy than, say, corporation lawyers. I learned to respect Kimball's thorough preparation for this trial. I am not convinced, even so, that preparation was the only weapon in his armamentarium.

It was an interesting article. I was glad I had read it and glad the jury had not.

The first witness after the lunch break was the medical examiner who had examined the bodies on the floor of the lodge and later performed the autopsies.

Dr. Nath Kaul Chandra, called Pete by nearly everyone who knows him, is our county coroner. That is not a full-time job in a county the size of Alexandria County, and Dr. Chandra is on duty most of the time at the hospital, where he simply *is* the emergency room, besides being the finest neurosurgeon in southeastern Ohio.

He is Indian. He practices medicine here because we went looking for a doctor and, finding him, recruited him. His wife, in her sari, is an exotic, graceful sight on our streets and in our stores. We feel a little self-congratulatory about having Dr. Chandra here. He adds a cosmopolitan note to our little town.

Ken Simpson asked the questions that identified Dr. Chandra and qualified him as an expert witness.

"I direct your attention, Doctor, to the night of May 9 and 10 of this year. Were you called and asked to go to the Bailey lodge?"

Dr. Chandra preceded his answer with a small, short bow and polite smile—as he would preface his every answer to every question. "I was," he said.

He is of course dark-skinned. He is also compact. Small might be a better word, but that does not convey the fact that Dr. Chandra exudes an air of concentrated intelligence and energy packed in a diminutive person. A small voice comes from a small person. He speaks with an accent and uses the English language with careful precision.

"At what time did you arrive there?"

"It was approximately half past one o'clock in the morning of May 10."

"Were you asked to examine three bodies?"

"I was."

"Were you told who the bodies were?"

"I was."

"Who were you told they were?"

"I was told they were Congressman Charles Bailey, Miss Elizabeth Erb, and Mr. Donald Finch."

"Did you then examine the bodies?"

"I did."

"Turning first to the body of Congressman Bailey, whether or not that was the one you examined first, what did you observe?"

"I observed the body of a middle-aged man, partially dressed, lying on his side with his body drawn up in a fetal position, with a bullet wound which I then judged had punctured and shattered his sternum, which is the flat, narrow bone located on the median line of the front of the chest. The man was dead and had been so for approximately one hour."

123

"Referring to the body of Miss Elizabeth Erb, what did you observe?"

"I observed the body of a young woman lying face down, dressed in a white nightgown which was soaked with blood. I lifted the nightgown to see the wound and observed a bullet wound slightly to the right of the spine. The young woman was dead and had been so for approximately one hour."

"Referring to the body of Mr. Donald Finch, what did you observe?"

"I observed the body of a young man dressed in a light blue bathrobe soaked with blood. I opened the bathrobe to see the wound and observed a bullet wound to the left of the sternum and in the area of the fourth rib. The young man was dead and had been so for approximately one hour."

The members of the jury were transfixed by this testimony. It was the first description of the bodies they had heard. Murder can be a somewhat remote or theoretical concept until you hear a description of the dead body. That makes it immediate and personal. Their eyes shifted back and forth between Dr. Chandra and Miss Rheinlander, and I am sure they wanted to see how she reacted to this testimony. She reacted by lowering her chin, holding her hands flat together in front of her mouth and nose and keeping her eyes closed.

"Dr, Chandra, I refer you to the chart on the tripod. Do the letters *F*, *E*, and *B* accurately represent the position of the bodies as you remember seeing them?"

"They do."

"Did you subsequently perform autopsies on these three bodies?"

"I did."

Ken Simpson sat at his table, and now he opened a file, apparently one containing Dr. Chandra's autopsy reports. "Referring first to the body of Congressman Bailey, what was the cause of death?"

"The cause of death," said Dr. Chandra with his quiet, unemotional precision, "was a gunshot wound to the middle of the chest cavity, shattering the sternum and driving bone fragments into the heart and lungs. The bullet itself ruptured the pericardium near the top of the heart, penetrating and destroying the right auricle, and again rupturing the pericardium as it exited at the rear. The extreme pressure on the heart caused by the high-speed penetration of the bullet caused tearing of internal structures within the heart. The body cavity was immediately filled with blood."

Miss Rheinlander had opened her eyes and stared at Dr. Chandra. Her eyes were wet with tears, and she glanced repeatedly at her chief defense counsel.

"Would you say death was instantaneous?"

"Death is never instantaneous, sir. But it was as quick as any death possibly can be."

"Did you recover the bullet that caused the death of Congressman Bailey?"

"I did."

"Where did you find it?"

"It was on the floor. It had gone between two ribs of the back and through the silk jacket the congressman was wearing and was on the floor about four feet from his body."

"How do you know that the bullet you found on the floor is the one that killed Congressman Bailey?"

"It was stained with blood. The bullets that killed the other two victims remained inside their bodies. None of the bodies had more than one wound."

Ken drew a deep breath and sighed. He and I had seen the pictures, as had Kimball of course. The recollection of them made us all shudder.

"I hand you a bullet which has been marked as State's Exhibit B and ask you if it is the bullet you found on the floor near the body of the congressman."

Dr. Chandra accepted the bullet and frowned over it. It was a cylindrical hunk of lead, basically, though the front was flattened, giving the thing a vaguely mushroomlike appearance. "I did not find it, you understand. Deputy Johnson had found it and pointed it out to me. This is, I believe, the bullet that killed Congressman Bailey."

"Returning then to Miss Erb, what was the cause of her death?"

Dr. Chandra's testimony was quiet and precise. A bullet had struck the young woman's seventh dorsal vertebrae, which contact deformed it and sent it tumbling into her right lung, where it did extensive damage. If she had received immediate medical attention she might have survived. As it was, she bled to death before anyone could help her. The bullet remained in the body, stopped by a rib, and the physician was able to identify it—State's Exhibit C.

As to Finch, a bullet had caused extensive heart and lung damage. He had died very quickly. Dr. Chandra identified the bullet—State's Exhibit D.

Lloyd George Kimball walked over to the diagram of the lodge and stared at it for a moment, as though he had just noticed something on it that he had not noticed before. He stood beside the tripod and chart as he cross-examined Dr. Chandra.

"Doctor, is it part of the standard autopsy procedure when examining a person who has died of a gunshot wound to look for gunpowder residue on the skin?"

"It is."

"Did you perform any test for the presence of gunpowder residue?"

"I did."

"How is that test performed?"

"One applies a chemical that will change color in the presence of gunpowder residue."

"Will that test detect invisible traces of gunpowder residue?"

"Yes, it will."

"What was the result of your tests, Dr. Chandra?"

The little doctor bowed slightly as always and said, "I found no trace of gunpowder residue."

"What does that mean, Dr. Chandra?"

"It could mean two things: first, that the shot was fired from some distance away, second, that all the gunpowder residue was captured on the fabric of the victim's clothing and none penetrated to the skin."

"Is it true or not true that the gunpowder residue is more likely to reach the skin if the fabric of the clothing is light, also that there is only one layer of it?"

"That is true."

"And the congressman was wearing . . . ?"

"A thin silk jacket."

"Miss Erb?"

"A light cotton nightgown."

"Mr. Finch?"

"A terry-cloth robe."

"Are you aware, Dr. Chandra, that no trace of gunpowder residue was found on any of these items of clothing?"

"I have been so told."

"What does that lead you to conclude, Doctor?"

"That the shots were fired from some distance away."

"You testified that Congressman Bailey was shot through the heart, Mr. Finch was shot through a lung and the heart, and Miss Erb was shot through the spine and lung. If it was the shooter's intention to kill those three people, he could hardly have aimed more accurately, could he?"

"No, sir," said Dr. Chandra simply.

"Did you ascertain the blood-alcohol levels of the three victims?"

"I did."

"What was the percentage of alcohol in the blood of Miss Erb?"

"It was point-zero-nine per cent."

"How would you characterize that blood-alcohol level, in the context of whether or not she was intoxicated?"

"I would not describe her as intoxicated. That amount of alcohol in her blood is consistent with her having had a cocktail or two before dinner and perhaps a glass of wine or two with dinner. The law defines point-one-zero per cent as 'under the influence' for the purposes of driving a car, and she was slightly below that percentage."

"Mr. Finch?"

"Mr. Finch was point-one-two. I would describe that as seriously intoxicated, though not so much so as to make him unable to walk and so forth."

"Congressman Bailey?"

"He was point-one-four. He was definitely intoxicated."

"Were you asked to go to the county jail and take a blood sample from Miss Rheinlander?"

"I was."

"Did you examine her blood for alcohol?"

"I did."

"What did you find?"

"Miss Rheinlander's blood-alcohol level was point-one-one."

"At what time did you take that sample?"

"About three o'clock."

"Would her blood-alcohol percentage have diminished during the past two or three hours, assuming she had been drinking until midnight or so?"

"Yes, she would have assimilated some of the alcohol."

"Is it correct to say, then, that at the time when the fatal shots were fired Miss Rheinlander's blood-alcohol level was *at least* point-one-one and probably higher?"

"That is correct."

"It certainly couldn't have been any lower."

"That is correct."

"State law defines point-one-zero as impaired, so much so that a person should not drive a car. Correct?"

"Correct."

"At point-one-one a person would be somewhat more impaired, right?"

"Right."

Kimball walked away from the tripod and returned to the defense table, taking a stand in front of it. It is a good forensic tactic to move around the courtroom a little. It makes the jury a little more alert.

"Dr. Chandra, did you examine the body of Miss Elizabeth Erb to determine whether or not she had experienced sexual intercourse within the last hour or so of her life?"

"I did. That is standard autopsy procedure when examining the body of a woman who has been murdered."

"In your opinion, had she experienced sexual intercourse within the last few hours of her life?"

"No."

"How about Donald Finch?"

"He had experienced a very recent sexual emission. The *vesiculae seminales* were almost empty."

"What of the condition of his penis?"

"The skin was somewhat inflamed, as was the glans—suggesting the organ had been vigorously palpitated not long before his death."

"How about Congressman Bailey?"

"His *vesiculae seminales* were similarly almost empty. His penis was in a similar condition."

"Thank you, Dr. Chandra. That is all I wanted to ask you."

Ken Simpson understood the significance of these last questions. "Dr. Chandra," he asked, "could those two men's recent sexual emissions have been the result of masturbation?"

"Oh, yes," said Dr. Chandra.

Ken Simpson called Deputy Sheriff Margaret Vogt. After identifying her, he began his questions:

"Mrs. Vogt, how many women are deputies to Sheriff Dan Phelps?"

"I am the only woman deputy."

I have not before described Margaret she was a hard, wiry woman, thirty years old, given to wearing too much makeup: a deputy with complete dedication to her job, to the point where she had no sense of humor about it whatever. Her husband is a town policeman, her father is a highway patrolman, her grandfather was sheriff of Alexandria County. She carried a nine-millimeter Beretta automatic in her holster and had fired it twice in the line of duty.

"Since you are the only woman deputy, you have been in charge of Miss Rheinlander a good deal, have you not? I mean, you move her from the jail to court and back and so on."

"Right."

"Would you say you have come to know her pretty well?"

Margaret stared for a moment at Marietta Rheinlander. "I guess I know her reasonably well."

"As a result of your contacts with her, having her in your custody, observing her demeanor, and hearing her talk, have you formed an opinion as to whether or not Miss Rheinlander has a hot temper?"

"If Your Honor please," said Kimball curtly, rising to his feet. "The question calls for an opinion. Mrs. Vogt is not an expert witness on the question of whether or not a person has a hot temper."

"It is Ohio law, Your Honor," said Ken Simpson, "that a nonexpert witness may give opinion testimony on a matter within the common observation and experience of mankind."

I quieted both lawyers with a lifted hand. "Members of the jury," I said, "the lawyers need to argue a point of law. This may be as good a time as any for you to have a break. The bailiff will escort you to the jury room, and as many as wish may also go to the bathroom. We will call you back as soon as this point of law is decided—in no more than five minutes, I am sure."

When the jury was out of the courtroom, I nodded to Kimball and let him resume his argument. We remained on the record, and Alice Tutweiler went on pressing the keys on her stenotype machine.

"If the court please," he said, "the Supreme Court of Ohio ruled on this question in the case of Baltimore & Ohio Railroad Company versus Schultz, 43 Ohio State Reports 270." He turned to his assistant, Megan O'Reilly, who handed him a buckram-bound volume of the reports of the decisions of the Supreme Court of Ohio. "The supreme court has most emphatically held, Your Honor, that a nonexpert witness cannot give opinion testimony as to whether or not a person was angry, drunk, sick, in love, or insane, but can only testify to facts that might lead the jury to reach such a conclusion."

Ken Simpson had an open law book in front of him as well. "It has been held by a court of appeals, Your Honor—State versus

Moore, 74 Ohio Law Abstract 116—that a law-enforcement officer has sufficient experience with intoxicated persons to express a competent opinion as to whether or not a person is drunk. By the same token, a law-enforcement officer has sufficient experience with such states of mind as temper to express a competent opinion as to whether or not a person has a hot temper."

Ken's problem of course was that he had not, and probably could not, suggest a motive as to why Marietta Rheinlander would have wanted to kill Congressman Bailey and the other two. He wanted to make it appear that she killed Bailey in a fit of temper, after some furiously bitter quarrel, then killed Erb and Finch because they were witnesses. There were holes in that theory, but it wasn't even much of a theory if he could not establish that Miss Rheinlander had a violent temper.

Kimball spoke, "May I, Your Honor, read a paragraph from American Louisiana Pipeline Company versus Kennerck, 103 Ohio Appeals 133? The court ruled, 'Where it is practical to place palpably before the jury the readily perceptible facts supporting their opinions, non-expert witnesses should be restricted in their testimony to such facts, unaided by the mere opinions of the witnesses.' If Mrs. Vogt has observed facts from which the jury might conclude that Miss Rheinlander has a hot temper, let her testify to those facts and let the jury reach its conclusions."

I ruled. "Mr. Simpson," I said, "I am going to sustain the objection. Your witness may testify about facts that may lead the jury to conclude that the defendant has a hot temper."

"If the court please," said Kimball. "While the jury is out, I would like to raise a relevancy objection against any testimony to the effect that the defendant Miss Rheinlander pushed or shoved Mrs. Vogt. That is prejudicial and does not tend to prove anything that need be proved."

"I overrule you on that one, Mr. Kimball," I said. "The jury is entitled to hear testimony to the effect that the defendant has a hot, or violent, or uncontrollable temper."

"Please reserve an objection for the defense," said Kimball—

meaning he thought maybe he had just caught me in an error that would be helpful to him if he had to appeal the case.

When the jury was again in the box, we returned to the question Ken Simpson had asked before Kimball raised his objection. I had ruled that we could not hear Margaret Vogt's opinion on Miss Rheinlander's temper, so Ken had either to drop the subject or ask what facts Margaret had observed that might lead the jury to think Miss Rheinlander had a hot temper.

We were going to hear about the pushing incident.

"Mrs. Vogt, has the defendant at any time when she was in your custody committed an act of violence or aggression?"

"Yes, sir."

"Tell us about it."

"When I got her to the jail on the night of May 9, morning of May 10, I just put her in a cell. It was too late to take mug shots of her or fingerprint her. Anyway, she was crying and . . . well, I guess it's not too much to say she was hysterical. It was no time to try to take pictures of her or fingerprint her. I got Bess Whittlig out of bed and—"

"Identify Bess Whittlig."

"Bess is married to one of the deputies. She and her husband live in the apartment in the jail building. She cooks the food for the prisoners, and she's sort of night jailer when we have a woman in jail. Anyway, I got Bess out of bed and told her one of us was going to have to watch this woman all night."

"By 'this woman' you mean the defendant Miss Rheinlander?"

"Right. She was so upset I was afraid she'd try to hurt herself."

"All right. Go on."

"Bess watched her two hours, then I watched her two, and so on. Dr. Chandra came in and drew a blood sample, but otherwise Miss Rheinlander was not taken from her cell during the rest of the night. In the morning Bess gave her some breakfast, which she didn't eat. Then I told her she'd have to be photographed and fingerprinted. I took her out of the cell, and we did that. Then Bess came in again, 'cause I guessed we might have some trouble with what came next."

"Which was?"

"She had to be searched—meaning strip searched. We took her in a room where it was private, and I told her she'd have to take her clothes off. She said she'd be damned if she would. I told her she would, one way or another. She sort of backed away, shaking her head, and I reached out and took ahold of her arm. That was when she gave me a shove."

"Was it a hard shove?"

"Hard enough to throw me off balance. I fell back against the wall and kind of slid down the wall till I was almost down on the floor. Bess was scared and stepped back."

"Objection," said Kimball. "The witness knows that Bess stepped back. She does not know she was scared."

"Sustained."

"What did you do then?"

"I got up. I said to Miss Rheinlander . . . I don't know what words I used exactly, but I told her she was in trouble. I told her to get her clothes off and get 'em off now. She did it. She stripped. It was a body-cavity search, you know. Do I have to explain that?"

"No."

"Okay. She cooperated. She made it clear she didn't like it. She cried all the time, but she did what we told her. Then I made her take a shower, and we dressed her in some blue denims and took her back to her cell."

"Has there been any other incident of temper or violence?"

"I guess that depends on how you look at it."

"Describe any other incident or incidents that the jury might think represented incidents of temper or violence."

"Well . . . one time—she'd been in jail two weeks, I guess—I was putting her back in her cell after she'd been to court. I have a habit— I suppose it's a habit—of sort of taking a prisoner by the elbow and leading her into her cell. That time she jerked her arm away from me and said, 'Keep your hands off me! I know which way is in.'"

Ken turned a page in his yellow legal pad. "All right," he said. "When did you first see, or meet, Marietta Rheinlander?"

133

"That was on the night of May 9, morning of May 10. I was called to the Bailey lodge to take her into custody."

"Describe the incident."

"When I got there, she was sitting in the back of one of the cars, behind the screen. Her hands were cuffed behind her back. She was crying."

"What did you do?"

"I went in the house to find the sheriff and asked him what he wanted me to do. He told me to take her into town and lock her up. I asked him if she'd been formally arrested and read her rights and so on. He said yes, but he told me to do it again, because he didn't think he'd actually told her she was charged with murder. I went back to the car, got her out, told her she was under arrest for the murder of Congressman Bailey and the two other people, and read her her rights."

"How did she react?"

"She was hysterical. She screamed."

"Then what did you do?"

"I took her by the arm and led her over to my car. I put her in the back, behind the screen. Then I started the car and drove her into town."

"Did she talk to you during the drive to town?"

"Yes. She cried all the time, but she did say a few things. She told me she was in love with Congressman Bailey and couldn't possibly have killed him."

"What else did she say?"

"She asked me if I was going to put her in jail, and what kind of place was the jail, and what were we going to do to her? I told her we would put her in jail and hold her for trial. She asked me again what kind of place the jail was. I told her it wasn't a nice place but that it was clean and nobody would hurt her there."

"What else did she say?"

"She asked me if I'd stop and take the handcuffs off her, or at least let her have her hands in front. I told her we only had a few minutes more to go. She said the handcuffs hurt. I said they'd be off in five minutes. Then she kind of got quiet and cried some more."

"What else did she say?" Ken persisted.

"Well . . . when we got inside the town, she seemed to take an interest in the lights of the town. She sat up straight and looked around. Then she said, 'I guess I've really fucked up, haven't I? How could I have been so stupid! Jesus God, I've really fucked up.'"

Ken stared at his legal pad for the better part of a minute—for dramatic effect, of course. Then he sighed and said, "Thank you, Mrs. Vogt. I am sure Mr. Kimball has some questions."

8

Lloyd George Kimball remained seated, and for a long moment he stared at Margaret Vogt, then for another long moment he studied some notes on his yellow pad.

During the testimony of Margaret Vogt, Marietta Rheinlander had flushed and frowned, and twice at least she had wiped tears from her eyes with one finger—whether because she was tormented by her memories of her first hours in custody or because she thought the testimony damaging, I could not guess.

Ken Simpson sat impassive. I suspected he thought he had shot his best gun and had little left to do to make his case.

Kimball had cut some holes in the fabric, but the case for the prosecution remained strong. Marietta Rheinlander had been seen with the murder weapon in her hand. It bore her fingerprints, no one else's. She had attempted to flee. And then, in custody, she had made a statement, maybe inculpatory and maybe not, but surely suggesting she was guilty. Besides which, she had displayed a hot temper.

I was anxious to see how Kimball would handle the testimony of Margaret Vogt.

He had, of course, known how she would testify. He'd had time to prepare a defense. The question was, what sort of defense would he use?

"Mrs. Vogt," he began, "how long have you been a deputy sheriff of Alexandria County?"

"Nine years," said Margaret.

"Is it correct to say you have been a deputy for all of your working years?"

"Well, I worked as a waitress two years before I got to be a deputy."

"But, deputy is what you wanted to be, all your life?"

"I wanted to be some sort of law officer."

"In your nine years' experience, have you had many occasions to take custody of, and process into the jail, women who were charged with serious crimes, crimes that would produce long terms of imprisonment if they were found guilty?"

"Yes, sir. A good many times."

"What kind of crimes?"

"Well, murder only once before. But armed robbery. You get convicted of that, you go away for a long term. Burglary. Arson. Child abuse."

"Is it true then that you have seen and heard many women react to being arrested and charged with a serious crime?"

"I guess you could say many. Twenty-five or thirty."

"In your experience, would you say that the defendant Miss Rheinlander acted very differently from other women arrested, being locked up, and facing serious charges?"

This was a risky question for Kimball to ask. What if Margaret had answered that Miss Rheinlander did act differently, more violently? How could he prove otherwise? I think it is a compliment to Margaret Vogt that Kimball had confidence she was honest and professional and would answer the question forthrightly.

"I don't suppose she acted very different from most other women," said Margaret impassively.

"It's a tough deal, isn't it?" asked Kimball. "I mean, to find yourself arrested, your hands locked behind your back, then to find yourself confined in a cell, knowing you're going to be charged with a very serious crime. That's tough, isn't it?"

"It has to be a nightmare," said Margaret.

"And then early the next day, after the woman has spent a sleepless night inside a barred cell, she confronts an order that she strip herself naked. You've described how Miss Rheinlander reacted: that she gave you a hard shove. What do you think that represented, an ungovernable temper or a woman stressed to her limits by her situation?"

"Objection! That calls for an opinion and a conclusion."

"Mr. Kimball . . . ?"

"I withdraw the question, Your Honor."

He might as well. He'd made his point.

"Mrs. Vogt," Kimball continued, "when Mr. Simpson asked you questions, he excused you from describing just what a body-cavity search is. I wish I could, as well. But I'm afraid I'm going to have to ask you to explain to the jury what a body-cavity search is."

If there were two of the twelve jurors who did not know, I would be surprised. But you could see the jury tense to receive this titillating bit of testimony. Even mature and somber members of the jury unconsciously leaned forward and listened intently.

Margaret Vogt sighed. "Experience has proved," she said, "that a few people—very few—will try to smuggle into a jail or prison something they shouldn't have. It can be anything from diamonds to finance the bribing of somebody, to narcotics, to poison to commit suicide. They can carry it in any of the orifices of the body. This means that people like me have to search them in all those places. So we look in their mouths, in their nostrils, in their ears . . . and in their private parts."

Kimball nodded. "And that is how you were required to search Miss Rheinlander, was it not?"

"That's what we had to do."

"I'm sorry, but I have to ask you to describe to the jury just what you had to do."

Margaret Vogt hesitated for a moment, maybe waiting for an objection. Then she said, "Well, we made her open her mouth and pull her lips back with her fingers while she shined a flashlight inside. Then we looked up her nose, then in her ears. And then . . . well . . . she had to spread her legs and use her fingers to pull herself open, fore and aft, so we could see inside her private parts."

"How did Miss Rheinlander react to this experience?"

"She cried."

"Did she refuse or try to fight you off?"

"No, sir. She did what she was told."

"Incidentally, Mrs. Vogt, at what stage in her menstrual cycle was Miss Rheinlander on that day? If you know."

"She was menstruating. We provided tampons for her."

"All right. After you searched her, what happened?"

"I told her she had to take a shower. She did. After that, I gave her a pair of jeans and a blue-denim jacket and put her back in her cell. She could wear her own clothes after we'd searched them, and I handed her some of her own clothes half an hour or so later."

During all of this testimony, Marietta Rheinlander covered her face with her hands and bent over the table. She knew, as I did, that tonight this would be the highlight of every news story about her trial, as in fact it would remain for weeks.

"The matter of her jerking her arm away from you and demanding that she be allowed to walk into her cell on her own," said Kimball. "Was that unusual?"

Margaret shook her head. "No."

"When you bring Miss Rheinlander to court from the jail and when you take her back again, you handcuff her, do you not?"

"Yes."

"And fasten the handcuffs to a chain around her waist."

"Yes. That's right."

"How does she react to being chained that way? I mean, does she resist it, or does she cooperate?"

"She cooperates. She's patient about it."

Kimball rubbed his hands together. "Considering the amount of stress and all the rest of it, she has not been a terribly unusual prisoner, has she?"

Ken objected, of course. I allowed the answer.

"I guess not," said Margaret. "Once we got past the first few days she settled down and accepted what she had to."

It was time to take the afternoon break.

I sat in my office with a can of Diet Pepsi. Dick Winter came in. Like many others in town—in town? in the world—he had developed a fascination with this trial and had taken time off from his busy practice to come into the courtroom and sit inside the bar, watching intently.

"Y' missing something if you aren't paying any attention to that young lawyer Megan O'Reilly," he said to me.

I admit I had given little attention to Lloyd George Kimball's junior associate. I had taken her for a mousy little girl, which in itself was wrong, because she— well, in the first place mousy little girls did not work as attorneys at Kimball and Associates. Anyway, she was not mousy. Her dark eyes snapped at questions and answers, and she scribbled furiously on her pad and handed Kimball her notes, which he invariably read. She kept in front of her an Ohio trial evidence manual, and when Kimball raised an objection, or Ken Simpson raised one, she opened the manual to the right page, so Kimball would have the rule and explanatory case notes before him. She had a small stack of case reports volumes on the table, too, with slips inserted at the pages where there were cases Kimball might want to read from, as he had done during the argument on opinion evidence.

"She's not bad to look at either," Dick said.

"I guess she isn't," I said.

There we were, two old men appraising a young professional woman on the basis of her looks. That's what's called sexism. I guess Dick and I are too old to discard the habits of a lifetime. In our defense, our first thoughts *had* been about her professional ability.

"You and I," said Dick reflectively, "can't imagine what it must be like to practice law the way those people do."

"I can't imagine being paid $75,000 my first year out of law school," I said.

"I can't imagine the demands that must be met to earn that $75,000. The hours . . . I looked her up in Martindale–Hubbel. She's a graduate of the Michigan Law School, class of 1989. What you want to bet she works a sixty-hour week?"

"It's what you call a career," I said. "You and I just make a living."

* * *

We returned to the courtroom.

Lloyd George Kimball stood in front of the jury box, with a hand on the rail. "Mrs. Vogt," he said, "I would like to return to your testimony about statements made by Miss Rheinlander on the way from the Bailey lodge to the county jail. Her statement was 'I guess I've really fucked up, haven't I? How could I have been so stupid! Jesus God, I've really fucked up.' What did you take those words to mean?"

"Objection," said Ken Simpson. "It is for the jury to decide what the words meant. The question calls for an opinion."

"Sustained," I said.

"Mrs. Vogt," said Kimball, "did you—do you now—consider those words ambiguous or unambiguous?"

"Objection."

"We will let the witness testify as to whether or not she thought the words were ambiguous," I ruled.

Margaret sighed and said, "I suppose the words were ambiguous."

"In other words, they were susceptible of two interpretations and maybe more. Isn't that right?"

"Yes."

"Miss Rheinlander could have been referring to a number of things. Correct?"

"Yes."

"She was not necessarily confessing to murder—"

"Objection!"

"I am going to sustain, Mr. Kimball," I said. I turned to the jury. "Members of the jury, you have heard the words spoken by Miss Rheinlander. In fact, you have heard them twice. It will be for you to determine what those words meant, what Miss Rheinlander intended to express."

Kimball stood frowning for a moment, glanced at Miss O'Reilly as if to ask if she had any suggestions, then said, "Thank you, Mrs. Vogt. I have no further questions."

*   *   *

At this point I would not have been surprised if Ken Simpson had rested for the state. I imagined Kimball thought he would. But Ken had a surprise for us.

"The state now calls Mrs. Bess Whittlig," he said.

Bess is a plump little woman, blonde, attractive. She was sworn and took her seat on the witness stand, tugging her skirt down, visibly nervous. She was one of the witnesses most disturbed by the television cameras.

"Mrs. Whittlig, tell the jury what your duties are with respect to the county jail."

"I cook the meals," she said. "That's mostly what I do. When we've got a woman in jail, I go back and check 'em every so often. When somebody is checkin' in and has gotta be strip searched, I go back and watch, 'cause there's supposed to be two witnesses there when that's done."

"You mean, of course, when a woman is searched."

"Oh, yeah. I never seen a man strip searched. Wouldn't wanta."

She said it so innocently that a surge of laughter spread across the courtroom.

"Did you witness the strip search of the defendant Marietta Rheinlander?"

"Yeah. I was there when Margaret searched her."

"Did you see the defendant Marietta Rheinlander give Margaret Vogt a shove?"

"Yeah."

"Please describe the demeanor of Miss Rheinlander at that time?"

"Huh?"

"Was Miss Rheinlander angry, so far as you could tell?"

"I'd say she was pretty mad, yeah. She didn't want to take her clothes off."

"All right. Miss Rheinlander has been in your jail for something like five months now, right?"

"That's right."

I should stop here and explain that Ken would ask no questions about some special privileges Marietta Rheinlander had been allowed: her meals from outside, her radio, and so on. He and Kimball had met with me on Friday before the trial started, and we'd reached some agreements. One agreement was that no mention would be made of any of this. That kind of talk could prejudice a jury, and I would not allow it.

It had been agreed, too—normal procedure—that the jury was not to see the defendant in handcuffs or under any other form of restraint. Nothing of the kind was even to be brought into the courtroom. The general idea is that seeing a defendant wearing restraints tends to make a jury think that person is dangerous, and guilty. It had surprised me when Kimball had asked Margaret Vogt about handcuffs and the belly chain. He had balanced the sympathy he thought he'd get for his client against the negative impression he risked creating.

"Would you say you've gotten to know her reasonably well?"

"I guess I've got to know her pretty well. I take her in her meals. I stand and talk with her when I can."

"During these talks, did she ever say anything to you about the murders?"

"Yes, sir."

"What did she say?"

"She told me she killed those folks and figured she'd have to spend the rest of her life in prison."

"NO!" Marietta Rheinlander shrieked. *"I never said any such thing! NO! She's lying!"*

Both Kimball and Miss O'Reilly grabbed the defendant by the arms, or she would have jumped to her feet. They hovered over her, joined by Bob Mitchell, her local counsel. She shook her head wildly and whispered shrilly to Kimball. I heard the words, "liar, liar." I heard her sob.

The crowd in the courtroom did stand, some of them, and some

143

reporters struggled their way toward the doors. Miss Rheinlander's mother began to cry. Her husband clutched her to himself and patted her back.

I rarely use my gavel, but I used it now. "The court will be in order," I barked. "Order! Everyone sit down."

It took two or three minutes to bring the courtroom to order. I rapped the gavel and pointed with it to some clusters of people who were talking.

When the room was quiet again, I spoke to Kimball. "Mr. Kimball, do you feel you can proceed?"

His client wept. She seemed unaware now of what was going on.

"May I approach the bench, Your Honor?" Kimball asked. "With Mr. Simpson."

I nodded, and the two lawyers came to the bench. I indicated to Mrs. Tutweiler that we were off the record.

"I need hardly tell you that this comes as a complete surprise," Kimball said in a low voice the jury could not hear. He nodded at Ken. "Congratulations, Mr. Simpson," he said sarcastically. It was the first sign of emotion I had seen from Lloyd George Kimball. "I need some time to analyze this and prepare a cross-examination. I would appreciate a recess until tomorrow morning."

I spoke to Ken. "How much more do you want from this witness?"

"Just one or two more questions," he said.

"I suggest we hear the answers to those questions," I said to Kimball. "Then I'll give you your recess."

Kimball nodded. "Let me have a couple of minutes to calm her down," he said.

I nodded. He went back to his client and spoke earnestly to her. She looked up and at first seemed hardly to recognize him or know where she was. Then she began to nod. Kimball looked up at me and nodded. I gestured to Ken Simpson.

"Mrs. Whittlig," he said, "I would like for you to tell the jury, to the best of your recollection, the exact words Miss Rheinlander used when she told you she committed the three murders."

"She said, 'I done it, you know. I done somethin' awful.'"

"Did Miss Rheinlander discuss this matter with you once or more than once?"

"Uh . . . more than once."

"What else did she say to you?"

"She asked me about the Ohio Reformatory for Women. She said she figured she'd have to spend the rest of her life there and wondered what kind of place it was."

"Did she say anything else whatever to you on the subject of the murders?"

"No, that was it."

"Thank you, Mrs. Whittlig. No more questions."

"At this point," I said, "the court will stand adjourned until nine o'clock tomorrow morning."

While I was still hanging up my robe and checking the weather through the window in the jury room, the defense team and their tearful client hurried in. Marietta Rheinlander was distraught, almost hysterical. I hastened to leave these people with some privacy, but as I opened the door into the clerk's office, Margaret Vogt walked in, and I could not help but witness a little scene I thought was telling.

Margaret was carrying the handcuffs and belly chain. Miss Rheinlander looked at them with a stricken expression, and Margaret said to her, "Give me your word you'll be good, and we'll leave these off this time." Miss Rheinlander nodded tearfully, and Margaret put the manacles and chain in her shoulder bag. In fact, that was the last we saw of the chain. On subsequent days, Margaret handcuffed her prisoner but did not use the chain.

I worked in my office for an hour or so, then Linda joined me, and we walked down the street to the Alexandria House for a drink or two in the bar before we went home for dinner. Glen Myers was there. So was Dick Winter. A reporter approached me and wanted to ask a question, but I told him I simply could not talk about the case.

We sat down on bar stools, and Glen turned to me and said quietly but very emphatically, "There is something fishy about what Bess Whittlig said."

"I agree with that," said Dick Winter.

Linda and I ordered our drinks: Beefeater martinis on the rocks with twists. The *Newsday* reporter had noticed that we drank martinis, but he had overlooked the fact that they were Beefeater martinis, which makes a world of difference. We know about these things, even in the wilds of the Ohio Valley.

"Tomorrow," said Glen Myers, "we are going to find out what kind of lawyer Lloyd George Kimball really is. I wouldn't want to be Bess Whittlig, facing the cross-examination she's going to get in the morning."

A commentator for Court TV said something similar, as we watched at home a couple of hours later. Calling Bess Whittlig "a surprise witness," the commentator said her testimony had shocked the defense team, which had obviously been unprepared for it.

A New Jersey trial lawyer, appearing as an expert to explain points of law and matters of strategy, said, "I have to be skeptical. It's obvious that Lloyd George Kimball and his associates have prepared for this case very thoroughly, and they've prepared the defendant, too. I just can't imagine that she would have confessed to a jailer and not told her lawyers about it."

"Well, Mr. Kimball has his work cut out for him tomorrow, doesn't he?"

"Tomorrow is when he earns his fee," said the New Jersey lawyer.

Bess Whittlig may have seen that report on Court TV. She had surely heard from somebody anyway that she faced a difficult ordeal in the morning. When she took the stand to face cross-examination, she was tense and flushed and clasped her hands tightly together.

Miss Rheinlander was wearing again her cream-white linen dress, and she looked drawn. I knew that her lawyers had been at the jail with her for most of the evening.

Lloyd George Kimball did not stand up to question Bess Whittlig. He sat at the defense table, his elbows on the table, his hands pressed flat together.

"Mrs. Whittlig," he said, "please repeat for the jury the words you claim Miss Rheinlander spoke to you about the murders. Tell us again exactly what she said."

Bess turned down the corners of her mouth and nodded. "She said, 'I killed 'em.'"

Kimball shook his head. "That's not what you testified yesterday. Do you remember what you told us yesterday?"

Bess lifted her chin. She opened her mouth but hesitated for a moment. "Not the exact words, I don't remember."

"All right. Let's read what you said yesterday. Will you do that for us, Mrs. Tutweiler?"

Alice Tutweiler had been alerted that she would be asked to read this portion of her transcript, and she read:

> *"Question*, MR. SIMPSON: Mrs. Whittlig, I would like for you to tell the jury, to the best of your recollection, the exact words Miss Rheinlander used when she told you she committed the three murders.
> *"Answer*, MRS. WHITTLIG: She said, I done it, you know. I done somethin' awful."

"Thank you, Mrs. Tutweiler. Now, Mrs. Whittlig, when Mr. Simpson asked you for Miss Rheinlander's exact words, you testified yesterday afternoon that she said, 'I done it, you know. I done somethin' awful.' Now you are testifying that she said, 'I killed 'em.' Which was it, Mrs. Whittlig? Mr. Simpson asked you for the exact words. This morning I asked you for the exact words. You did not answer with the same exact words. So, I ask you again, what were Miss Rheinlander's exact words? Do you want to give us a third version?"

Bess blinked tears from her eyes. She stared at Ken Simpson as if she thought he might raise some objection and help her. We waited for an answer. Kimball did not prompt her. He just looked at her calmly, with an air of patience, and waited for her answer.

"I had it right the first time," she said finally, her voice breaking.

"All right, then," said Kimball. "We are settled about it, right? Miss Rheinlander said, 'I done it, you know. I done somethin' awful.' Is that your recollection and your testimony?"

"Yes."

Kimball turned to his client and said something. I could see what the jury could not see: that he smiled as he made his quiet comment.

Well he might. He had just poked a big hole in Bess Whittlig's testimony. It was obvious, and the jury knew it without his even having to argue it, that the educated and sophisticated Marietta Rheinlander would not have said, "I done it."

"Mrs. Whittlig, you don't much like Miss Rheinlander, do you?"

Bess shrugged. "I got nothin' against her."

"Has she been in any way a special burden to you, beyond what other prisoners in the jail are?"

"Not particular."

"How does she like your cooking?"

"She don't eat it."

The agreement had been that *the prosecution* could not mention the fact that Marietta Rheinlander was allowed to receive meals delivered to the jail by the kitchen at the Alexandria House. Nothing prevented the defense from raising it. If Kimball wanted to take the risk, that was his business—and I supposed he had considered the question carefully and reached a conclusion.

"She doesn't?"

"No, her dinners and suppers come in from the Alexandria House hotel."

"Special food . . ." said Kimball quietly.

"Right. She gets special dinners and suppers—which includes bottles of wine. In the jail. I guess she can afford it."

"Mrs. Whittlig, how would you describe the food you serve to the prisoners in the Alexandria County jail?"

"It's the best I can do for the money I'm allowed to pay for it," said Bess defensively.

"I am sure it is," said Kimball. "But would you say it might be a little . . . fattening? I mean, considering that a prisoner gets no exercise. Might it be that your meals—the best you can do, considering the allowance the county makes to pay for them—are a little heavy on starch and fat?"

"I do the best I can," said Bess sharply.

"We understand you do," said Kimball. "But . . . do other prisoners ever receive extra food from their families? Like fruit and candy, which are too expensive for you to buy?"

"Yeah."

"Do families bring radios in?"

"Yeah."

"And Miss Rheinlander does have a battery-powered radio in her cell?"

"Yeah."

"Does she receive *any* privileges that are not allowed to other prisoners?"

"I never seen anybody get their dinners and suppers from the hotel before."

"If another prisoner could afford to have meals brought in from a restaurant, would the sheriff not allow it?"

"I don't know. He told me I had to let *her* have 'em."

"He said you *had* to let her have them. Does that mean you would not have allowed her to receive those outside meals otherwise?"

"Whatta ya mean?"

"If it were up to you, would you let her have outside meals?"

"No."

"Why not?"

"Who's *she*? Why should she have somethin' special?"

"If it were up to you, would you allow prisoners to receive things like fruit and candy and cigarettes from their friends and families?"

"That's different."

"How is it different?"

"Well . . . I don't know exactly. It's just different."

"How is it different?" Kimball asked again, his voice hard and challenging.

"It's just different."

"Did you tell the sheriff you didn't like it?"

"Yeah."

"And what did he say?"

Bess drew breath. She is not stupid, and you could almost see the wheels going around in her head. She guessed Kimball had called Dan Phelps last night and asked him. "He said I had to do it."

"Whether you liked it or not?"

"Yeah."

"And you *don't* like it?"

"Well . . ."

"Did you ever tell anybody that you don't like it?"

"I guess I might have mentioned it to somebody."

"Did you ever tell anybody you don't like Marietta Rheinlander?"

"Uh . . . no. I don't mind her. She's . . . interestin'."

"Thank you, Mrs. Whittlig."

Ken Simpson rose. "Mrs. Whittlig," he asked, "have you ever known a prisoner in the county jail to be allowed to drink wine or beer or any other form of alcohol during his or her imprisonment?"

"No, I never hearn of it."

"Thank you, I have no further questions. Your Honor, the State rests."

9

At this point in the trial, Lloyd George Kimball might have moved for dismissal or a directed verdict of acquittal. That he didn't demonstrated that he knew Ken Simpson had made out a strong case against his client. If he had made such a motion, I would have overruled him, as he knew.

No. The case had to go to the jury.

In the glare of television lights. Under the eyes of cameras. Marietta Rheinlander was of course the focus of attention. Much of the time a camera was on her, even though the cameras were both behind her and could not televise the expressions on her face except when she turned to speak with one of her lawyers.

She faced me, and I could see her face most of the time. So could the jury, though they saw her in profile. I remarked earlier that her face was perhaps more expressive than was good for her. It told too much and spoke this morning of heavy weariness, even of resignation, also of fear. You have to think about it. This woman was accustomed to living well, even luxuriously, to the company of sparkling companions, to a variety of stimulating events. This woman had spent the past five months in a six-by-eight-foot cell, most of the time alone. She faced a triple life sentence—assuming I did not sentence her to death.

It is not fashionable—the current phrase might be, I suppose, not "politically correct"—to acknowledge the fact that the punishment for crime falls heavier on some people than it does on others. In my experience as a lawyer and judge, I've seen men in the county jail who were not terribly distressed to be there. For them, confinement in a jail or prison is an inconvenience and not much more. They sit around in dirty T-shirts, comparing tatoos, smoking unfiltered cigarettes, swapping stories, and forming homosexual liaisons. Circumstances that would be a horror for me are not much more than an annoyance to them. I've seen men lose their tempers in the courtroom and kick a chair or table because they've just been sentenced to a three-to-five. But they are not terrified. They've been there before. I've seen other men dissolve in tears at the terrifying prospect of three to five years in a penal institution. Don't tell me the punishment is the same, just because it's the same three-to-five in each case.

Punishment for crime is supposed to deter. But it does so only in a limited sense. Our chief punishment is confinement, but confinement is not punishment to a certain class of men and women. What can I hope to accomplish by sentencing an inveterate automobile thief to a term in the penitentiary? Probably nothing. You and I don't write hot checks, because the idea of being locked up in a place like that scares us to death. The auto thief goes on stealing cars because he finds it more inconvenient to be without wheels than to do a short stretch in the crowbar hotel.

Oh, on this subject I'm not democratic, not egalitarian, not politically correct. But I'm telling the truth. Confinement in the county jail was living hell for Marietta Rheinlander. That's why I'd told Dan Phelps to let her have outside meals, including bottles of wine.

The prospect of spending a minimum of twenty years—and realistically probably many more years, since she was on trial for three murders, not just one—confined in the women's reformatory had to be almost more than she could bear.

I am not robbing this story of suspense when I tell you I was strongly disinclined to sentence Marietta Rheinlander to death, even if she were convicted of three murders. I am not robbing it of suspense because you know what happened, it being so notorious a case. There was some editorializing to the effect that if ever a defendant deserved a death sentence that defendant was Marietta Rheinlander; but her life was not really seriously at stake in this trial. At the end the decision and responsibility would be mine, no matter if the jury did find she killed Elizabeth Erb to eliminate her as a witness, and I would be entitled to consider mitigating circumstances as well, such as that Miss Rheinlander had no prior criminal record. I had no intention of sentencing her to death. I couldn't send that word to her, but I think Lloyd George Kimball was perceptive enough to know it and had probably told her.

If I had wanted to do her a kindness, a death sentence would have been kinder than three life sentences. It would have been preferable, anyway, except for the protracted ordeal of repeated and repeated appeals that follow death sentences in this country today.

I have gone through old court records. In 1870, say, a man convicted of murder on October 25 was hanged on November 5. I remember a case in the 1950s when a couple kidnapped and killed a little boy, were caught and brought to trial, convicted, exhausted their appeals, and died in a gas chamber, all within three months. Too fast. But in my judgment, a capital case should be thoroughly and carefully tried, the judge intervening to see that every right of the defendant is asserted and recognized, even if his counsel fails to raise points he should raise; conviction should be followed by an exhaustive examination of the trial record by the several appellate courts, and every argument should be heard and considered and ruled on. No more than one year should pass between conviction and either reversal or execution. Let it be done once, let it be done right, and let it be finished.

As a judge I cannot say that I will never impose a death sentence. I have to say that I will apply the law the state legislature has enacted. I can say, though—and do say—that I will apply it where the enormity of the crime clearly requires it. That is not because I entertain wimpish sympathy for murderers. It is because the eternally drawn-out appeals process we now have leaves the convicted person hanging in limbo for too many years. It is cruel and unusual punishment.

It punishes, too, the people who have to administer the system. And in that context, let me say that I do not condemn lawyers who bring repeated appeals and petitions for habeas corpus. If you represent a person under a death sentence, you are ethically and morally obligated to do everything the system allows to save your client's life. What else can you do, bearing that responsibility? It's not the defense lawyers who are at fault; it is the system.

To sentence a murderer to life imprisonment is adequate punishment and as good a deterrent as the death penalty—provided that a life sentence *means* life. In some states it means a whole lot less. I am as outraged as the next person when I hear that some murderer has been released on parole after serving six or seven years. If that were the way it was in Ohio, I would impose death sentences.

Anyway, Marietta Rheinlander sat in my courtroom contemplating her personal hell—life in prison or death in the electric chair—and it showed, as it was bound to show.

That morning as he rested his case, the strain on Ken Simpson showed, too. He didn't know I would not impose the death sentence he was asking for. I couldn't have told him any more than I could have told Kimball. Having rested his case, he was suddenly burdened with the horror of what he was asking this jury and this judge to do. He had been honest when he said in his opening statement that he hoped he would never have to ask for the death penalty again. He had to do it—a triple murder—but he was oppressed by it. He was thirty-one years old, and he was going to argue that a woman be clamped in an electric chair and put to death by the application of electric current. It was his duty.

That is another argument against the death penalty: what it does to the people who have to administer the law. Suppose I had sentenced Marietta Rheinlander to death and she was executed, and then, two years later, ten years later, we learned she had not been guilty after all. What would that dreadful knowledge have done to me? What would it have done to Ken Simpson? To the members of the jury? To the governor who denied executive clemency? To the warden who supervised the execution?

People who simplistically argue for the death penalty think of it in terms of the criminal and the victim. They don't think of the people who have to carry the penalty into effect. I doubt most of them could pull the switch, if it came to it. I'm not sure I have much respect for those who could. Executioners do what they have to do because they hold offices that entail that duty and know that if they don't do it somebody else will. It has a damaging impact on every one of them.

Lloyd George Kimball called his first witness.

"The defense calls Det. Lt. Robert Dugan."

The man who now took the witness stand was a bulky individual in a dark blue suit, who moved somewhat clumsily as he crossed the front of the courtroom, took the oath, and sat down.

"State your name, please."

"Robert Dugan."

"What is your profession or occupation?"

"I am a detective first grade, Manhattan South, New York Police Department."

"Mr. Dugan, what is the law of New York relative to the ownership of pistols?"

Dugan had a big square face. He was, I suppose, what in New York is called a typical Irish cop. "We have what is called the Sullivan Law," he said. "Under that law, it is illegal to own a handgun in the state, anywhere in the state. That's to own it, even in your own home."

"Are there exceptions?"

"You can apply for a license."

"Did you, Mr. Dugan, at my request check the records to determine whether or not Miss Marietta Rheinlander has such a license or ever applied for one?"

"Yes, I did. She does not have a license and never asked for one."

"I would like you to examine a revolver that has been marked as State's Exhibit A. We have heard testimony to the effect that the fingerprints of the defendant were found on the grips and trigger of this pistol, but none were found on the cylinder or any other part of the weapon. What is more, none were found on the spent cartridges that remained in the pistol after it was fired. In your judgment, based on your experience as a police investigator, could a person have loaded this pistol without leaving fingerprints anywhere but on the trigger and grips?"

"No, sir. No way. Unless the person wore gloves."

"In your experience as a New York City detective, is it usual or unusual for a murder weapon to bear fingerprints only on the trigger and grips and nowhere else?"

Ken Simpson frowned, obviously thinking of objecting, but he did not and allowed the answer.

"I'd say that's *very* unusual. You often see a pistol with no finger-prints on it at all—meaning somebody had been careful to see it had no prints on it—but fingerprints on the grips and trigger only—" Detective Dugan shook his head. "I've never seen a case like that."

"Mr. Dugan, would you call this an *accurate* weapon?"

"No, sir. This pistol has got a five-inch barrel. It's designed to shoot somebody at close range. It's a personal-defense weapon or a close-range deadly weapon."

"Would this pistol kick or buck when it's fired?"

"Yes, sir. To some extent it would."

"Testimony in this case has shown that each of the three murder victims was killed by a single bullet fired into a vital organ of the body. Does that impress you as exceptional marksmanship?"

"Objection," said Ken Simpson. "That calls for an opinion."

"Mr. Simpson," I said, "do you challenge Detective Dugan's quali-fications as an expert witness?"

Ken pondered for a moment. "I . . . I suppose not."

"Well, if he's an expert witness, he's entitled to state an opinion," I said. "I will overrule the objection."

Dugan was obviously an experienced witness. He had waited patiently and had his answer ready. "That depends on the range and whether or not the victims were standing still or moving," he said. "But I would say, based on my experience investigating literally hundreds of deaths caused by firearms, that it would be very unusual for someone to be able to fire that accurately. You have to assume that the people were moving."

"I object to the assumption," said Ken Simpson.

"Members of the jury," I said. "Please take note that the witness has testified that he *assumes* the victims were moving. We have had no evidence that the victims were moving or not moving."

"Mr. Dugan," said Kimball, "two of the victims, Congressman Bailey and Donald Finch, were shot in the front of their bodies, while the third victim, Elizabeth Erb, was shot in the back. In your experience, does that suggest the victims were moving, at least that Miss Erb was attempting to flee?"

"Objection. The answer would be nothing but speculation."

I sustained the objection. Kimball had made his point.

"Detective Dugan, there has been testimony to the effect that a period of one second or more elapsed between each of the first three shots. In your professional experience, do people being shot at stand and wait to be hit, or do they move?"

"Objection!"

"We'll hear this answer to this question," I said.

Dugan had been prepared and knew every question he would be asked. "In my experience," he said, "they try to escape, if they have the time."

Kimball stood nodding and apparently pondering, as if trying to decide if he had more questions. He ran his hand through his white hair. "I believe that's all, sir," he said.

Ken Simpson rose. "Detective Dugan, in your experience are people being shot at normally in a state of shock?"

"Yes, sir. I think that would be usual, or normal."

"Terror?"

"Yes, sir."

"Which might freeze them in their tracks for a short time?"

"Yes, sir."

"Thank you. No further questions."

Kimball stood for redirect. "Do you think Miss Erb was shocked and frozen in her tracks, considering that she had turned her back on the gunman?"

"Your Honor! There has been no evidence that Miss Erb *turned*

157

her back. She may have been standing with her back toward . . . toward the person who shot her."

I looked at Kimball and couldn't help but smile. He smiled, too, shrugged, and said, "I guess that's a point well taken. I withdraw the question. And I have no more questions for the witness."

The man was skilful in arguing his case in his questions, getting his points before the jury even when he invited objections I had to sustain.

He had a facility, too, for making the jury think he and they had some little secrets together. Sometimes when Ken Simpson was asking a question, Kimball would smile almost invisibly at the jury: a smile that came more from his eyes than from his mouth.

"The defense calls Mr. Richard Lysander."

Lysander was a tall, gaunt black man with a bony face, close-clipped hair, and extraordinarily long arms and big hands. He wore a dark blue suit with narrow lapels and a narrow black tie.

"Mr. Lysander, will you please tell the jury where you are employed and in what capacity?"

"I am employed at La Guardia Airport," said Lysander in a rich dark voice. "I am assistant director of airport security."

"How long have you held that position?"

"Eight years, approximately."

"What did you do before that?"

"I have always been employed in airport security," said Lysander. "I was at first a uniformed guard. Then I was several times promoted."

"As assistant director of airport security at La Guardia, are you in charge of such things as the magnetometers that check passengers as they pass into the concourses, the X-ray machines that check luggage, and so on?"

"Yes. During my work shift, I am the supervisor for all the personnel that operate that equipment, and it is my responsibility to see that all such equipment is in working order and that all prescribed security measures are in fact taken."

"I now hand you a document which will be marked Defense Exhibit B and ask you to identify that document."

"This is a partly used airline ticket."

"Please give the jury the details of that ticket."

"It is a ticket for 'M. Rheinlander,' for USAir Flight 127, New York La Guardia to Pittsburgh, then USAir Commuter Pittsburgh to Parkersburg, West Virginia, on May 5, 1992. That part of the ticket was used. The coupons for the return flights were not used."

Kimball took the ticket and handed it to Ken Simpson to examine. Ken waved it off, and Kimball handed it to Alice Tutweiler to be tagged.

"Mr. Lysander, would it have been possible for Miss Rheinlander or any other person to carry a pistol aboard a USAir flight leaving La Guardia Airport on May 5, 1992?"

"No, sir. Not on her person or in carry-on baggage, or in checked luggage."

"If you know, Mr. Lysander, would the same checks have been performed at Pittsburgh?"

"Unless she recovered her luggage at Pittsburgh, it would not have been X-rayed a second time. She would have passed through another magnetometer at the entrance to the concourse and could not have carried a pistol through on her person or in her carry-on luggage."

"Thank you, Mr. Lysander. That's all."

Ken Simpson had no questions.

Megan O'Reilly got up and left the courtroom, following Richard Lysander. He had traveled all the way from New York to spend three minutes on the witness stand, and I imagine she went out to thank him, maybe also to be sure he had been adequately paid for his expenses.

The defense then called a private investigator named Leroy Van-Kamp. So-called private detectives are not a class that appeal to me. The brave and honest private eye is a staple of bad fiction and is to be found only in bad fiction. The archetypal private investigator is a sleazy paid snoop. I had seen Leroy VanKamp in my courtroom before, and I suppose if I had to face one of the ilk at all, I could face VanKamp better than others.

As unkempt and seemingly disoriented as Columbo, he was a man of sixty who had made a doubtful living all his life taking money for spying on people. Myopic, he squinted at the world through thick bifocal glasses, which he adjusted on his nose, not with his fingers, but by lowering his jaw to stretch his cheeks and raising his eyebrows. Oddly, he made an effective witness, mainly I suppose because he impressed juries as too stupid to lie. Some called him Porky, an allusion to Van Camp's pork and beans.

He worked out of Cincinnati. The small towns of southeastern Ohio offered no employment for private investigators, except two or three of the dullest of them.

"Mr. VanKamp, did you at my request make an effort to locate a gun shop from which Miss Marietta Rheinlander might have purchased a pistol?"

"Yes, I did."

"How did you do that?"

"I used the yellow pages for every town within fifty or sixty miles of here and identified all the gun shops and sporting-goods shops. Then I asked around in the different towns, asking where a person could buy a pistol. Then I carried Miss Rheinlander's photo to every one of those shops and asked if anyone recognized her as a person who'd bought a gun there."

"With what result?"

"None of them had sold her a pistol."

"What else did you do at my request?"

"At each shop I showed them a photo of the Smith & Wesson and gave them the serial number. In Ohio they don't have to keep track of the serial numbers of the guns they sell, and most of them don't. None of them had any record of this serial number. None of them had sold *any* Smith & Wesson thirty-eight revolver in the past several months."

"Thank you, Mr. VanKamp."

Ken Simpson remained seated, smiling with an air of tolerance at the somber Porky VanKamp. "Mr. VanKamp," he said, "do you really believe you covered *all* the gun shops within fifty miles of Alexandria?"

"I could have missed one or two. Not more."

"Of course, the pistol could have been sold by an individual to an individual, and you'd have no way of checking that. Isn't that so?"

"I guess that's so."

"Thank you, Mr. VanKamp."

The jury wasn't much impressed with what we'd heard so far of the case for the defense. Neither was I. Kimball was covering small points he felt he had to make. I expected it would all amount to something before long. I also expected some heavy dramatics before the trial was over.

"The defense calls Cyrus Burge."

Burge was an employee of Smith & Wesson, the company that had manufactured the revolver. Kimball's questions brought out his qualifications: that he had worked for Smith & Wesson for thirty years, that his duties at the company involved receiving firearms that had failed in some way or had been damaged and replacing damaged or faulty parts. He was, in short, a highly qualified gunsmith and an expert witness.

"Mr. Burge, have you at my request examined the Smith & Wesson revolver I now hand you, that has been marked as State's Exhibit A?"

Burge, a solemnly intense man whose light hair lay on his head like a vinyl cap, peered at the pistol through silver-rimmed eyeglasses and glanced at a note he had on a small piece of paper. He was comparing the serial number on the gun with the one he had written down. "Yes, sir," he said, nodding. "This is the revolver I examined at your request."

"When was that pistol manufactured, if you can tell?"

"The serial number indicates it was manufactured in 1953."

"In what condition is that revolver?"

"This revolver isn't safe to fire," said Burge somberly. "There's a hairline crack in the cylinder."

161

"What can you tell, if anything, about how many times that pistol has been fired?"

Burge shoved forward the release and let the cylinder fall out to the side. "This pistol," he said, "has fired at least a thousand rounds, and I'd guess more like two thousand, maybe even three."

"How can you tell?"

"Condition of different parts. Metal has been eroded in the chambers by the explosions of so many cartridges. That's how it comes to be cracked, too. Also, the firing pin has been shortened by the same thing. It's punched through a lot of primers."

"How would this wear affect the accuracy of this pistol?"

"Very badly, except for one thing. The barrel has been replaced. It wasn't replaced by us. We'd have engraved a mark in the steel, to show. It was replaced by somebody else."

"Could the owner have replaced the barrel himself?"

"Yes and no. Yes, in the sense that anybody can remove a barrel and install another one. No, in the sense that we won't sell parts to anybody but a qualified gunsmith."

"In any event, the barrel is . . . would you say relatively new?"

"I'd judge that no more than five hundred rounds have gone through this barrel. What's more, the riflings aren't pitted, which means the pistol has been cleaned after it was fired. This revolver has been well cared-for in one way, but that crack in the cylinder could have cost somebody a hand if it had exploded."

"For what use was this pistol manufactured, Mr. Burge?"

"It's a police weapon. It's standard in many urban police departments—or used to be. It's a personal-defense weapon."

"What would you say about its accuracy?"

"It's accurate enough at the short range at which it's intended to be used."

"Mr. Burge, if you were going to fire this pistol at a target, say four or five yards away, and wanted to hit a target, say eight inches in diameter, would that be a difficult shot?"

"I'm going to have to object," said Ken Simpson.

"I will allow the answer," I said.

"You'd have to take careful aim with both hands," said Burge.

"Thank you, Mr. Burge."

Ken nodded. "I thank you, too, Mr. Burge. Your testimony has been very interesting. But let me ask you this— Suppose your range was, say six feet, and your target was eight inches in diameter. How difficult a shot then?"

"The closer you get, the easier," said Burge.

"Would there be anything extraordinary about hitting an eight-inch target at six feet?"

"Nothing extraordinary," said Burge solemnly.

"Thank you."

"I have one or two more questions, Your Honor," said Kimball. "Mr. Burge, suppose we had three eight-inch targets, one six feet away, one ten or twelve feet away, and one twelve to fifteen feet away. Would it take pretty good shooting to hit all three of them?"

"That would be pretty good shooting," said Burge.

"What if the three shots were fired in rapid succession, say no more than one second between each two?"

"That would be really fancy shooting," said Burge.

We took the mid-morning break.

I sat down at my desk with a mug of coffee and looked through the mid-morning mail. A woman from the clerk's office came in with a fax that had arrived.

Someone in Chicago—someone with a name I did not recognize—had clipped an article from the Chicago *Tribune* and faxed it to me.

Some reporters arriving in Alexandria, Ohio to cover the murder trial of socialite art-dealer Marietta Rheinlander expected to spot Carrie Kennicott shopping on Main Street or George Babbitt selling real estate. They have been disillusioned. In the first place there isn't any Main Street. The streets of the town are mostly named for the New England towns from which the settlers came, so we have Salem Street, Worcester Street, Quincy Street, and Waltham Street.

What is more, the town is the site of a fine small college, Alexandria College, with a faculty of more than a hundred and a student body of about twelve hundred. The college lends the town a cosmopolitan air it would otherwise lack.

When the rich and famous go to trial in small cities and towns, earnest young prosecutors are often overwhelmed by crafty big-city trial lawyers. Not this time. The prosecutor, Kenneth Simpson, is only 31 years old, but he is not intimidated in the least by his famous opponent and has been quietly building a strong case against an increasingly frightened Miss Rheinlander.

Simpson is the son of the town's Chevrolet dealer, was well educated at good colleges, and is an interesting mix of the ingenuous and the shrewd. Watching him work in this courtroom, one has a sense he is condescending to the jurors, some of whom are in fact ingrained small-towners, yet he does it so deftly that they do not guess it. He plays the innocent small-town boy, and even the jurors who probably understand it's a facade probably also find it an endearing act—if I guess correctly.

Being prosecuting attorney is not a full-time job in Alexandria County. Simpson practices law as well. His wife is not present in the courtroom to watch him try his famous case, because she is in his office, answering the telephone. She is, in fact, his secretary, though she is herself a graduate of Western Reserve University where her husband studied law. The town admires their partnership in building a practice everyone expects to be highly successful.

Back in the courtroom, Lloyd George Kimball began to call a succession of character witnesses. The questioning of character witnesses proceeds according to a fixed formula.

The first character witness was Mrs. Myra Loewenstein.

"Mrs. Loewenstein, are you personally acquainted with the defendant, Miss Marietta Rheinlander?"

"I am."

"How long have you known her?"

"About twelve years."

"Do you know other people who know her?"

"Yes, I know many other people who are friends of Marietta."

"On the basis of that acquaintanceship, have you been able to form an opinion of her reputation for telling the truth?"

"Yes, she has an excellent reputation for telling the truth."

"On the same basis, have you been able to form an opinion of her reputation for being a law-abiding citizen?"

"Yes, she has an excellent reputation for being a law-abiding citizen."

Ken Simpson could have cross-examined Mrs. Loewenstein. He could have asked her how close a friend she was of Marietta Rhein-lander. He could have asked her if she would be willing to lie to help her friend Marietta Rheinlander. He could have asked her if she knew anyone who held a different opinion about the reputation of Marietta Rheinlander. But none of this would have been of much value.

The reputation evidence was not of much value, really. A jury would not acquit Miss Rheinlander simply because there was incontrovertible evidence that she had a good reputation. Still, Kimball had to put it in. It was a minor part of his case but still an essential part.

He called eight character witnesses. They included personal friends, men and women, and business associates. They were a group of handsome, well-dressed people, glistening with respectability, meant to be seen as the kind of people Miss Rheinlander ordinarily associated with. It was interesting, though, that none of them was comfortable with his or her appearance as a witness. They were nervous, even frightened. None of them had seen their friend since she came to Ohio and wound up being arrested for murder, and they were apprehensive about seeing her. They tried not to stare at her. She stared at them, anxious to make eye contact with each of them—and she couldn't. When they were finished, they hurried out of the courtroom, only glancing at her with weak little smiles.

The fact was, all these people were embarrassed to face their friend, now a prisoner in a jail. All of them would, if asked, vehemently protest her innocence; in fact, they sincerely wanted her acquitted, even if she were guilty; but they were awed, cowed, by the *trappings* of her ordeal: the cell where she had slept last night and would sleep tonight, the handcuffs they had seen in pictures, the courtroom with its stern-faced judge and coldly curious jury, the lights and cameras. They couldn't look at the woman's eyes and give her a friendly, encouraging smile. They wanted to, but they couldn't.

Although there were eight character witnesses, none of them took more than a few minutes, and we were finished with them before we broke for lunch.

10

What Kimball had presented during the morning was boilerplate; to mix metaphors, it was the nuts and bolts of his defense. Everyone was interested to see what tack he would take when he came to the essence of his case.

His first witness of the afternoon both surprised and perturbed me. I had begun to suspect what Kimball was going to do, and the testimony of Barbara Milligan confirmed my suspicion.

"Miss Milligan, please tell the jury where you live."

"Huntington, West Virginia."

The witness was a small, pretty girl: blonde, wearing an unfortunate pair of white-framed tear-shaped spectacles. She sat in the witness chair constantly tugging at her skimpy gray skirt, having too late decided that it showed too much of her legs.

"Where are you employed?"

"With the firm of Wilcoxen, Branch & Bailey."

"Is that the law firm with which Congressman Bailey was associated?"

"Yes, sir."

"Was Miss Elizabeth Erb one of your fellow employees at that firm?"

"Yes, she was."

"Did you have any other relationship with Miss Erb—I mean, other than that you worked in the same office?"

"We were best friends. She was my roommate. We shared an apartment."

"Do you also know David Ogle?"

"Yes, I do."

"What is, or was, the nature of your relationship with David Ogle?"

"When he came back from Washington he would sometimes come to our apartment for a drink. He'd bring a bottle of Scotch or whatever and sometimes something to eat, and we'd sit around and talk."

"What was the nature of the relationship between Elizabeth Erb and David Ogle?"

"Well, I don't know what he thought of her, but I know she was in love with him."

"How do you know that?"

"Because she told me she was. All the time. He made her very sad."

"Why or how did he make her sad?"

"Because there couldn't be anything between them."

"Why not?"

"Because he's gay."

It was what I expected, but I may have been one of only two or three people in the courtroom who did; and the crowd first gasped, a simultaneous roar of a gasp, followed by a loud eruption of chatter. I banged my gavel.

Ken Simpson was on his feet. He could not speak until I restored order, but when I did, he said, "Your Honor, I strenuously object to any further testimony along this line. I see what Mr. Kimball is driving at. It is totally irrelevant to the question of whether or not Miss Marietta Rheinlander shot and killed three people. It—"

Kimball interrupted. It was the first time he was so rude as to do so. "If the court please," he said with iron-jawed firmness, "the line of inquiry I have now opened is one hundred per cent relevant to the question of whether or not *someone else* murdered Congressman Bailey, Miss Erb, and Mr. Finch. Absolutely none of the prosecution's evidence so much as *suggested* a motive for the defendant Miss Rheinlander to murder those three people. I intend to prove a clear motive for any one of several other people to have committed the crime."

"We showed a motive!" Ken burst out. "He wanted to be rid of—"

For the first time I interrupted an attorney with my gavel. I seized it by the head and pointed the handle at each of the lawyers. *I* was

168

going to talk. I glanced around the courtroom. Some reporters had run for the telephones. Others were jabbing fingers at the keyboards of their laptop computers, writing copy they would soon transmit by phone to their wires and newspapers. I looked for a moment at the jury, which sat bewildered.

"Mr. Kimball," I said sternly, "I am going to be very upset with you if you have opened this can of worms only as a distraction."

"I personally assure you, Your Honor, that my motive is anything but that. Anything but. I am opening an essential element of the defense."

I had been afraid he was. A trial that had already been uncomfortably notorious was about to become ten times more so.

"I cannot," I said, "exclude relevant evidence that may tend to exculpate the defendant. I have no choice but to overrule your objection, Mr. Simpson, and allow the defense to proceed on this line."

During the outburst in the courtroom and the exchange between the lawyers and me, Barbara Milligan had sat flushed and confused, staring this way and that, tugging on her skirt.

"Miss Milligan," said Kimball gently. "How do you know that David Ogle is a . . . a homosexual?"

"Because he told me he is."

"Your Honor," said Ken, who had remained standing and now shook his head and spoke with an air of wounded patience. "That is naked hearsay."

Kimball had anticipated this objection, too. "If the court please," he said smoothly. "There is a recognized exception to the hearsay rule for statements made by a person as to his own health, his condition, his state of mind, and so on. If A says to B, 'I am suffering from cancer,' B can testify to that. If it is not direct evidence that A has cancer, at the very least it is evidence that A thinks he has, which goes to his emotional state and so on."

"What has that got to do with hearsay about a person's sexual predilections?" Ken demanded scornfully.

"There is another exception to the hearsay rule that applies," said

Kimball. "Mr. Ogleby's statement that he is gay is a statement against interest and so admissible. Why, Your Honor, would Mr. Ogleby *say* he was a homosexual unless he was? And if he was, that fact would seriously impact his state of mind on the night of May 9 as well as his state of mind when he testified in this courtroom."

The law of evidence is arcane, and no element of it is more arcane that the hearsay rule and its exceptions. I ruled. I am not certain I ruled correctly. Lawyers have told me I did. Lawyers have told me I didn't. I've had a score of letters, about evenly divided, citing cases. "The objection," I said, "will be overruled. It is a close thing maybe, but considering what is at stake here, we will hear all evidence that falls reasonably within the rules."

Kimball nodded and turned to Miss Milligan. "Please describe the circumstances in which he told you that."

"Well . . . we were all pretty good friends, all three of us—I mean him and Betty . . . uh, Elizabeth, and me. So one night when we were in the apartment and she hadn't got home yet, I just told him he was making her awful unhappy. That's when he told me."

"What exactly did he tell you?"

She drew a deep breath, then spoke in a reluctant but resolute voice. "He said he and Congressman Bailey were lovers and he was committed to the congressman."

A gavel was not enough to bring the courtroom back to order this time. Reporters charged for the doors. People were on their feet, some yelling in shrill outrage that the witness was lying. I banged the gavel and banged the gavel. Hearing the clamor, two deputies came in from the clerk's office, two state highway patrolmen from the hall.

"Clear the courtroom!" I ordered. I pointed at Miss Rheinlander's parents. "Except for those two people." I identified two who had stood and yelled. "Get them out of here," I said, pointing with the handle of the gavel. Three or four reporters grinned at me and made signs indicating "Who, me?" They were right. They had sat quietly. I pointed at them and told the officers to let them stay.

It took five minutes to straighten it out, and when we had done it, only twenty spectators remained in the courtroom. Sitting in chairs inside the bar of the court, Dick Winter, Pete Varner, and Glen Myers remained. Linda sat in the second row, on the opposite side from the Rheinlanders. I ordered the officers to guard the doors and called a ten-minute recess.

"Ladies and gentlemen of the jury," I said when we were again in session, "you must not be influenced by the disgraceful demonstration that interrupted us a few minutes ago. Now. The line of defense Mr. Kimball is going to pursue is one we may find embarrassing. It may indeed be damaging to some people's reputations. But the gravity of the matter before this court is such that we cannot deny Miss Rheinlander the right to raise any defense she and her counsel see fit. Mr. Kimball may be able to prove certain things. He may not. It will be for you, when you have heard all the evidence, to decide whether or not the things suggested are true and what they mean to the chief question, which is of course whether or not Miss Rheinlander is guilty. I charge you to keep open minds and not be prejudiced by suggestions you may find distasteful."

The jury listened somberly, and I believed they understood and would act accordingly. I turned to the courtroom, to the cameras in fact. "For the balance of the afternoon, this courtroom will remain closed to those who were excluded a while ago. They may watch the proceedings on the television screens that are to be found all over town. I have this to say to the members of the news media. Any reporter who bolts for the door again will find his or her credentials lifted. Some of you may find it preferable to watch the trial on television. Then you can file reports whenever you wish. You will not leave this courtroom until the court is in recess.

"So far as people who choose to stand up and scream epithets, you had better understand that the next one of you who does will be taken in custody and conveyed to the county jail. The *minimum* penalty for disrupting this trial will be forty-eight hours' confinement and a fine of one thousand dollars.

171

"Mr. Kimball, does the defense offer any objection to the rulings I have just made?"

"No, Your Honor."

"Let the record show that the defense offers no objection."

It was not inconceivable that the defense might have argued later that I had violated the defendant's constitutional rights by closing the courtroom to the general public. I wanted it on the record that Kimball did not object.

Ken Simpson was on his feet most of this time, waiting to offer an objection. "Surely the witness's last statement is excludable as hearsay," he said quietly.

Kimball spoke. "Once again, Your Honor, the evidence goes to the state of Mr. Ogleby's mind."

I nodded. "I am compelled to agree." He wanted to establish a motive for David Ogleby—or maybe someone else—to have killed Congressman Bailey. I could not deny him the right to try, though, once again, I am not absolutely certain I ruled correctly. I earned my pay as a judge that day. "Proceed, Mr. Kimball."

"Miss Milligan, when we were so rudely interrupted by the outburst in the courtroom, you had just testified that Mr. Ogle said to you that he and Congressman Bailey were lovers. Will you please tell the jury the exact words, the best you can remember them, in which he said that?"

Barbara Milligan was thoroughly nonplused by what had happened. "He . . . well . . . he told me he couldn't be in love with Betty 'cause he already had a lover, and when I asked him who, he said Mr. Bailey."

"Then what did you say, and what did he say?"

"I said I couldn't believe that, and he said something like, 'For God's sake, doesn't everybody know?' "

"To the best of your understanding, what did he mean by 'everybody'?"

"Well, not the whole world. Just us. I mean, the people in the office, us who were close to things. People who were around them a lot and saw things."

"Miss Milligan, did David Ogle ever say to you that he was *in love* with the congressman?"

. She shook her head. "Yes. He said he was in love with Congressman Bailey."

"Did he say the congressman was in love with *him*?"

"No. He didn't say either way, that he was or he wasn't."

"Miss Milligan, did Betty Erb ever tell you that she did or did not have an intimate sexual relationship with David Ogle?"

"She said she didn't. She said he wouldn't. She thought maybe if she could get him to do that she could win him over. But he wouldn't. That was what made her so unhappy."

"Did she tell you anything about her trip to the Bailey lodge on May 9?"

"She said she was going. She said she hoped it would be a time when maybe she could get Mr. Ogle to cotton up to her more."

"'Cotton up'? Old-fashioned expression. Is that exactly what she said?"

"That's what she said."

"Miss Milligan, do you have any direct knowledge of the sexual predilections of Donald Finch?"

"No, sir."

"Thank you, Miss Milligan."

Ken Simpson was left in a dilemma. If he did not cross-examine the witness, he seemed to be accepting the truth of her testimony. But if he did cross-examine her, what could he ask? It was obvious that she was not likely to be shaken in her testimony, and cross-examination would only serve to allow her to repeat what she had already said. He made what I thought was the correct choice. He did not cross-examine.

No end of surprises. Kimball's next witness entered the courtroom wearing a Roman collar and black suit. He was sworn as a witness and took the stand.

"Will you state your name, please?"

"Francis X. O'Donnell."

"You are, I believe, *Father* O'Donnell. And you are a Jesuit priest, is that correct?"

"That is correct."

Father O'Donnell had ruddy skin, close-clipped white hair, big blue eyes under bushy white brows, and a face as square and solid as a brick.

"Father, please tell the jury what position you presently hold."

"I am dean of the Graduate School of Arts and Sciences, Georgetown University."

"How long have you held that position?"

"Four years."

"Father O'Donnell, did you know Donald Finch?"

"Yes, I did. He was a student in our graduate school."

"Did Donald Finch affiliate himself with any particular organizations that you know of?"

"Yes, he did. He was a member of the Alliance for Gay and Lesbian Rights."

Even in the courtroom I had so firmly subdued, this created a murmur—which I was able to silence with a hard glance.

"Father O'Donnell, was Donald Finch a homosexual? I mean, was he such to your personal knowledge?"

The priest shook his head. "I have no means of knowing."

"It is a fact, I suppose—is it not?—that a young man could be a member of the Alliance for Gay and Lesbian Rights and not himself be gay."

Anticipating Ken Simpson's cross-examination, Kimball was asking Ken's main question and cutting it off. Besides, by this question he appropriated for himself a mask of careful fairness.

"I suppose that's possible," said Father O'Donnell with a mien that clearly told the jury he thought it possible maybe—but highly unlikely.

"I thank you, Father. I have no more questions."

Ken did not cross-examine. Kimball had asked the one question he would have asked, and there was nothing left for him to inquire

about. It is always a little risky to cross-examine a clergyman anyway. Ken had no choice but to sit looking a bit sulky and let the
testimony in.

Kimball's next witness was another surprise. Her name was Felicia
Longlea. Personally, I know next to nothing about what is called
"society." I don't look at the society pages of our local newspaper,
much less at those in the New York *Times* or Washington *Post*.
When Felicia Longlea entered our courtroom and was sworn as a
witness, I saw only a tall, slender woman, erect and attractive, with
confident poise. I would find out as I read press accounts of our trial
that Felicia Longlea was as prominent a socialite as Washington,
indeed as the nation, offered.

Her late husband, an inventor-industrialist, had made a fortune
from his patents on what is called a copy-machine "engine"—that
is, the innards that make the whole thing work, which may be found
inside the boxes bearing various brand names. He was a heavy
contributor to the Republican Party and had spent the last years
of his life serving as United States ambassador to Belgium and
Switzerland, where Felicia Longlea, nee Skipwith, who had inherited
a respectable fortune of her own, made a reputation as hostess of
elegant diplomatic parties paid for out of the family money, not the
State Department appropriation.

Widowed in 1986, she became known as the most desirable match
in Washington. The man who became Felicia Skipwith Longlea's
second husband would have married a dark-haired, dark-eyed, handsome, charming, accomplished, intelligent woman—with a multimillion-dollar fortune. When she was seen at sumptuous parties on the
arm of the second-term congressman from West Virginia, a man
hitherto not very well known, the two of them became the subject
of—I adopt the language of my sources—breathless gossip.

If any member of the jury knew any of this, I much doubt. It is the
kind of thing small-town people in the Ohio Valley don't know much
about. Or care much about.

Felicia Longlea, in contrast to the eight character witnesses who
had appeared in the morning, nodded cordially to Marietta Rhein-

lander; and, concealing the gesture from the jury, gave her a thumbs-up signal.

"Mrs. Longlea," Kimball began, "did you know the late Congressman Charles Bailey?"

"Yes, I did." She had been told to speak to the jury, and she did, nodding for emphasis, and—as best I could judge—making eye contact with one juror after another. "I knew him for about five years before his death."

"How would you characterize the nature of your relationship with Congressman Bailey?"

"Our relationship was intimate. We slept together."

"Did you ever sleep with Congressman Bailey at his lodge here in Alexandria County, Ohio?"

"Yes."

"Please describe the occasions."

"He used to have what he called his cronies' parties. The guests would be prominent political people, from West Virginia and Capitol Hill. He held these parties annually. In 1987 and 1988 I came here with him and spent the night with him in his room."

"Was that known to his guests?"

"Absolutely. He played cat who swallowed canary."

"Would this have been known to the housekeeper, Mrs. Merritt?"

Felicia Longlea shrugged. "I have no idea what his household staff may have known or not known."

"Mrs. Longlea, you are a wealthy woman, are you not?"

"I suppose so. That's what the newspapers say of me."

"They also say that you are beautiful and intelligent and so on. It is easy to see why Congressman Bailey should have been attracted to you. Will you tell us why you were attracted to him?"

Ken Simpson interjected before she could answer. "Your Honor, is there any possible relevance in this?"

"I am afraid we are going to have to find out," I said.

"Mrs. Longlea . . . ?"

She blew away a breath she seemed to have held. "Chuck Bailey," she said, "had a reputation as a coming man. He was a good-looking young congressman. Money behind him, it seemed. He had time. It looked as if he would likely become a senator. It was not impossible he would become a candidate for president of the United States, say in 1996 or 2000. He was engaging, charming, an interesting companion . . . What more can I say?"

"Did you fall in love with him?"

"No. Not quite that. Yet. But I could see something out there in the distance. I was widowed. He was single. It would have been no scandal if we had married. And I might become First Lady."

"Did you have any reason to believe he was thinking along the same lines?"

"He was ambitious," she said. "I knew he didn't think the presidency was out of reach. I talked to him a month before he died. He was watching the governor of a small southern state, Arkansas, moving toward the Democratic nomination. If Governor Clinton of Arkansas had a good shot at the nomination, why not Senator Bailey of West Virginia? Why did it belong to Jay Rockefeller? He thought he had a chance. A remote chance maybe and not for a few more years, but still a chance."

The frankness with which the woman talked was impressive. Her *presence* on the witness stand was impressive. She testified that she slept with Congressman Bailey, and she was not perceptibly reluctant to tell it, not in the least embarrassed. Barbara Milligan had tugged at her skirt. The skirt of Mrs. Longlea's exquisitely tailored light blue wool suit exposed six inches or more of her dark-stockinged legs above her knees, and she was conspicuously unconscious of it. Not once did she pull at her hem. I did not notice her even glance at her legs. She was forty-four years old—as I would learn by later reading—and comfortable with herself.

"Mrs. Longlea," said Lloyd George Kimball, "I apologize for this, but I am going to have to ask you to testify to a few of the details of your intimate relationship with Congressman Bailey."

"Do you assure me this is relevant to your defense, Mr. Kimball?" I asked.

"I assure you it is, Your Honor. Absolutely."

By now the reporters turned out of the courtroom would have found television sets that could be tuned to Court TV. They would be cursing themselves for having gotten shut out of what promised to be the most stimulating afternoon of the trial.

"Mrs. Longlea," said Kimball, "I now ask you to describe, in the most modest terms you can, the nature of your intimate relations with Congressman Bailey."

This question embarrassed Felicia Longlea no more than any other. If I guessed correctly—and I now know I did—all that really troubled her about testifying from the witness stand was that she could not smoke a cigarette. I could see what the jury couldn't: that she kept rubbing her interlaced fingers back and forth together. She needed a drink, or she needed a cigarette. It was a cigarette.

She blew a sigh and shrugged. "I slept with Charles Bailey maybe fifty times," she said quietly to the jury. "In bed. All night. Nude. And of those fifty nights, I don't think we made love, meaning had sexual relations to a climax, more than six times. The truth is, he really didn't want to. He didn't really enjoy it when we did do it. And, frankly, he wasn't any good at it."

"I am sorry to have to ask this question, Mrs. Longlea, but was it difficult for Congressman Bailey to achieve an erection?"

She nodded emphatically, and Kimball asked Mrs. Tutweiler to record that the witness had answered affirmatively.

Mrs. Longlea expanded her answer. "I did things I thought would help him. I mean, I showed myself to him in skimpy underthings. And so on. It didn't help."

"Did he offer you any explanation?" Kimball asked.

"Only to say he had always been that way, that he had always had difficulty in performing like a man."

"How did you react to his telling you that?"

"I told him he ought to see a doctor. I *urged* him to see a doctor. I told him he was sexually dysfunctional but that it could be cured."

"How did he react to that?"

"He just sort of smiled at me."

"Did this cause a rupture between the two of you?"

"Not for a long time. He was charming. He was attentive. We went places together and were seen. It generated newspaper publicity. He liked that, and I'm not going to say I didn't."

"Is it your judgment that he liked the idea of having an open and notorious relationship with a prominent woman?"

"Objection!"

Kimball smiled. "If Mr. Simpson will not have it simply, then we'll go through it. Mrs. Longlea, when you came to the Bailey lodge here in Ohio, did Congressman Bailey make any effort to conceal from his friends that he was going to sleep with you?"

"Not at all. To the contrary."

"Be specific, please."

"Well . . . on those nights, his friends would be playing cards, drinking, joking, laughing, and so on. Chuck each time took me by the arm and called out, 'Well, g'night, fellas. See you in the morning!' And he led me around the corner and into his bedroom. I was embarrassed. I thought we could be a *little* more circumspect. To speak the truth, I felt like a *trophy* those nights, like a *conquest*, and I was sure they would all spend the next hour talking about me."

"Did he do anything of the kind in Washington?"

"Yes. And in Virginia, in my home. In my house, he sort of played that he was the host. My husband was dead, and he played like he replaced him. He offered people drinks from my bar. And when the guests left, he'd be standing in the door with me, patting me on the fanny, like he was my husband, making it very clear that *he* wasn't leaving, he was staying."

"Then what would happen?"

"Then we'd go to the bedroom, and he couldn't. Or wouldn't."

"What caused you to discontinue your relationship with Congressman Bailey?"

"He wouldn't see a doctor. He said we didn't have to have an intimate relationship. He asked me if that was the only thing I cared about. He said some men just didn't care that much about that aspect of life. He said many women didn't either."

"And . . . ?"

"Well, this woman did. I told him he could either have his dysfunctionality treated or I couldn't continue with him. He didn't, and I didn't."

"Did you ever identify the specific cause of his dysfunctionality?"

"No."

Lloyd George Kimball stood in the center of the floor and for a full minute seemed to ponder on what his witness had just said—time for the jury to ponder on it too, before Ken Simpson got his inning. "Thank you, Mrs. Longlea. I am sure this has been embarrassing for you, and we are grateful to you."

The lifestyle of the rich and famous. Marietta Rheinlander and her defense team had the money to seek out and find their witnesses, wherever they might be. This afternoon we had heard a dean from Georgetown University and a prominent Washington socialite. There may have been witnesses somewhere who would have contradicted some of what these witnesses said, but Ken didn't have the resources to go looking for them.

Ordinarily . . . Let's get this one straight. Ordinarily it is the prosecution that has the advantage in resources. Police departments and sheriffs' offices will always help the prosecutor, any way they can. I am proud of our sheriff's department, which will help the defense, at least to the extent of not concealing evidence, but not every sheriff or chief of police will do it.

I remember a case. I was a young lawyer, admitted to the practice only two or three years, and I was appointed to defend an indigent. He was in the county jail, almost a derelict and almost certainly guilty of the armed robbery with which he was charged. His alibi was that when the robbery was committed he was in a beer joint in Louisville, Kentucky, drinking with others of his kind. He didn't know their names, just Jeff and Joe and Will. There was no way I could go to Louisville and go through the bars on Saturday night, looking for Jeff and Joe and Will. I was being paid forty dollars by the county, for defending this man. I couldn't hire a private eye to go to Louisville for me. What was more, I couldn't call the Louisville police department and ask them to look for Jeff, Joe, and Will. But the prosecution could have. A call from the Alexandria County, Ohio, prosecuting attorney to the chief of police in Louisville would have generated some kind of police search for Jeff, Joe, and Will. (I think. Maybe the chief in Louisville would have turned out to be a rare exception. The exception would have been rare.)

The point? Maybe there *was* a Jeff, Joe, and Will. Maybe my client-by-appointment *was* innocent. I doubt it. But I will never know. The poor devil went off to serve his ten-to-twenty-five and wasn't eligible for parole until after seven. And maybe Jeff, Joe, and Will sat around in their Louisville bar and wondered whatever happened to their friend.

It wasn't that way for Marietta Rheinlander. She had the re-sources—Kimball had the resources—to locate witnesses and fly them to Ohio. We had just heard one, an important one.

I took the mid-afternoon break.

Ken Simpson stood up and faced the witness. He had a difficult, delicate job here. The defense had taken a turn he had not expected, and he was not prepared for it. When Barbara Milligan had suddenly testified that David Ogle was a homosexual, Ken had been as sur-prised as Kimball had been when Bess Whittlig testified that Marietta Rheinlander confessed.

Cross-examining this poised, engaging woman was going to be as touchy as cross-examining the priest. There could be no doubt but that most of the jurors were fascinated with her. If she had been appealing for nothing else, she was appealing for her perfect candor.

"Mrs. Longlea, do you know whether or not Congressman Bailey was sexually dysfunctional with other women? Was it with all women? Or was it just with you?"

"He said he had never been able to perform the sex act very easily or very successfully. Since he was well over forty years old when I met him, I assume I was not the first woman he ever tried to make love to."

Ken clasped his hands together and pressed them against his

chin. "Do you know . . . as a matter of fact and not as a matter of speculation, if he was dysfunctional with women because he preferred to have intimate relations with members of his own sex?"

"Are you asking me if he was gay?"

"Yes, *if you know.*"

"He never told me he was."

"Did you ever observe any *facts*, like any conduct on his part, that told you he was?"

"No."

"So in fact you don't know if he was."

"No."

Ken should have stopped. Instead he pressed the witness, irritated her, and what he got he had coming. "So it is not your testimony that Congressman Charles Bailey was a homosexual?"

"It is my testimony that he *acted* like one," she said acerbically. "I have in my life gone to bed with only a very few men, and when I have they've all been able to perform—except Chuck Bailey, and he didn't even want to."

Leave well enough alone is a cardinal rule of cross-examination. Ken had been doing all right. She had testified that the congressman had never told her he was a homosexual and that she had never observed any conduct of his that told her he was. His final question produced an answer he surely didn't want. I hope the experience taught him something.

"Mrs. Longlea," he said now, "I noticed that you and Miss Rheinlander exchanged greetings when you came in. Are you friends?"

The witness turned up the palms of her hands. "I believe I would say we are acquaintances."

"How long have you known her?"

"I met her a year or so before I met Congressman Bailey, as a matter of fact. I bought a work of art from her."

"Do you see her often?"

"Once or twice a year."

"In what context do you see her?"

"I go to her gallery to see works of art. I've also had dinner in her apartment, where she shows works of art."

"Were the three of you ever together—I mean, yourself, Miss Rheinlander, and Congressman Bailey?"

"No. Never. In fact, I was quite surprised when I read in a newspaper that she and Chuck Bailey had become a pair."

"Did you ever talk with her about Congressman Bailey?"

Ken was taking a risk here. He was fishing. He had no idea what might be the answer to these questions.

"No, I never mentioned him to her. She never mentioned him to me."

He came out all right that time, but I thought he had better stop. He did.

I recessed until Friday morning.

Thursday evening of every other week is Linda's bridge night. The fourth Thursday of the month is also the night when the local Masonic Lodge meets. I am no longer so faithful a Mason that I go to every meeting, but I try to make about half of them. I am a past master of our lodge, so have done my duty to the lodge.

The lodge meets at seven. The meeting was over by eight-thirty.

As I have mentioned, one of the duties of a judge is to inspect the county jail periodically. When I make my occasional visits, I let them be a surprise. I have never found anything much wrong at the jail, but I figure there is little point in an inspection if it is announced in advance. So that night on my way home I stopped by the jail.

Deputy Larry Whittlig, Bess's husband, answered the buzzer. We walked through. I did my usual inspection, looking into the kitchen first, checking for cleanliness. As usual I told Larry to go back to his rooms. I want to talk to the prisoners out of the hearing of the jailers.

There were eighteen men in the jail that night. All but four of them were housed in a sort of dormitory, a big barred cage with twenty cots, four basins, four toilets. Four—hard cases in Larry Whittlig's judgment—were in individual cells. I stood outside the bars and talked with the prisoners. None of them had any complaints about the jail. What they wanted to tell me was that they shouldn't be in there, that the legal system was stacked against them, and so on. I'd heard it all before.

I walked around the corner and into a short corridor where the two women's cells were located. Miss Rheinlander was in the first one.

She was lying on her cot, reading a paperback book. She was dressed in soft faded blue jeans and a gray sweatshirt. When she saw me, she got up, paused to smooth her blanket and pillow, then came to stand at the bars.

"Everything all right?" I asked her.

I'd inspected the jail five or six times since she'd been here, and I always asked the same question.

"I've asked for a bigger bulb in the light," she said, rubbing her eyes. "It was a hundred watt, and when it burned out they put in a sixty."

"I'll take care of that."

Her cell was decent. If it can be humane to lock a person in a cell month after month, this one is humane, though the inch-thick bars and solid steel walls and ceiling would securely contain the strongest gorilla. It is small but not cruelly small. The toilet is of stainless steel and has no wooden seat. The tiny basin has but one tap: cold water. The walls and the bars are painted with shiny potato-soup-colored enamel, much of it chipped off, leaving dark pits. The cell is kept clean. That is to say, *she* was made to keep it clean, to mop the floor twice a week, including the floor of the corridor outside, to use a brush in her toilet basin, even to use a dust rag on the bars and cross-braces. The floor was so clean that she kept some of her clothes under her cot, together with her books, art supplies, and radio. She was required to fold those clothes neatly, also to line up her toothbrush, toothpaste, hairbrush, and comb in an orderly line on the little shelf above the basin. She was required to make her cot each morning, tucking in the blanket and squaring her pillow in a military manner. If she mussed the cot by sitting and lying on it, she was to smooth it before she left it.

I am not aware that she ever protested any of these rules, which may have seemed petty to her. I think she understood she was better off confined in a neat, clean cell than in an untidy clutter. It was less damaging to the spirit.

Miss Rheinlander closed her hands loosely around two of the bars and stood looking at me with a sort of quizzical weak smile.

"Glen Myers asked if he could come by and visit you," I told her. "I told him I doubted you'd much want to see anybody after a day in court and the time you must spend with your lawyers in the evening."

"He's been kind. I'd like to see him. I guess I won't be here much longer, one way or the other."

"No . . ." I said. "You won't be here much longer . . . one way or the other."

She closed her eyes, and that squeezed a small tear out on each cheek. "I'm scared," she whispered.

What could I say? What in the world could I say? "I can only tell you," I promised her, "that I will do everything I can to be sure it will be fair. Lawful and fair."

She nodded and whispered, "Thank you."

11

"The defense now calls to the stand the defendant, Marietta Rheinlander."

Often there is speculation about whether or not the defense will call on the defendant to testify. I don't think there was any doubt in this trial. Lloyd George Kimball *had* to call her.

It is risky. Once a defendant takes the stand, it opens questions of veracity. In this case no question was going to arise about the defendant's prior criminal convictions. She didn't have any. But in many trials it is a crucial issue. If the defendant doesn't take the stand, the prosecutor cannot bring before the jury his past criminal record—usually; there are exceptions—but once the defendant takes the oath to be truthful and testifies, then the prosecution is entitled to talk about things that cast doubts on veracity, including past criminal activity. In the case of Marietta Rheinlander I didn't know what doors Kimball opened by calling her to testify. We would see.

She had been alternating all week between a white linen dress and a pink cashmere suit. This was a day for the suit. With that chic and expensive suit she wore a single strand of pearls and no other jewelry. She wore this morning a light touch of pink lipstick, and she had darkened her eyebrows and her lashes very sparingly.

Harold McCluskey held out a Bible, and she put her left hand on it. I noted that my sixty-five-year-old clerk was not nearly as tall as the woman on trial.

"Do you solemnly swear," he asked in his parchment voice, "that the testimony you are about to give in the cause at hearing will be the truth, the whole truth, and nothing but the truth, as you shall answer to God?"

"I do."

"Take the stand."

She stepped up the one short step and sat down in the black-leather-upholstered armchair. Harold adjusted the microphone for her.

I must confess that I suppose I had become too sympathetic to this woman. Even if she were guilty of the crimes charged against her, she had about her such an air of pathetic helplessness, of bewildered anxiety, that I had to form for myself a determined resolution not to rule too much in her favor.

I think I was influenced by the parallel between Marietta Rhein-lander and Felicia Longlea. Absent the ordeal Miss Rheinlander was experiencing, she and Mrs. Longlea were all but twins: women of the same social class, sharing many of the same interests, sharing even an interest in the same man. Felicia Longlea retained the poise and confidence Marietta Rheinlander had possessed before the night of May 9, 1992.

I confess too much. But, as you will see, I had virtually no influence on the outcome of the trial. I confess a sympathy for the defendant that could not and did not help her.

"Please state your full name for the jury," said Kimball. He remained seated at the defense table.

"Marietta Rose Rheinlander."

"It is *Miss* Rheinlander, is it not?"

"Yes. I have been married twice and divorced twice, and in each instance the court returned my maiden name."

"Have you any children, Miss Rheinlander?"

"No."

"Where do you live?"

She drew a breath and frowned, maybe a little confused by the question. "Since May I've lived in the Alexandria County jail," she said. "Otherwise, 590 Park Avenue, New York."

"What is your business or occupation?"

"I am an art dealer, part owner of a gallery in New York. I also show and sell art in my apartment."

"Do you specialize in any particular type or style of art?"

"Yes, I specialize in what used to be called the New Realism—that is, art that is representational, in which you can recognize actual people and things, rather than abstract art."

"Do you make a living as an art dealer?"

"Yes. I have other resources, but I had built the business up to a point where I could live comfortably on the income it produced."

"Is it a fact that you are independently wealthy?"

"I suppose you could say that. I inherited from my grandfather."

"How old are you, Miss Rheinlander?"

"I am forty."

Kimball got up and stepped to a point just in front of the jury box. "Miss Rheinlander, did you shoot and kill Congressman Charles Bailey?"

"No, I did not," she said firmly. This was a moment she had waited for, and her face flushed. She clasped her hands tightly together, and you could see her shoulders stiffen.

"Did you shoot and kill Elizabeth Erb?"

"No, I did not."

"Did you shoot and kill Donald Finch?"

"No, I did not."

Kimball nodded, as though her answers had settled all the issues in the trial and he felt complete satisfaction. He walked back to his table and sat down.

"When and where did you meet Congressman Bailey?"

"I met him in Washington in December of 1988. I had gone down to Washington for the opening of a show at the National Gallery, and he was there. Senator Moynihan was there, and he introduced us."

"Did you immediately begin to see him?"

"No. I didn't see him again for several months. Then he came into my gallery in New York. He reminded me that we'd met, which I remembered, and he asked if I would have lunch with him. I did, and after that I saw him regularly."

"Did the relationship between you develop into a love affair?"

"Yes, it did."

"Did you fall in love with Congressman Bailey?"

"Yes."

"And did he fall in love with you?"

"Yes."

"How do you know he did?"

"He told me he was in love with me. Repeatedly."

"What other evidence did you have that he was in love with you?"

"He proposed marriage."

I had opened court that morning by reminding the reporters and spectators in the courtroom that I would tolerate no outbursts in the courtroom, had said again that anyone who disrupted the trial would be jailed and fined, and had repeated my ruling that reporters who left the courtroom other than during recesses would not be allowed to return until a recess. The answer Miss Rheinlander had just given produced a murmur and some more of that furious pecking away at the keyboards of laptop computers, but I was not compelled to rap my gavel.

"When did he propose marriage?" asked Kimball. He now rose and stood behind his table, leaning forward on his hands. He had a sense that changing postures or moving from one place to another in the courtroom alerted the jury and emphasized some parts of testimony.

"At Christmas, last year, 1991. And he gave me an engagement ring."

Lloyd George Kimball leaned over, reached into his briefcase, and took out a small manila envelope. He opened it as he walked forward and handed it to Miss Rheinlander. "Is this the ring he gave you?"

She took the ring from the envelope and stared at it for a moment. "Yes, it is."

He reached for the ring. "If the court please, we offer the ring in evidence as Defense Exhibit C."

Alice Tutweiler tied a tag to the ring and wrote on the tag. Kimball offered the ring to be examined by Ken Simpson, who looked thoughtfully at it for a moment, then handed it back.

Kimball offered the ring to me, and I took a look at it. Inside, it was engraved: C.B. & M.R. 12/25/91. I don't know how many carats the diamond was, but it was a big stone, set in heavy gold. Congressman Bailey had spent a lot of money on that ring.

Kimball now handed the ring back to Miss Rheinlander and asked her to read the inscription. She did, in such a low voice that he asked her to repeat.

"Were you wearing this ring on the night of May 9, 1992?"

"Yes."

"Was it taken from you at the jail?"

"Yes."

"May I assume you accepted his proposal of marriage?"

"Yes."

The sight of the ring had affected her, obviously. Her answers were softer. If they had been anything more than a succession of yeses, accompanied by a nod, the jury would have had difficulty hearing. I leaned over and asked her if she would like to take a little break. She put her hands to her eyes and nodded. I recessed for fifteen minutes.

On the Huntington television station that night, David Ogle was interviewed by a respectful woman reporter. Some guidelines had been laid down in advance, apparently, because she did not mention the testimony of Barbara Milligan. She only asked him what he thought about what she called "the defense allegation that Congressman Bailey was engaged to marry the Rheinlander woman."

"It is preposterous. For him to have married a giddy New York socialite who had been married and divorced twice before would have ruined his political career."

The Barbara Milligan testimony had given the New York tabloid newspapers a new shorthand for Representative Charles Bailey. He was now THE CLOSET CONGRESSMAN! An editorial run in Sunday's *Daily News*, which someone sent me, said:

> Of course the Closet Congressman wanted a wife, the more prominent the better. A highly publicized wedding with the beautiful Marietta Rheinlander, thereafter being seen with her constantly, would have put a strong new lock on his closet door.

When we resumed, Miss Rheinlander appeared to have recovered her composure. Kimball pressed on, into a thorny field.

"Mrs. Longlea testified about what she called Congressman Bailey's sexual dysfunctionality. In your relationship with him, did you observe anything of the kind?"

"Yes. I knew he was gay."

"How did you know?"

"Because he told me he was."

Ken Simpson did not renew his hearsay objection.

"Mrs. Longlea testified that in the course of spending as many as fifty nights in bed with Congressman Bailey, she and he reached a satisfactory sexual climax no more than—what'd she say? Six times? Six times. Was that your experience?"

"No. At first it was, but . . . gradually he improved."

"For how long a period were you sexually intimate with him?"

"From, say March of 1989, until he died."

"Thirty-eight months, roughly. How many times a month did you and he sleep together?"

"At first, we didn't even do it every month. He'd come to New York to see me, or I'd go to Washington to see him, and sometimes we didn't even do it. I knew he didn't much want to."

"How long had you known him when he told you he was a homosexual?"

"A year, I suppose. About a year. We'd become very close, and he trusted me, and he had to explain to me why he found it so difficult to have sex."

"How did you react when he told you this?"

"I was not really surprised. But I was concerned. I went immediately to my doctor and was tested for the AIDS virus. I tested negative. I asked Charles to have himself tested, and he did and was negative. He told me he was not promiscuous. He said he'd never been in a gay bar in his life. He said almost no one knew he was gay."

"Did he name anyone with whom he'd had or was having a homosexual relationship?"

"Your Honor, I object," said Ken. "There has to be a limit to this hearsay somewhere."

"May we approach the bench?" asked Kimball.

When they stood before me and we were off the record, Kimball smiled at Ken Simpson and said, "Her answer is no, he never named anyone."

Ken shrugged. I overruled, and that is how she answered.

"Did you ever suspect anyone?"

"He had several young men on his staff. I suspected one of them was the man. But I didn't press the question. What I did press him to do was give it up."

"Did you urge him to see a doctor, as Mrs. Longlea did?"

"No. I thought maybe I could change him. And I did, too. He became more . . . functional. Not dysfunctional. When he proposed to me at Christmas, he promised he would break off every other relationship."

"Without going into great detail, how did he become more functional?"

"His problem had been that he couldn't have an erection. By the time he proposed marriage, he could have one relatively easily, and we had an almost normal physical relationship."

"Had he in fact broken off entirely with whoever was his male companion?"

"Objection," said Ken. "The only possible answer is hearsay."

"Miss Rheinlander," I said, "can you answer the question on the basis of any knowledge other than what the congressman told you?"

She shook her head. "I only know what he told me."

"Well, we're going to have to put a limit on the hearsay," I said. "Which we had better do right now. The objection is sustained."

Kimball switched smoothly to a slightly different topic. "Did you and Congressman Bailey have sexual relations on the night when he was killed?"

"No. I was menstruating, and he didn't like to have relations at those times."

"Did he, though, achieve an erection that evening?"

"Yes. By then he could get an erection just by looking at me. And he did, definitely. I offered to . . . do something for him, but he said no, it would be all right."

I paid considerable attention to the jury during these questions and answers. The trial had taken a turn none of them could have expected when they agreed to serve. The only one who seemed to be troubled by it was Mrs. Emily Lee, the wife of the superintendent of schools. With her chin down, she stared grimly from under her brows, with the corners of her mouth turned down. She glanced up at me from time to time, as if wondering why I didn't put a stop to it. I suspect she had not yet settled in her mind the relevance between what she was hearing and the crime that had been committed. The other members of the jury listened stolidly, gravely. Most of them, I think, had begun to understand the defense.

"Miss Rheinlander, let us now turn to the events of the week of May 3, 1992. When did you first decide to come to Ohio and stay in the Bailey lodge?"

"As soon as I heard that Charles was going to be there on the weekend. Frankly, I didn't like for him to stay for a weekend in the lodge alone with some of his staff members. I suspected that one of them might be his companion—or, as I hoped, former companion—and I thought it might be well if I were here with him. It was also true that I'd had a hard week or two, traveling, hanging a show, working long hours, and I decided that coming out a few days before he did would give me a restful time. Also, coming five days early sort of concealed my other purpose."

"How did you obtain a key to the lodge?"

"I didn't need to obtain a key. I had a key. Charles had a key to my apartment in New York, and I had a key to his apartment in Washington."

"The prosecutor and I have stipulated that Defense Exhibit A, which is a key found in Congressman Bailey's luggage in his room at the lodge, is a key to your apartment." Kimball turned and spoke toward Ken Simpson. "And Mr. Simpson has also kindly agreed to stipulate that two keys found in your purse are keys to the lodge and to Congressman Bailey's apartment in Georgetown."

Stipulation means that two sides have agreed something is a fact, eliminating the necessity of calling witnesses to prove it. Without the stipulation about keys, Kimball would have had to employ locksmiths to examine the locks and keys to these several places and compare them to the keys the sheriff had in his property cabinet, then to testify.

"Miss Rheinlander, you arrived in Alexandria on Tuesday, May 5. What did you do the balance of the week, until Congressman Bailey arrived?"

"Rested mostly," she said. "I contacted one of my distant cousins, who invited me to dinner at his house. He owns a boat, and he and his wife took me on a long ride up and down the river. They showed me the house where my great-grandparents lived. I walked around the town a bit. I had dinner one evening at the Alexandria House. I drove around the county one afternoon. I stopped at an old family burial ground and walked in to read the old headstones."

"Did you meet someone at the little cemetery?"

"As a matter of fact, yes. A man who turned out to be a professor from Alexandria College drove up, with a young woman. He seemed a little disturbed to find me there, so I introduced myself. I thought maybe he was afraid I'd come to steal a headstone or something. But it turned out he was a professor of art, and he'd brought a student to the burial ground to photograph her nude among the headstones, which he thought would be an interesting juxtaposition. He told me this after I introduced myself as an art dealer—"

"Your Honor," Ken Simpson interrupted, "does this have any relevance?"

"Does it, Mr. Kimball?" I asked.

"We'll move on, Your Honor," he said. "Miss Rheinlander, was Congressman Bailey glad to see you? Was he glad you were at the lodge?"

"Yes, he was. Very definitely."

"What makes you think he was? Let's not say that he told you so, which would be hearsay, although I think admissible hearsay. Tell me how he *acted* toward you."

"He kissed me . . . fondled me. He was very affectionate."

"When Mr. Ogle testified, he said there was tension between you and the congressman that afternoon. Is that true?"

"It is not true."

"He testified that at one point you told the congressman to go to hell."

Marietta Rheinlander had not smiled since she seated herself in the witness chair, but now she did: a measured, bitter little smile. "Mr. Ogle has no sense of humor," she said. "Or maybe no experience with normal, affectionate human relationships."

Ken Simpson started, as if he were about to make an objection; but he and I were in the same position—neither of us able to think in an instant what the objection might be. A lawyer cannot simply say, "I object." He must give a reason. Before Ken could think of a supporting reason, she continued.

"Charles and I loved each other. And when two people love each other and are confident of each other, they engage in foolish bantering. Each knows the words don't mean what they seem to say. Yes, I told him to go to hell. And he told me I'd had too much to drink, as Mr. Ogle also reported. Two loving people can talk to each other that way, and neither takes offense."

This had been rehearsed, I had no doubt. The jury may have sensed that, too. They may also have sensed that what she was saying was true. This woman may have been subdued by imprisonment and anxiety, but she was not conquered. She was not declawed, and by her little comment that Ogle maybe had no experience with normal, loving human relationships she had drawn sharp claws right down his face.

"Mr. Ogle also testified," said Kimball, "that at least once during the afternoon he saw the congressman squeeze your breast. Did he normally do that when he was feeling tense or brittle?"

"I wouldn't say he squeezed my breast. I would say he fondled it. That again may be a distinction beyond Mr. Ogle's experience and understanding. And no, he didn't do it when he was tense or angry. Charles could be tense and brittle and irritated, and he had his ways of showing it. That was not one of his ways."

"Mr. Ogle and Mrs. Merritt testified that you and Congressman Bailey took your dinner alone in the bedroom you were sharing. Mr. Ogle testified that he heard angry shouting between you and the congressman during the course of the dinner hour. Mrs. Merritt testified that she heard no such thing, but of course she was several rooms away. Was there in fact angry shouting between you and Congressman Bailey while you were alone with him in the bedroom?"

"No. None whatever."

"What in fact took place between you and the congressman during that time?"

"We ate our dinner, drank our wine, talked, watched television."

"Were you undressed?"

"Yes, completely."

"What did you talk about?"

"For one thing, we talked about his running for the United States Senate. He thought he had a good chance of beating Senator Byrd in the 1994 Democratic primary."

Lloyd George Kimball stood and walked close to the jury box. It was a signal that he was about to ask something important and wanted his witness to be able to talk to him and to the jury without glancing back and forth.

"I ask you now . . . to tell the jury . . . what happened."

Marietta Rheinlander drew a deep breath. You could see that she understood starkly that this was the most important moment of her testimony, maybe the most important of her trial. I don't quite know how to describe her face. What I saw did not show on television. I know the jury saw. In a subtle way, the muscles of her face relaxed—collapsed, you could say—leaving her face oddly soft, so that expressions of emotion appeared only faintly, as though seen through layers of sheer silk, all dramatic lines softened. Her voice was firm but strained.

"I was not conscious of the time, exactly," she said. "We lay together on our backs, propped up a little against the pillows. Charles had a firm erection. I held it in my right hand but didn't do anything more. Both of us had drunk a good deal, and he'd had a long day, traveling, working, and we sort of dozed. The television was on. Some kind of documentary, as best I can recall. We weren't paying any attention, and neither of us had the ambition to get up and turn it off.

"At some point he got up and went to the bathroom. When he came back, he went to the sliding glass doors that opened from the bedroom on the north side of the house. He said he'd heard some kind of noise outside. Then he said he was going out in the living room and look out the big doors toward the pool. He pulled on that Japanese jacket. I laughed at him and said he couldn't go out in *that*, it didn't cover his buns or anything else. He laughed, too, and out he went."

"What time was that?"

"I'm not sure. It must have been pretty close to midnight. I don't know how long he was gone. I tried to focus on the television, but I realized I couldn't keep track of what somebody was saying. I was dozing, slipping in and out.

"Then I heard the shots. I was terrified. I couldn't imagine what I was hearing. I grabbed my panties, that were lying on the nightstand on my side of the bed, and got into them as I hurried toward the door. I opened the door and stumbled over Charles's body. I didn't know that's who it was, but I was afraid for the worst. Then I saw two others on the floor. I didn't know who they were.

"I saw the pistol lying on the floor, close to the body that turned out to be Donald Finch. Then I saw someone outside the big doors between the house and the pool. Lights were showing in the Merritts' suite on the opposite side of the pool, and I could see a figure—the figure of a man, I thought it was—moving around the pool, going west, as I understand the directions out there. I ran for the pistol, grabbed it up, and fired it toward the man, or figure, I saw. I knew I didn't hit anybody. The figure I saw disappeared around the corner of the house and out of sight."

Kimball possessed another skill I had noted once before: that of receiving a witness's testimony as if it suddenly cleared up everything and left nothing to worry about. He stood there in front of the jury box, nodding, displaying a posture and expression that said as clearly as any mime could make it, So there, that settles that, and I'm glad to hear it.

"What happened next?" he asked.

"I was in a state of shock," she said in a voice that had now become oddly fluid. "I suppose my eyes became better adjusted to the dim light, and I realized that the bodies I was staring at were Charles and Finch and the little secretary from Huntington. Then the bedroom door on the southeast end of the house burst open, and David Ogle came running out. I was standing there with the pistol still dangling in my hand, and I let it drop to the floor. I was all but naked, and I ran back into the bedroom to cover myself."

"Go on."

She sighed loudly. "While I was dressing I realized that I'd been seen standing over the bodies with a pistol in my hand, that my fingerprints were all over the pistol. I did something stupid. I ran out through the sliding glass doors of the bedroom, got into my rented car, and took off."

"Why?"

"Panic," she said simply.

"Miss Rheinlander, how many shots did you fire?"

"Three."

"Had you ever fired a pistol before in your life?"

"No. Not even once. I had never touched a pistol before in my life. I only knew what the trigger was because I'd seen pistols fired in the movies and on television."

"You drove away from the house. Would you judge you were too drunk to drive?"

"Yes. I don't think I'd have run the car off the road if I hadn't been."

"Is it correct that you were not injured when the car went off the road?"

"I wasn't hurt. Just shaken up a little."

"What did you do?"

"I took my suitcase out of the car and started walking back to the lodge. Then I saw the lights of a car coming, and I walked back into the woods to be out of sight. When I saw the markings on the car, saw that it was a police car, I stepped out where I'd be seen."

At this point I called the two attorneys to the bench and went off the record.

"Mr. Kimball," I asked, "we have another hour or so before noon. Do you think you will finish direct examination of Miss Rheinlander in that time?"

He nodded. "Another hour. Yes, Your Honor, I think so."

"Then we can begin cross-examination after lunch. That may be finished before the day is over. Now we have a question. Will there be other witnesses?"

"I have no plans to call anyone else," said Kimball.

"Rebuttal, Ken?" I asked.

"I won't know until I've cross-examined."

"All right. My inclination would be to be in session tomorrow, Saturday, for final argument and the charge to the jury. I don't see why Miss Rheinlander should have to sit in jail until Monday, wondering what her fate is. On the other hand, I suppose you'd like to have the weekend to prepare final argument, right?"

"I certainly would, Your Honor," said Kimball. "And I know Miss Rheinlander will endure the weekend gladly to give me that time to prepare."

"All right. Tomorrow, Saturday, we'll hear the end of cross-examination if necessary and any rebuttal witnesses—or, for that matter,
surrebuttal witnesses—we need to hear. We'll hear final argument
on Monday, and I'll charge the jury. Plan on two hours apiece, max,
for final argument. Right now, we'll take fifteen minutes."

Linda had sat in the courtroom again this morning and listened to
the testimony. She came into my office and sat down with me during
the break, and we drank cups of coffee.

"I believe every word she says."

My wife has a dignity that would give her a better judicial appearance than I have. She acquired it when her hair turned gray. Before
that she could look a little frivolous, though I never thought she was
that. She almost never spoke to me about cases before the court,
and I was surprised that she did now.

I tried to dismiss her statement, as lightly as possible. "Please.
You must not improperly influence the judge."

"I didn't believe that Ogle when I heard him, before I knew what
he is."

"Before you heard somebody *say* what he may or may not be," I
said. "I cannot entertain an assumption that, even if what Barbara
Milligan says is true, that means the man is a liar."

My darling wife smiled wickedly. "What do you want to bet half
your jury entertains that very assumption?"

"I have more faith in juries than that," I said.

"Spoken like a judge and lawyer. We must always *assume* juries
are honest, thoughtful, sincere, and correct. That's how we evade
responsibility for their decisions."

"I'm glad the case is being tried to a jury," I said. "I'd hate to have
to try the case without a jury."

"Between husband and wife, how would you decide right now?
I've never asked you that about a case before, but I'm asking now.
How would you decide?"

200

"Linda, I honest-to-God don't know. You can't ignore the evidence against her."

"When you told me last night about seeing her at the jail and how scared she is, dammit, my heart went out to her."

"What if she killed three people?"

"She didn't," said Linda firmly.

"This conversation," I said, "is so improper it could get me reversed. It could get me thrown off the bench."

Linda lifted her chin and again smiled wickedly. "Who's to know? Isn't it still the law that a wife can't testify against her husband? Isn't there something—what's it called?—privity within marriage?"

I grinned. "If you buy a fur coat after this trial, I'll know that Lloyd George Kimball paid you a fee for influencing the judge."

Back in the courtroom, Kimball addressed the questions arising from his client's statements in custody.

"Mrs. Vogt testified that you made the following statement to her while you were in the police car on your way to jail. 'I guess I've really fucked up, haven't I? How could I have been so stupid! Jesus God, I've really fucked up.' Miss Rheinlander, tell us what you meant by that statement."

Marietta Rheinlander's face reddened, though it retained its flaccid character, as if it had lost the ability to express deep emotions. Her voice was low as she said, "I was in the back of a police car. I'd been in the first car for half an hour or so, I guess. Now I was in a second car, and I knew I was on my way to jail. My hands were handcuffed behind my back and had been for all that time. I was frightened. I have never been so frightened, and I was thinking about what I'd done to get myself into such a position. I knew. I'd tried to run away. I'd picked up the gun and put my fingerprints on it. They were going to find my fingerprints on it. If I hadn't touched it— if I hadn't touched the gun, and if I hadn't tried to run away, I don't think they would have arrested me."

"Now. Mrs. Whittlig testified that while you were in jail you made to her the following statement—'I done it, you know. I done somethin' awful.' Did you make such a statement?"

"I did not. She is a liar."

That flat statement produced a gasp in the courtroom.

"Can you describe Mrs. Whittlig's general attitude and demeanor toward you during the time you have been a prisoner in the jail where she is cook?"

"She's made it very plain she doesn't like me."

"How has that manifested itself?"

"Well, for example, when the light bulb burned out in my cell, she replaced it with one with a lower wattage, that makes it hard to read at night. I've had to ask several times before I got a bar of soap, until finally my mother, when she came to visit, brought me soap. I get my evening meals from the hotel, true, but I get my breakfasts and lunches from her. I get cold coffee. I get stale doughnuts. And so on. I don't know what other prisoners get."

"Let's turn to the occasion when you gave Mrs. Vogt a shove. Tell us about that."

"It was the day after I was arrested. I was frightened and confused. I'd never been in jail before. When she told me I had to strip naked, I became very angry. She grabbed my arm. I shoved her away from me. It was a stupid thing to do."

"After you did that, what happened?"

"She told me I'd made a big mistake and told me to strip right now. I did, and then she put me through the most humiliating thing I have ever known or heard of in my life."

"The body-cavity search."

"Yes."

"How would you describe your relationship with Deputy Margaret Vogt at the present time?"

"Objection. Irrelevant."

"We'll hear the answer."

Miss Rheinlander looked at Margaret Vogt, who was sitting in the courtroom, inside the rail. The defendant was in her custody, her responsibility. "I've learned that . . . she's just doing her job. And I think she understands I'm living through absolute hell."

Score! That appealed for the jury's sympathy, and I think it worked.

"She testified," said Kimball, "that since the shoving incident and another minor incident you have been altogether cooperative with her. When she brings you to the courthouse and takes you back to jail, she puts handcuffs on you, doesn't she?"

"Yes."

"And fastens the handcuffs to a chain around your waist?"

"Yes."

"How do you feel about that?"

"How would anyone feel about it? It's a horrible thing to have to live with. But it's what she has to do. It's nothing personal."

"If the court please . . ." said Ken.

"I believe, Mr. Kimball," I ruled, "that you have made your point."

Kimball nodded, smiling faintly at me, more with his eyes than his mouth. "One final question, Miss Rheinlander. Tell the jury once more. Did you shoot and kill Congressman Charles Bailey?"

She shook her head. "No. I was in love with him. He was in love with me. Why would I want to kill him? How *could* I kill him?"

12

Marietta Rheinlander had done herself no harm by her testimony. "Well-rehearsed lines well spoken," said Pete Varner as we sat down for lunch at the Alexandria House.

Although she would have been welcome, I know, my wife did not join me at my customary table. No woman ever sat down with us. That wasn't our choice; it was theirs. Linda said she just wouldn't feel comfortable. In fact, we had a new young woman lawyer in town, and she didn't join us either. Old customs die harder in small towns than in big cities.

"The cross-examination is going to be an ordeal," said Dick Winter.

"The key to the trial," said Glen Myers. "If Ken can't crack her some way, I think she bailed herself out this morning."

"Want to start a pool on how long the jury will be out?" Pete asked, only half facetiously.

"Please, gentlemen!" I laughed. "Not in the presence of the trial judge!"

"Kimball has done something that may be very clever or may be very stupid," said Dick. "I mean, introducing this business of homosexuality into the trial. Remember something. Only two witnesses have testified that Bailey was one."

"Three," said Glen.

"No," said Dick. "Felicia Longlea testified that he acted like one. She did not say he was. She said he was inept in the manhood department, which made her think maybe he was. She did not say he was or that he told her he was. In fact, if you think about it, Barbara Milligan said Ogle told her *he* was gay. She didn't say he told her the congressman was. The only witness who said he was is . . . Marietta Rheinlander. The defense is taking a hell of a risk."

"How so?" asked Pete.

Dick paused while the waitress put our drinks on the table. I don't drink a lunchtime martini when I am presiding in the courtroom and so had iced tea. Since Dick and Pete would be in the courtroom watching the trial, instead of seeing clients and so on, they had whiskeys. Glen, of course, had his noon martinis, no matter.

"Well, obviously," said Dick, "the idea is to establish a motive for someone else to have shot Bailey, maybe Ogle himself. The trouble is, what Miss Rheinlander has testified to gives *her* a motive for killing the congressman. Ken didn't establish much of a motive, but she did, in her own testimony."

"I shouldn't be listening to this," I said.

"If I didn't have perfect confidence in your objectivity, I wouldn't talk this way in front of you," said Dick with a puckish grin.

"Well, I want to hear how you figure," Glen said.

"All right. You're Marietta Rheinlander. You're in love with this guy. He's gay, but you've devoted yourself to straightening him out. He's proposed marriage and given you a ring. You don't want him to come to Alexandria without you, because you suspect Ogle—or maybe Finch—is or has been his gay companion. In the bedroom he won't have sex with you, but he gets a hard on. He leaves the bedroom. After a while you wonder why he doesn't come back. You walk out into the hall and find him with Finch, the two of them going at it. Remember, he and Finch both had emissions in their last hour or so. You run back in the room and grab a pistol. In the meantime, Elizabeth Erb has come into the living room, maybe on her way to Ogle's bedroom, since she's in love with Ogle and hoped on this weekend she could get him to 'cotton up' to her. You come out and shoot the two gay lovers. Elizabeth's a witness, so you kill her, too. You empty the pistol into the night to establish a story that you shot at an intruder."

Glen laughed. "You should write for television, Dick."

Dick shrugged. "Hey. However you write the scenario, she's created a motive. Her lover had a sexual emission just before he died.

He didn't have it with her. She caught him *in flagrante delicto*. It had to be with Finch."

"Maybe *Ogle* caught him *in flagrante delicto* with Finch."

"Wait a minute," said Glen. "Whoever did it had a pistol with no fingerprints on it—"

"Guys!" I said. "Will you stop it? I have to *try* this case."

And they stopped.

During the afternoon it become obvious that Ken Simpson had been thinking along some of the same lines.

Miss Rheinlander sat again in the witness chair, facing him with apprehension she could not disguise. As Glen had said, how she handled herself on cross-examination was likely going to be the key to the whole trial, and she knew it. She was not calm. How could she have been calm? She sat with her hands clutched. Her face was bright pink. She glanced at me, and I saw fear.

"Miss Rheinlander," Ken began, "there has been innuendo to the effect that Congressman Bailey was a homosexual. He—"

"I object strenuously, Your Honor, to the word 'innuendo,'" said Kimball, rising to his feet. "There has been direct, positive testimony to the fact of his homosexuality. No innuendo."

"If the court please," said Ken, "an attempt has been made to destroy the reputation of a man whose reputation prior to his death had been for nothing but devotion to public service—"

I interrupted. "Mr. Simpson," I said sharply—maybe too sharply; maybe I revealed myself—"Congressman Bailey's reputation is a matter for concern, but what is at stake in this courtroom is the defendant's life. If you have evidence to the effect that the congressman was not a homosexual, let's hear it. If on cross-examination you can demonstrate that the defendant has misrepresented the fact, let's hear you do so. I will sustain Mr. Kimball's objection to your use of the word 'innuendo.' Prove it is baseless innuendo, Mr. Simpson. Prove it, if you can."

Well . . . that's me, on television, in the newspapers, in the news magazines. "Prove it is baseless innuendo, Mr. Simpson. Prove it if you can." I am afraid I damaged Ken's case. But a word like "innuendo" does a lot of damage, and you can't let it pass.

Ken was surprised, and I thought at the time he was more than a little hurt by my ruling and the tone I had given it. He glanced at the lawyers sitting inside the bar—Dick Winter, Glen Myers, Pete Varner—as if to appeal to them. But he was a trial lawyer, trying the most important case in the early years of his career. Like a quarterback whose bomb pass has just been dropped, he had to go on.

My judgment was wrong. He knew exactly what he was doing; and if he looked hurt by my ruling, it was a part of his act as a clever lawyer.

"You have testified, Miss Rheinlander, that Congressman Bailey told you he was a homosexual. Correct?"

"That's what he told me."

"Are you aware, as a matter of fact and not as a matter of guess or speculation, that he ever said the same thing to anyone else?"

Marietta Rheinlander pondered for a moment, then said, "I have never spoken with anyone else who told me Charles had told them he was gay."

"You heard the testimony of Mrs. Longlea. Am I correct in summarizing that by saying she suspected he was gay but she never knew as a matter of fact?"

"That's right. She suspected it because—"

"Well, never mind why she suspected it, but she could not testify as a matter of fact that he was. Isn't that right?"

"We both heard her testimony, Mr. Simpson."

"Right. And she did not testify that he ever told her he was a homosexual. Right?"

"We heard her, Mr. Simpson."

"Miss Rheinlander. She did not testify he ever told her he was a homosexual. Do you argue about that?"

"I am not arguing. I only say we heard the testimony. You remember what she said. I remember what she said."

This little showdown scored a tie, so far as I could evaluate it. He wanted to make her admit something. She never did admit it. I had a sense there would be many of these confrontations.

"Miss Milligan testified that Mr. Ogle told her he was gay. Did Congressman Bailey tell you Mr. Ogle was gay?"

"No."

"Did the congressman ever name to you any other man or woman and tell you that person was a gay or lesbian?"

"No."

"But the congressman told you *he* was gay?"

"Yes, he did."

"Did you ask him to identify his gay companion or companions?"

"Yes, I asked him."

"And what did he say?"

"He never named anyone. He assured me he was not promiscuous and had never had more than one gay lover at a time, but he never named a man."

"Did you press him about that?"

"Yes, I did."

"But you didn't get an answer?"

"I never got an answer."

"You have testified that you suspected members of his congressional staff. Was that Mr. Ogle and Mr. Finch?"

"Yes."

"Why them?"

"Because they traveled together. Because he was alone in their company rather often."

"Did anyone ever tell you that either of those two men was homosexual?"

"No."

"But you suspected it."

"I suspected it."

"On any other basis than that they and the congressman were alone together from time to time?"

She considered that question for a long moment, then said, "On no other basis that I can think of."

"Then why them? Why couldn't his gay lover have been a man in leather clothes and chains?"

"Because that's not the kind of man Charles would have associated with in any case," she said firmly. "Because these two were nice-looking, respectable-looking, intelligent, well-spoken young men."

Score! Ken had asked the wrong question. Cross-examination is a dangerous process.

Ken decided to change the subject. That was a good idea. So far he wasn't doing too well.

"Miss Rheinlander, what was the name of your first husband?"

"Timothy Gibbons."

"Do you remember the date January 18, 1974?"

"I can't say that I do."

"Was Timothy Gibbons received at the emergency room at Roosevelt Hospital on the evening of January 18, 1974?"

"I remember he went to the emergency room. I don't remember the date."

"Do you remember why he went to the emergency room?"

"Yes . . ."

"Why?"

"He had a cut on his head that was bleeding too much. We'd had a quarrel, and I'd hit him with a glass pitcher. It broke and cut his head. I wrapped his head in a towel and took him to the emergency room in a taxi."

"Were you questioned by the police?"

"Yes."

"How did they dispose of the case?"

"They called it 'domestic violence' and let it go, since he did not want to press it."

"'Domestic violence.' You hit the man with a glass pitcher. How long was he in the hospital?"

"Overnight. He had a slight concussion and—"

"Were stitches required to close the wound?"

"Yes. Four stitches."

"Did you yourself require any medical treatment as the result of this quarrel?"

"No."

"On the night of May 5–6, 1992, you were arrested and put in jail. Was that the first time you had ever been arrested and put in jail?"

"No."

"Tell us about the other times."

"There was only one other time. During an anti-Vietnam War protest in Northhampton, Massachusetts, I was arrested and held in jail overnight."

"You were a student at Smith College at the time?"

"Yes."

"How many Smith students took part in that protest?"

"I don't know. Hundreds. With boys from Amherst and girls from Mount Holyoke."

"How many were arrested? How many were in the jail with you that night?"

"Two. Maybe three."

"Out of hundreds of protesters, only two or three were arrested. Why were you one of those two or three?"

"I hit a policeman."

"Why did you hit a policeman?"

She shrugged. "I was stupid."

"Is that all? Were you perhaps also angry?"

Marietta Rheinlander drew a deep breath. She nodded. "I was also angry."

"When you are angry, Miss Rheinlander, you seem to have a propensity for striking out at people. Do you not?"

"I don't think two incidents make a propensity."

"Then the incidents with Deputy Margaret Vogt do not show a propensity either?"

"If you say so."

"When you were arrested in Northhampton, were you hand-cuffed?"

"Yes."

"With your hands behind your back?"

"Yes."

"So when you had that experience here, it was not the first time, right?"

"No, it wasn't the first time."

"At the jail in Northhampton, were you strip-searched?"

"Yes."

"A body-cavity search?"

"Yes."

"So what Deputy Margaret Vogt did was not your first experience with that, either. Right?"

"That's right."

"You were not, then, in a great panic because you were about to experience a humiliation you could not imagine. You had experienced it before. Right?" ·

"Having experienced it before did not make me fear it any less."

"How, incidentally, did you get out of jail in Northhampton?"

"My father came and posted bond. I was fined, and he paid the fine."

Ken Simpson was effective during this series of questions and answers. He sat at his table, turning over sheets of his legal pad, as though he had all the questions written there, which he didn't. He had some notes that suggested the topics. He spoke in a bland voice, as if to suggest to the jury he was just eliciting acknowledgment of a few damaging facts that the defendant should have acknowledged during her testimony-in-chief.

Marietta Rheinlander was miserable. Obviously, she didn't want to talk about any of this. She kept glancing at her counsel—showing the jury, unfortunately, that she *was* unhappy and hoped he would somehow interrupt and stop this slicing away at her flesh.

Lloyd George Kimball sat back with his legs crossed, his arms crossed on his chest, miming a man who finds something routine, boring, and inconsequential. He knew it wasn't. What Ken was doing had to hurt.

"Miss Rheinlander," said Ken, "you have testified that you and Congressman Bailey were engaged to be married. Was there ever a public announcement of the engagement, say in a newspaper?"

"No."

"Did you have an engagement party?"

"No."

"You wore the ring he gave you. Correct?"

"Yes. Always."

"To how many people, to the best of your recollection, did you say that ring was an engagement ring?"

"I am not sure."

"Well, Miss Rheinlander, the ring is a beautiful ring, expensive I am sure, and I am sure you cherished it. But it is not a traditional engagement ring, is it?"

That point had occurred to me. It was a gorgeous ring, gold, set with a huge diamond; but, so far as I am an authority on such things, it did not look like an engagement ring. It looked like an opulent and maybe somewhat impersonal piece of jewelry.

"I am not sure what you consider a 'traditional engagement ring,' Mr. Simpson," she answered.

"Let's put it this way," said Ken. "Would the average person, say the average woman, look at that ring and say, 'Oh look, she's gotten engaged!'?"

"Whatever the average person might say, it was my engagement ring," said Marietta Rheinlander, steely cold.

This was touchy ground, and Ken moved on. "Was it generally known, among your acquaintances and his, that you were engaged?"

"No. We had agreed to keep the matter . . . not a secret. We had just decided not to announce it until his campaign for reelection began. Then we would announce it, and I would appear with him at a few political meetings."

"Did your father and mother know you were engaged to be married to Congressman Bailey?"

"Yes, they did."

"Who else knew?"

"A few of my closer friends."

"What about the congressman's friends?"

"I am not sure who he had told."

"Do you think David Ogle knew?"

"He testified that he didn't."

"Donald Finch? Elizabeth Erb?"

"I don't know whether they knew or not."

"Did either of them congratulate you?"

"No."

"Now, Miss Rheinlander, I would like to inquire of you about some checks that you wrote. Specifically, I refer first to a check written by you on your financial management account with Shearson Lehman Brothers. Will you first explain to the jury what a financial management account is?"

"A financial management account is an account in which you can deposit both cash and securities. In fact, your personal manager will buy and sell securities as you order. It differs from an ordinary stock brokerage account in that you can write checks on it."

"All right. Now, on December 5, 1991, you wrote a check payable to Congressman Bailey in the amount of $30,000. Can you explain that? What was the check for?"

"It was a contribution to his 1992 reelection campaign."

Ken Simpson drew a breath and frowned. "Miss Rheinlander, were you not aware that federal law limits the amount of money a person can contribute to any one congressional campaign and that the limit is $1,000?"

"I wasn't aware of it at the time. I've become aware of it since."

"On March 19, 1992, you wrote another check to Congressman Bailey, in the amount of $22,000. What was that for?"

"I understood that to be another campaign contribution."

"Did you not *then* know that such a contribution would be unlawful?"

"No."

"And on April 10 you wrote still another check to Congressman Bailey, for $10,000. Was that another campaign contribution?"

Miss Rheinlander's face gleamed bright pink. "Yes," she said simply.

"Over a period of about five months you gave the congressman $62,000. Is it your testimony that you believed these were campaign contributions?"

"Yes. He told me his reelection campaign might cost half a million dollars or more and that he would need help from his friends."

"When did you learn that these were illegal contributions?"

"Only after I was in jail here and began to confer with my lawyers."

"Do you know what Congressman Bailey did with the $62,000?"

"No. I assumed it was in a campaign fund."

"Do you know whether or not he reported these contributions to the Federal Elections Commission?"

"I know now that he didn't. I didn't know it at the time."

Ken rose and walked forward. "Miss Rheinlander, I hand you the check you wrote on December 15, which your counsel kindly provided so we wouldn't have to issue a subpoena to obtain it. Is that in fact your check, bearing your signature?"

She nodded. "It is."

He reached for the check. "I ask that this document be received as State's Exhibit E."

Kimball waved it off, and the court stenographer marked it. Ken handed it back to Miss Rheinlander.

"Please look at the endorsements on the back," he said. "Where did the congressman deposit this check?"

"In the Chase Manhattan Bank."

"In New York City?"

"Yes."

"Is there any indication that the check was deposited to a special account, say a campaign fund account?"

"No. He simply endorsed it and deposited it."

"When did you first see this canceled check?"

"In January, I suppose. I'm not sure."

"Did you not notice that he had deposited your check to a personal account, not to a campaign account?"

"I supposed he kept a separate campaign account with Chase Manhattan. He lived in Washington and in Huntington. An account in New York was unusual, and I supposed it was where he segregated his campaign funds from other money."

"Did you ask him about it?"

"No."

Ken led her through the same kind of questions about the other two checks. Bailey had deposited her $62,000 in a personal account in a New York bank. The other two checks became State's Exhibits F and G.

He returned to his table, opened a manila envelope, and took out several more checks. He handed one to Miss Rheinlander.

"You have never seen that check before, I assume. Can you nevertheless identify it?"

She studied the check for a moment. "This appears to be a check written by Charles. That is his signature."

"On what account, Miss Rheinlander?"

"On his account in the Chase Manhattan Bank."

"Payable to whom?"

"Payable to Georgetown Property Management Associates."

"In what amount?"

"$2,500."

He handed her three more such checks. The four checks became State's Exhibits H, I, J, and K. Although she did not know who Georgetown Property Management Associates were, she did not contest Ken's assertion that Bailey had been paying his rent out of his Chase Manhattan account.

"So it wasn't a campaign fund account, was it?"

"Apparently not," she conceded.

"Is it still your testimony that your $62,000 was a campaign contribution?"

215

"That is what *I* understood it to be."

"Miss Rheinlander, you are a businesswoman, I believe. Do you insist you were so naive you—"

Kimball interrupted. "Mr. Simpson can argue his case tomorrow, Your Honor," he said.

"Since you did not get to finish your question, I am not sure if it was argumentative or not," I said to Ken. "Do you want to finish it?"

"I'll drop it, Your Honor. I do have one more question along this line. Miss Rheinlander, was Congressman Bailey in chronic financial hot water?"

"Not to my knowledge."

We took the afternoon break.

I could not determine if Ken Simpson had changed his entire trial strategy or had had the same idea all along. Until now it had appeared that he had treated the case as the murder of a fine, honest public servant by a woman with a vile temper. Now he seemed to be developing a tactic that Bailey had exploited, maybe even abused, Marietta Rheinlander. A weakness in his case had been motive. Maybe he was now going to portray Bailey as a manipulative man who had taken Miss Rheinlander's money, exploited her sexually, and continued to betray her confidence.

I was told later that during this break, Miss Rheinlander excoriated her counsel for allowing her, as she put it, to be skinned alive.

It was an interesting afternoon.

In the courtroom again, we settled down for more cross-examination of the defendant. She remained flushed, conspicuously tense.

"Miss Rheinlander, did you give Congressman Bailey any other money? I mean, did you give him any in addition to the $62,000 in three checks?"

216

"No."

Now Ken returned to a subject I had hoped we'd heard the last of.

"Miss Rheinlander, you have testified that Congressman Bailey told you he was a homosexual. You have testified that you believed he had a gay lover, or maybe more than one. Were you jealous of the congressman's gay lover, whoever he was?"

"I never thought of it that way."

"How *did* you think of it?"

"We were going to be married. I wanted him to give up any other sexual intimacy."

"Other than with you?"

"Yes, of course. Isn't that what marriage is about?"

"*Did* he give up other sexual intimacy?"

"I only know what he told me, which you objected would be hearsay."

Ken should have smiled. But he didn't. "I'll waive the hearsay rule for this question. What did he tell you?"

"He told me he had given up all other intimate sexual relations."

"You have testified that on the night when he was murdered he did not have sexual relations with you. Dr. Chandra testified that the congressman had an emission not long before he died. Can you explain that?"

"No, I can't."

"He couldn't have had intercourse with Elizabeth Erb, because she had not experienced intercourse in the hour or so before she was murdered—as Dr. Chandra testified. Donald Finch, on the other hand, had had an emission within the last hour of his life—again, as testified to by Dr. Chandra. Isn't it likely then that Congressman Bailey had a homosexual experience with Donald Finch?"

Miss Rheinlander glanced at Kimball, as though she expected an objection. Kimball could have objected on the ground that the question only called for her to speculate. He didn't. He let her answer.

"I don't know if it's likely or not," she said.

217

"What's the alternative?"

"There are several alternatives," she said. "Donald Finch could have had an experience with David Ogle. Charles could have, also. Another man or woman could have come into the house from outside. Donald Finch and Charles Bailey could have masturbated. Elizabeth Erb could have fellated either one of them, or both."

Ken pretended to study his notes. "Miss Rheinlander . . ." he said quietly, his head still down. Then he raised his chin. "You testified that on the night of the murder you were menstruating and that the congressman did not like to have sex with you when you were. You testified that you—I believe your words were, 'I offered to do something for him.' What did you offer?"

Her face tightened. "To give him oral sex," she said crisply.

"To switch to the term you used with respect to Elizabeth Erb, you offered to fellate him, is that correct?"

She closed her eyes and nodded. "That's correct."

"Had you done that before?"

"Yes, once."

"Did you dislike doing it?"

"I hated it. But I loved him."

"You had only done it once?"

"Once or twice."

Ken stood up. He puffed out his cheeks as he blew a loud sigh. "Miss Rheinlander, do you have a friend named Lois Lucas?"

"Yes."

"Who is Lois Lucas?"

"She went to college with me. She lives in Pittsburgh now. Her husband is a part owner of the Pittsburgh Pirates."

"Did she know Congressman Bailey, too?"

"Yes. Her husband's family has known the Bailey family for many years. They were in the same business: coal mining."

"After you were arrested, did Lois Lucas make a statement to the Pittsburgh *Post-Gazette*?"

"Yes."

"What did she say?"

"She said Charles probably deserved whatever happened to him."

"And she was so quoted?"

"Yes."

Marietta Rheinlander's composure was quickly dissolving. Once again, Lloyd George Kimball was trying to pretend this was all routine and meaningless, but the act was transparent. Ken, on the other hand, was a little too eager, in my judgment: a little too aggressive.

"Why do you suppose she said the congressman deserved whatever happened to him?"

"I'll object to that, Your Honor," said Kimball. "The question asks Miss Rheinlander to speculate on what Mrs. Lucas's motive may have been."

"Sustained."

Ken stepped to the center of the floor between the witness stand and the jury box. "What did you tell Mrs. Lucas about your physical intimacy with Congressman Bailey?"

Marietta Rheinlander shook her head. "Nothing . . ."

"Well, we've served a subpoena on her, and she can be here to tell us herself, tomorrow. I will try to help you refresh your recollection. Did you tell your friend Lois Lucas that the congressman was a difficult man to satisfy?"

"I . . . I guess I said something to that effect. We were all friends, and she made something of a joke about it."

"Did you ever suggest to her that Congressman Bailey was a homosexual?"

"No."

"Did you . . ." He turned, went back to his table, and picked up a sheet of paper. I don't know if it was a written statement from Lois Lucas or not. I doubt it. "Did you ever say to Mrs. Lucas any words to this effect: 'Charles is a difficult man to satisfy. He makes me do terrible things.'?"

For a long moment she sat there staring at him, until, just before he appeared about to prompt her, she nodded and spoke very quietly. "I told her something like that."

"Did you tell Mrs. Lucas that in order to—to use your own term, 'to get him up,' you had to fellate him regularly?"

"I didn't use the word 'regularly,' " she said hoarsely.

"Did you use words like 'often' or 'frequently'?"

She nodded. "Words like that, I guess."

"When you testified a few minutes ago that you had only done it once or twice, you were not telling the truth, were you?"

"I didn't want to talk about it. I didn't want to admit doing something like that."

"Of course, you wouldn't want to admit having shot three people, either. Would you?"

"Objection," said Kimball lifelessly.

I sustained the objection. It didn't make any difference.

"In your conversation with Mrs. Lucas, you told her about other things you did for the congressman, to 'get him up.' Didn't you?"

"Yes," she whispered.

"We needn't go into them," said Ken. "But would you have denied them if I had asked you about them this afternoon?"

"Objection."

"Your Honor," said Ken, without waiting for me to rule. "I have no further questions of this witness."

He had caught her in a lie. That was all he wanted. It was all he needed.

Lloyd George Kimball rested his case. He had no more witnesses, no further evidence. Ken said he would have one rebuttal witness, tomorrow.

I spoke to the jury. "Ladies and gentlemen, you are going to have the weekend off, mostly. I'm sorry we can't let you go home. We will hear a witness in the morning and then recess until Monday morning. You will hear the arguments of counsel then, followed by my charge. I anticipate that you will begin your deliberations Monday afternoon."

It was time to go to the Alexandria House for a drink. As Linda and

I walked through the courthouse on our way out, we encountered Margaret Vogt leading Marietta Rheinlander to the car. The woman looked exhausted, beaten, and afraid. Her hands, cuffed together of course, were clenched into tight fists. Her shoulders were hunched, and her chin was down. She stared at her handcuffs or at the floor and did not look up.

13

I will not recite the conversation over drinks at the Alexandria House bar that evening. The usual cast of characters was present. Their views differed. Some thought Ken had made conviction all but certain when he caught Marietta Rheinlander in a lie. Others thought he had failed to prove his case and that she would be acquitted on that basis, whether she was guilty or not. Others thought the case against her had been weak from the beginning and could in no way justify a conviction.

The interesting thing about this division of opinion was that—beyond any question whatever—the same division had to exist among the jurors.

"A hell of a lot is going to depend on final argument," said Dick Winter, the most experienced and most successful trial lawyer in Alexandria County.

That was true, though I wished it were not so. I would rather juries reach their conclusions on the basis of the evidence, without reference to the arguments of counsel.

Actually, of course, appealing though the idea might be, you couldn't turn a case over to a jury without giving the lawyers opportunity to argue the significance or insignificance of various parts of the evidence. Final argument is an important right, for both sides of a case, and cannot be taken away.

That evening, Linda and I listened to a commentator on Court TV:

"Judge McIntyre told the jury this afternoon that it would have the case Monday afternoon. That means he is sharply limiting the arguments of the prosecutor and the defense attorney. In big-city trials of this nature, it is not unusual for each side to be given a full day to argue, and often even more. Deborah Fairchild is an experienced criminal defense lawyer in New Jersey. Tell us, Mrs. Fairchild, is Judge McIntyre risking reversal by imposing so tight a limit on final argument?"

The New Jersey lawyer, who was a public defender, answered:

"No, I don't think so. This has not been a complicated trial, if you review it. I cannot imagine an appellate court saying the lawyers were entitled to more than two hours. You do realize that the defense can appeal a conviction but the prosecution cannot appeal an acquittal. If Miss Rheinlander is convicted, I would expect Lloyd George Kimball to argue on appeal that he was not given enough time to argue. But I don't think that will prevail."

We convened on Saturday morning.

The rebuttal witness was no great surprise. Ken Simpson had recalled David Ogle.

"I have only one or two very simple questions for you, Mr. Ogle. Are you a homosexual?"

"Absolutely not," said Ogle indignantly.

"Did you ever tell Barbara Milligan, or suggest to her, that you are a homosexual?"

"Absolutely not."

"Was Congressman Bailey in financial difficulty?"

"Yes. He was heir to a small fortune, but he spent a lot of money. He lived well in Washington, kept a nice home in Huntington, and kept the lodge here, too. He went through a lot of money and from time to time was hounded by people he owed."

"Thank you, Mr. Ogle. I have no further questions. I imagine Mr. Kimball may have some."

"Questions, Mr. Kimball?" I asked.

"A few, Your Honor," said Lloyd George Kimball.

Ogle's hostility toward Marietta Rheinlander and her lawyer could not have been more obvious. If he wanted to be an effective witness, which I am sure he did, he should have suppressed himself. He was, as I have remarked before, a tall, handsome man. He exuded calm self-confidence. This morning he glowered.

Kimball remained seated at his table and pretended that questioning Ogle was a routine matter, only a matter of disposing of a minor annoyance.

"May I suppose it is your testimony as well, Mr. Ogle, that Congressman Bailey was not a homosexual?"

"He most assuredly was not. The suggestion that he was is outrageous!"

"What about Donald Finch?"

"I couldn't say about him. I will tell you this. He wouldn't have been employed by us if we had thought he was."

"How is that? Are we to understand you and the congressman denied employment to homosexuals?"

"We didn't want them around the office. They cause dissension."

"Do they indeed? Homophobia, Mr. Ogle?"

"Whatever you want to call it, Mr. Kimball."

Lloyd George Kimball stood and walked to the witness stand, carrying with him two photographic prints. He handed one of them to Ogle and asked him if he could identify it.

"This seems to be a picture taken the night of the murder. Yes. I'd gone back into my room and pulled on a sweater."

Kimball offered the photograph as Defense Exhibit D. "So that is you, taken on the night of May 5, 1952. Mr. Ogle, I ask you to look at your left hand, and what is often called 'the ring finger.' Are you wearing a ring on that finger?"

Ogle stared at the photo. "Oh, I guess so," he said, feigning casualness but not quite bringing it off.

"Well, I have an enlargement of that picture," said Kimball. He had it admitted as Defense Exhibit E. "Can you identify the ring in this enlargement, Mr. Ogle?"

Ogle frowned over the picture. "Yes. It's a ring I sometimes wear."

"A simple but heavy gold band, is it not?"

"Uh . . . yes. A gold band."

"You're not wearing it today."

"No. I've since lost it. I think it was stolen."

"Where did you get that ring, Mr. Ogle?"

"Oh, I don't recall exactly. I picked it up at an antique sale, as I recall."

"It wasn't a gift?"

Ogle shook his head. He was not the self-confident witness he had been a few minutes before. He was unable to hide the fact that he did not like this line of questions.

"Mr. Ogle, I now hand you a document I will ask the court to receive as Defense Exhibit F. Do you recognize that?"

Ogle stared at the little piece of paper. "No. I never saw this before."

Kimball offered it to Ken Simpson to examine, then to Alice Tutweiler. Ken shook his head but did not object.

"You never saw this document before, Mr. Ogle, but can you describe to the jury what it appears to be?"

Ogle shrugged. "It looks like a purchase order or bill of sale."

"Who selling what to whom?"

"Falcon Jeweler selling a ring to Charles Bailey."

"Have you ever heard of Falcon Jeweler?" asked Kimball.

"It's a store in Huntington."

"Huntington, West Virginia?"

"Yes."

"Within a block or two of the offices of Wilcoxen, Branch & Bailey?"

"I believe that's where it is."

"What is the date of the sale, Mr. Ogle?"

"September 7, 1991."

"How is the item described, Mr. Ogle?"

Ogle drew a breath and sighed, " 'One gold wedding ring.' "

"Is engraving designated, Mr. Ogle?"

"Yes."

"What was the engraving to be?"

Ogle squinted over the piece of paper, then read, "'cb–do, 9/17/ 91.'"

"Who was 'CB,' Mr. Ogle?"

"I have no idea."

"Charlotte Brontë, do you think?"

Ken Simpson shook his head. "Your Honor—"

"Do you know, Mr. Ogle?" I asked.

"No, sir."

"I'm afraid we'll have to leave it at that, Mr. Kimball," I ruled.

"And of course," said Kimball scornfully, "you would have no idea who 'DO' might be. Or the significance of the date."

"No. I have no idea."

"According to the canceled check on his account with Chase Manhattan Bank," said Kimball, "Congressman Bailey paid $800 for a gold ring, engraved for somebody. Is it your testimony you have no idea who the 'DO' in the engraving was?"

"That is my testimony," said Ogle brusquely.

"And of course the ring shown in the picture, which you have most unfortunately lost, had no engraving inside."

"It had none."

"What evil fortune that it has been lost or stolen," sneered Lloyd George Kimball. "I have no further questions of this witness, Your Honor."

Ken had no more questions, and that was the end of the evidence in *State* v. *Rheinlander*. The defendant was handcuffed and taken back to her cell for the remainder of the weekend. The lawyers— Ken to his office, Kimball and his two associates to their motel suite—went off to work on their closing arguments. I spent Saturday afternoon in my office, reviewing the charge I would give to the jury.

It was a beautiful autumn weekend, the kind of days the poet must have had in mind when he wrote of "October's bright blue weather." I put on an old sweatshirt and some comfortable faded old jeans and went out to rake leaves. Being a country boy, I could do with my leaves what city dwellers used to do but can't do any more—I raked them into a huge pile and lit a match to them. The blaze generated a white smoke that smelled delicious and is one of the things I always think of when I think of the fall of the year. A damned reporter came by and took pictures of me doing it, and a few papers ran one of his pictures.

I wasn't as comfortable as the caption suggested. I had much on my mind. Other people had much on theirs.

Think about the jury. They could see the beautiful days only from the windows of their motel. Under their charge, they were not supposed to discuss the case. They were not even supposed to think about it much, so they would not make up their minds before they heard the concluding arguments and the judge's charge. They were sequestered in a wing of the second floor of the Marriott Inn on the edge of town, where their windows overlooked the river: two in a room.

It is naive of us to suppose they did not think or talk about the case. What else would they be thinking about? Their television sets were tuned to football games that Saturday afternoon. The theory is that they concentrated on football games, or on books or crossword puzzles, and did not think about *State* v. *Rheinlander*. Theory.

Think about the defendant. She saw the glory of those two autumn days only through the bars of her cell and the bars of the window opposite. Among her thoughts, she must have wondered if ever again in her life she would have the privilege of shuffling through dry leaves and smelling the different odors of oak and maple. Her life, whether she would live or die or spend an absolute minimum of twenty years in a reformatory, hung on what those people in the Marriott Inn were thinking about. Most of them, she had to understand, had already made up their minds, though they had been told not to and would swear they hadn't.

Whatever they thought, it was beyond her control now. Everything was beyond her control. She lay on her neatly made little cot, inside her tidy little cell, and everything about her life, even when or whether or not she would be given food, was under the control of others. She must have felt utterly, totally helpless.

Glen Myers went to see her that Saturday night. He drew up a chair in the corridor outside her cell and sat and talked with her for an hour. They talked about the books he had sent her and about others they had read or wanted to read. When finally he had to leave, she put her face up to the bars and kissed him.

The Sunday New York *Times* was delivered. The Rheinlander trial remained front-page news. A part of the account by Victoria Baum:

> The evidence for and against Miss Marietta Rheinlander is in such close equilibrium that it is impossible to guess what the jury will do.
>
> The case against her is not fanciful. Her fingerprints and hers alone were on the death weapon. A paraffin test established that she had fired the pistol, though she never denied she did fire shots into the night. She may have had motive, not only in that she may have come upon the man she loved and trusted in a homosexual act, but also in that she had given him $62,000. Her testimony that she believed that money was a campaign contribution did not ring true. On Friday she was caught in a lie—on a tangential point, it is true, but still a lie.
>
> There are holes in the case for the prosecution. The chief witness for the prosecution, David Ogle, was also caught in a lie on the last morning of the trial—again, on a tangential issue, but still a lie.
>
> The difficulty for the defense is that conceivably the jury could convict Miss Rheinlander without the testimony of David Ogle. The rest of it is rather objective, technical evidence, which the jury might well find convincing without reference to the Ogle testimony.
>
> However the jury decides, clearly many questions will remain unanswered. We may never learn how an old Smith & Wesson revolver with a dangerously cracked cylinder found its way into the hands of Miss Rheinlander on the fatal night. We may never know for certain if Congressman Bailey was gay. The purpose of a criminal trial is to discover the guilt or innocence of a defendant, not to answer all questions.

14

Monday morning brought a small surprise. Lloyd George Kimball rose and asked to make a motion out of the hearing of the jury. I sent the jury to the jury room, and he made his motion.

"If Your Honor please, the defense moves that the indictment in the case of the death of Elizabeth Erb be amended to strike from it the allegation that she was killed to prevent her testifying as a witness. That allegation has to be proved beyond reasonable doubt like any other. For the allegation to stand, it must be proved that at least one of the murders occurred before Miss Erb was murdered, since obviously if she were the first one killed she couldn't have been a witness to anything. No evidence whatever has been offered to indicate in what sequence the three victims were killed. Since there is no evidence whatever on the point, I ask the court to amend the indictment."

His point was clear enough. If we amended the indictment as he asked, we eliminated the risk of the death penalty. It is Ohio law that murder in the absence of an aggravating circumstance is not punishable by death. Killing a person to prevent his testifying as a witness is an aggravating circumstance. Others are killing for hire, killing a police officer, and so on; there are eight specified aggravating circumstances.

Ken Simpson rose. "Your Honor, it is perfectly obvious that Miss Erb was not the first victim killed. There could have been no motive for killing her, except that she was a witness."

Kimball shook his head, his face a mask of tolerance. "What is obvious to Mr. Simpson is not evidence, Your Honor. There is no evidence of sequence."

I looked to Ken. "Can you cite any evidence?" I asked.

He thought about it for a moment. "None beyond the fact that it's obvious," he conceded.

I sighed. "Mr. Kimball is correct in saying that is not evidence. Since that allegation in the indictment is supported by no evidence, it must be stricken. The indictment will be so amended."

"Thank you, Your Honor," said Kimball.

"Mr. Kimball," I said, "is it your intention that the jury be informed of this amendment?"

"I suppose it must be, before it retires, Your Honor."

I think he made a mistake. He would have been wiser, in my opinion, to have left the matter alone. He had to know that if the jury returned a finding that his client murdered Elizabeth Erb to silence her as a witness, I would overturn it, since there was no evidence on the point. He would have been better off, I thought, to let the jury go out to deliberate, believing it had a case where the death penalty was possible. Some of the jurors might have been strongly disinclined to convict, thinking they might be sending Miss Rheinlander to her death. Of course, they might have been sophisticated enough to separate the issues, find her guilty of murdering the young woman but not of doing so to silence her.

His reason, I have to believe, was to relieve the worst cause of his client's anxiety. She looked that morning as if she were about to collapse. When I granted the motion, she closed her eyes and squeezed out tears. Kimball patted her shoulder.

"I should like to make another motion, Your Honor," said Kimball. "Ohio law defines aggravated murder as purposefully causing the death of another 'with prior calculation and design.' None of the evidence proves or tends to prove prior calculation and design. If Miss Rheinlander shot and killed those three people—which of course we continue vehemently to deny—it had to be without premeditation. It was in the passion of the moment. Nothing proves premeditation."

His point was easy to see. He had succeeded in eliminating the risk of the death penalty. Now he wanted to reduce the charge to simple murder, not aggravated murder—which is to say, he wanted to eliminate the minimum twenty-year sentence. If his client were convicted of aggravated murder, she would have to serve a minimum of twenty years before becoming eligible for parole—and it was unlikely she would be granted parole after serving the minimum sentence, considering that there were three murders. No wonder he didn't want the jury to hear this. It was a backup position.

I raised a hand to silence Ken Simpson and ruled without hearing his counterargument. "Mr. Kimball, unless your client found the pistol on the floor as she has testified, she brought it to the Bailey lodge. Or suppose the congressman brought it and it was in the bedroom. In that case, she had to return to the bedroom to get it. I think the precedents will sustain me that bringing the pistol to the lodge would certainly be sufficient evidence of prior calculation and design. You may argue the question of whether or not running back in the bedroom and grabbing it is sufficient evidence. You may in fact have to argue that question on appeal. But I am not going to withdraw the question from the jury. Your motion is overruled."

I doubt he was surprised. It was a nice try. I would have made it if I had been defending.

I brought back the jury. "Ladies and gentlemen, while you were out Mr. Kimball moved that an element of one of the indictments be deleted, on the ground that there has been no evidence to sustain that one element of that one indictment. I have granted the motion. You will not be asked to determine whether or not the defendant murdered Miss Elizabeth Erb to prevent her testimony as a witness to the other two murders. That amendment to the indictment removes the death penalty as an element of the case."

The jurors looked puzzled but relieved.

We proceeded to final argument. I charged the jury:

"Ladies and gentlemen of the jury, you are about to hear the final arguments of counsel for the prosecution and the defense. I ask you to listen carefully to what the attorneys have to say. They are entitled to point out to you what, in their view, is important evidence and what is not important, to call to your attention inconsistencies in the testimony, to point out what they regard as gaps in the evidence for either side. Final argument is an important right, both for the state and for the defendant. I ask you again, to listen attentively to what the lawyers have to say. I remind you, however, that what they say is not evidence. It . . . is . . . not . . . evidence. It is comment upon the evidence. Their comments may be helpful to you, or may not be. In the end, it is the evidence that must guide your decision. The purpose of final argument is to invite you to find some evidence important, other evidence not important; but in the end the decision is yours, as to what is and what is not persuasive."

Ken Simpson rose and stood behind the prosecution's table. It was the most important case he would argue in his entire professional life, probably: the one by which he would be remembered and judged. This morning he wore a dark gray suit with a faint white pinstripe, white shirt, regimental necktie in red and blue, and black shoes. Gone were the brown suits and brown shoes. I had to wonder if his wife, who is knowledgeable in such matters, had not urged this on him. Or maybe he had observed Lloyd George Kimball and decided he was a man worth emulating.

"Ladies and gentlemen of the jury," he said, "it is the obligation of the prosecution to offer to a jury as much evidence as can be accumulated to prove the guilt of the defendant. It is the obligation of the defense to overcome that evidence if it can, or to confuse the issues in the case by the introduction of irrelevant issues. If the defense has tried to confuse the jury, I do not condemn Mr. Kimball and his associates. They have not acted unethically. They have done their duty. If I were defending this case instead of prosecuting it, I would do just what they have done. If Mr. Kimball were prosecuting, he would do what I have done—though I acknowledge he would have done it much better."

Ken turned and smiled at Kimball, who nodded and returned his smile. It was a nice touch on Ken's part: the modest little acknowledgement of the senior lawyer's superior skills. A very nice touch.

Ken walked around his table and stood in front of it, his backside touching it and taking a little of his weight. "The facts of this case are about as simple as they could be, in any case we could imagine.

They are so simple and so conclusive that we don't have to look at any of the contradicted or disputed testimony. They are clearly established by testimony that has not been disputed."

That Ken had spent the weekend preparing was evident. He spoke without notes, his arms folded now as he faced the jury.

"The three victims of murder—Congressman Bailey, Donald Finch, and Elizabeth Erb—died from gunshot wounds inflicted by a specific .38 caliber Smith & Wesson revolver. Ballistic tests proved—and those tests have not been contested—that all three victims died as the result of being shot by that single revolver.

"That revolver bore fingerprints. Whose fingerprints? The defendant's: Miss Marietta Rheinlander's. No one else's fingerprints were on that pistol. A paraffin test proved that Miss Rheinlander had fired a pistol within a short time before that test was administered.

"Shortly after the murders, Miss Rheinlander jumped into her car and drove away at high speed. She would have escaped the scene of the crime—and we have no idea where she would have gone—except that she was not accustomed to driving on gravel roads and spun off into a ditch. She was found along the road, taken into custody by a deputy, and returned to the lodge."

Ken shrugged, throwing out his arms. That was his case. And a strong case it was, too. A jury could very well convict on that alone.

"Now, ladies and gentlemen of the jury," he went on, "a point has been strongly made that Miss Rheinlander was not accustomed to firing pistols and could not have fired three fatal shots with three rounds of ammunition alone. It has been assumed—and I submit to you that '*assumed*' is the correct word—that Miss Rheinlander fired at her victims from ten or fifteen feet away. You have heard testimony to the effect that her victims did not necessarily stand still and let her shoot them, that they more likely moved this way and that, trying to avoid being killed. Why should we suppose that Miss Rheinlander stood stock still in one position and aimed her pistol? If her victims likely moved, is it not at least as likely that *she* moved, stepping closer to this one and that, as she pulled the trigger? No, she did not move so close as to spray her victims with gunpowder residue. But what evidence suggests she did not move within three or four feet of each victim before firing? If she did that, her murders were no great feat of marksmanship."

Ken bore himself with the air of a man confident in his argument. Well he might have been, too.

"David Ogle testified that he came out of his bedroom and found the defendant Miss Rheinlander standing with the gun in her hand . . . and so on. The defense has suggested half a dozen reasons to wonder if Mr. Ogle is one hundred per cent truthful. But what difference does it make? Even if David Ogle lied throughout his testimony, the basic facts of the case remain, not dependent on his testimony: that a revolver bearing the defendant's fingerprints and hers alone, fired by her, killed the three victims. Those are all the facts we need to know, ladies and gentlemen—her fingerprints and hers alone were on the pistol. She fired the pistol. The shots from that pistol killed the three victims."

Marietta Rheinlander was grim and pale. The flush of tension and the gleam of perspiration that had so much marked her during the last two days of the trial were gone now. She was wearing the cream-white linen dress with the white cardigan sweater, so was almost without color.

Ken went on. "We have spent a great deal of time, ladies and gentlemen, listening to testimony as to whether or not Congressman Charles Bailey, David Ogle, and Donald Finch were or were not homosexuals. What difference does it make? None of you, I am sure, would acquit a murderer on the ground that the victim was gay. In any event, no one has suggested Elizabeth Erb was a lesbian. And if she was, what difference?"

He left his table and took up a station near the jury box. "Only one person in this courtroom, only one person who has testified, knows exactly what happened on the night of May 5, 1992. That person is Miss Marietta Rheinlander. If we are to believe her, she heard shots, rushed out from her bedroom, found a pistol lying on the floor, and fired it into the night, at some mysterious stranger who was running away.

"But can we believe her? I remind you, ladies and gentlemen—I am sorry to have to bring this up, but she testified that she offered the congressman fellatio that evening. She testified that *she had done so only once before* because she found the act so distasteful. On cross-examination, being reminded of what she had told her friend Mrs. Lucas, she admitted she had done it many times. She lied. I am sorry to have to put it so bluntly, but she lied—and if someone hadn't sent me the article from the Pittsburgh *Post-Gazette* and if I hadn't contacted Mrs. Lucas and taken her statement, Miss Rheinlander might have gotten away with it.

"She testified that she gave the congressman $62,000 as a campaign contribution. Miss Rheinlander is a businesswoman. She does not dispense money in such amounts lightly, we may assume. This is a campaign year. The newspapers have been full of stories about excessive contributions to candidates. She wants us to believe she gave Congressman Bailey a $62,000 campaign contribution, not knowing it was illegal. If you believe that, ladies and gentlemen, maybe you believe in the tooth fairy."

The jury was focused on Ken. He had their attention. He folded his arms.

"I said a moment ago that only one person really knows what happened on the night of May 5, 1992. Since we don't know, we are entitled to speculate a little. Let us suppose, ladies and gentlemen, that Congressman Bailey really was a homosexual. Besides Miss Rheinlander, two witnesses have suggested he was—that is, Mrs. Longlea and Miss Milligan. Let us suppose Donald Finch was. Miss Rheinlander had fallen in love with the congressman and had tried to win his love. She had tried to win a commitment from him that he would not engage in physical intimacy with anyone but herself. After all, as she herself testified, that's what marriage is all about, isn't it? He had proposed marriage to her and given her a ring. Yet, she wasn't quite confident in him and came to Ohio so he wouldn't be alone in the lodge with members of his staff. She did not, in other words, entirely trust him. She brought the pistol—or obtained it here in Ohio or West Virginia—because she was determined to have it out with Congressman Bailey, one way or another. She was careful not to put her fingerprints on the pistol or the cartridges, so she could say she had never touched it.

"Now. Here was a man to whom she had offered love. She had, in her own terms, 'done terrible things' to satisfy him sexually. She had given him $62,000. On the fatal night he was squeamish about having sex with a woman who was menstruating, even though he was aroused. He left their bedroom. After a while she went out looking for him. She found him in the living room, engaging in homosexual intimacy with Donald Finch. Enraged, she ran back to the bedroom and grabbed her pistol. Before now she had handled it only with gloves. Now, in her fury, she seized it and ran back to the living room with it. She has acknowledged that she had had too much to drink, so we may say she ran back to the living room in a *drunken* fury.

"Congressman Bailey and Donald Finch, knowing she was angry, had ceased to do what they were doing, and the congressman was on his way to the bedroom. As they reached the hallway, she stepped out and shot them both. Miss Erb, having perhaps heard angry words, had come from her bedroom to see what was the matter. She witnessed the shooting. In terror, she turned to flee. Miss Rheinlander shot her in the back.

"Realizing her fingerprints were on the pistol and maybe knowing what a paraffin test would prove, she went to the sliding glass doors that Miss Erb had opened to get in, and she fired three shots into the night."

Ken stood nodding. "Is that what happened? I don't know. I can't prove it. But the state has proved that Miss Rheinlander's fingerprints and hers alone were on the revolver that fired the fatal shots, also that she had in fact fired a pistol that night. The state has proved opportunity. The state has proved motive: love and jealousy and exploitation. The state has proved that Miss Rheinlander attempted to flee. The state has proved she is a woman of hot temper.

"With nothing more, ladies and gentlemen, that is enough to establish guilt beyond reasonable doubt. Were the words she spoke to Margaret Vogt an admission? Did she in effect confess to Bess Whittlig? You may decide those questions as you see fit. There is more than enough evidence to sustain a conviction, even without those admissions or confessions."

Ken walked back to his table and stood in front of it. "Three people are dead," he said solemnly. "Three people who deserved to live are dead. That's the whole point. That's why we have all been here for a week. That's why Miss Rheinlander has been in jail since May. Murder is the ultimate crime. And here we have, not just one, but three murders. A member of Congress, forty-eight years old. A graduate student, twenty-seven. A young woman, twenty-five.

"I think in particular of Elizabeth Erb, just a girl really, working as a secretary, getting her start in life, in love, maybe to no purpose, but with many, many years ahead of her to find happiness and satisfaction, to become the mother of children . . . shot to death with a .38 bullet in her back.

"Let's think about her. All of her hopes and dreams. And yes, all of her frustrations and sorrows. All of life. Suddenly taken from her. In an instant of anger. Or to silence her, so she could not testify here this week and tell us what she saw. Maybe she is in heaven. Let us hope so. We know one thing. She's not here. She is not in this world. She was blasted out of it. For no reason that had anything to do with her. Maybe Congressman Bailey abused and exploited the defendant Miss Rheinlander. Maybe Donald Finch was Miss Rheinlander's rival for the congressman's affections and passion. Miss Erb never harmed Miss Rheinlander, never exploited her. Yet, she is dead, too. And we can think of no other reason but that she was a witness. My mind has fixed itself on her, more than on the other two victims."

Ken's wife sat in the courtroom that Monday morning. She was as pallid as Marietta Rheinlander. Her eyes were wet with tears.

"Justice cries out, not for vengeance but for punishment. I am glad the death penalty has been removed as an element of this case. I was not comfortable about asking for it but felt that duty required it. You may now take this case to the jury room and deliberate on it, absent that emotional element. I believe that will make a difficult task a little easier.

"Do not be distracted, I beg you, by extraneous issues. Do not be distracted from the facts: that three people were murdered with a pistol that bore one set of fingerprints only, those of the defendant; that the paraffin test proved she had fired that pistol; that she tried to flee; that she had motive; that she lied to you from the witness stand. With those facts before you, ladies and gentlemen, I believe you will have no trouble in finding Marietta Rheinlander guilty of aggravated murder—and that beyond a reasonable doubt."

It was a powerful argument, a devastating argument, I thought. If the jury in fact focused its attention on the facts Ken Simpson had insisted they should, they might indeed have no trouble finding Marietta Rheinlander guilty of aggravated murder. The commentator on Court TV said the same.

We took fifteen minutes' recess before hearing the argument for the defense.

I saw Ken in the men's room. He was wiping his face with paper towels drenched in cold water. "Like a few minutes alone in my office?" I asked. He nodded, and I also asked, "With Stephanie?" She's his wife. He nodded again. "I'll find her and send her in," I said, and I went off to find her.

When we were again in session, Lloyd George Kimball rose to argue for the defense. He stood and spoke without notes: a tall, trim, handsome man with a ruddy face and white hair, wearing this morning another of his beautifully tailored suits, this one a dramatic black. He also wore polished Gucci loafers.

"I would like to begin, ladies and gentlemen of the jury, by reminding you of a fundamental principle of law. I will allude to it again later, but I should like for you to have it in mind as I speak to you on behalf of the defendant Miss Marietta Rheinlander. This basic principle of law is very old. It comes down to us through history, from the law of England, and is a significant right that belongs to every one of us.

"I refer of course to the fundamental principle that no person shall stand convicted of a crime until a unanimous jury finds that person guilty beyond a reasonable doubt."

He turned and reached for a book, which Megan O'Reilly had ready for him. It was one of the red volumes of the codified statutes of the State of Ohio. "This," he said, "is the law of Ohio, the Revised Code, and I read to you from Section 2901.05. 'Every person accused of an offense is presumed innocent until proven guilty beyond a reasonable doubt.' Subsection (D) defines reasonable doubt. ' "Reasonable doubt" is present when the jurors, after they have carefully considered and compared all the evidence, cannot say they are firmly convinced of the truth of the charge. It is a doubt based on reason and common sense. Reasonable doubt is not mere possible doubt, because everything relating to human affairs or depending on moral evidence is open to some possible or imaginary doubt. "Proof beyond a reasonable doubt" is proof of such character that an ordinary person would be willing to rely and act upon it in the most important of his own affairs.' "

He returned the book to Megan O'Reilly and moved closer to the jury box. "There is another way to state the principle. Until the state legislature adopted the section I have just in part read to you, a part of the official definition of reasonable doubt required that jurors be 'convinced to an abiding moral certainty of the truth of the charge.' "

He held out his hands, palms up. "I am going to say it another way. If you are confused by the conflicting evidence and are not sure what happened, then it is your duty to acquit. Ladies and gentlemen, what the law requires is certainty. If you are not *certain* the defendant committed the crime, you must acquit."

He returned to the defense table, glanced down at his client, then went on. "Mr. Simpson argued that only one person really knows what happened on the night of May 5, 1992. That person, he says, is

Marietta Rheinlander. But that is not true. Miss Rheinlander doesn't know what happened either. She was not present when the fatal shots were fired. She was still in the bedroom. She so testified."

He began to chop the air with both hands. I hadn't seen him gesture that way before. "Let me remind you, ladies and gentlemen, let me emphasize as strongly as I can that Miss Rheinlander testified she did not commit these murders—*and no one has testified that she did*. No one . . . has testified . . . that she did.

"The entire case against her depends on circumstantial evidence."

Ken Simpson was ashen as he watched and listened. I had ordered that Stephanie be allowed to sit inside the rail and just behind him. From time to time she reached forward and touched his shoulder.

Miss Rheinlander studied her lawyer with an expression of skepticism, as though she didn't think he was doing well enough. Her cheeks were now flushed, in contrast to the pallor of the rest of her face. She twisted a handkerchief, and from time to time she shoved it away impatiently and tried to keep her hands still.

"Many questions remain unanswered," said Kimball. "Why were Miss Rheinlander's fingerprints on the grips and trigger of the murder weapon but on no other part—and not on the cartridges? Mr. Simpson's theory seems to be that she brought the pistol to the lodge, being careful to wear gloves whenever she handled it so her fingerprints would not be on it—then, when she was ready to commit murder with it, she grabbed it in her bare hands and put her prints on the trigger and grips. Really, ladies and gentlemen, does that make sense? Is that a reasonable explanation? It is not, of course. Miss Rheinlander's explanation is reasonable: that she grabbed the pistol up from the floor and fired it at someone fleeing into the night.

"Paraffin test? Of course, the test showed she had fired a pistol. She *had* fired a pistol. She's never denied it. The question is: did she fire three shots, or six? The state's expert witness testified that the paraffin test could not make so fine a distinction. It proved that Miss Rheinlander had fired a pistol—but not how many times. Once again, there is no evidence but Miss Rheinlander's own testimony."

Kimball paused and looked down at his client, whose look of skepticism had by now vanished. I suspect she felt a faint trace of confidence as she listened to her lawyer's cultivated tones of reason and persuasion. He was good at what he was doing. The jury was rapt.

"Motive? What motive could Marietta Rheinlander possibly have had for murdering Congressman Bailey and his two young staff members? The scenario offered by the prosecution is that she emerged from her bedroom to find her fiancé engaged in homosexual intimacy with Donald Finch. Mr. Simpson offered no evidence whatever to sustain that scenario. It is a guess, pure and simple.

"Mr. Simpson has suggested also that the congressman had exploited Miss Rheinlander, taking money from her that she supposed was a campaign contribution and using it for personal expenses. Once again, you are asked to believe something for which no evidence has been offered. Miss Rheinlander testified that she gave the congressman $62,000, supposing it was a campaign contribution. It is true that it is illegal for a single contributor to give a single candidate for Congress more than $1,000, but we read every day about millionaires contributing hundreds of thousands of dollars to political campaigns. The distinction is that those big contributions are made to *party organizations* or political action committees— and they are entirely legal. Another distinction is that some state laws allow far bigger contributions to candidates for state and local offices. These distinctions are rather subtle, I think you will agree, and Miss Rheinlander may *well* have been unaware of them. In any event, she testified that she wasn't. No one testified that she was. On this point, too, you have her testimony under oath as your only evidence."

Lloyd George Kimball ambled across the well of the courtroom to the witness box, now empty, as though he were stretching his legs in a little stroll. "Let's suppose you were Marietta Rheinlander and came to Alexandria County, Ohio, carrying a pistol and bent on a confrontation, perhaps a deadly confrontation, with a man you had decided had abused and betrayed you. Let's suppose you had kept the pistol free of your fingerprints. Let's suppose you had decided to *kill* your lover. How would you do it?

"Would you pick up the pistol with your bare hands, step out into the living room of the house, where your lover was meeting with another man, for whatever reason, kill them both, then kill a witness—all this in a house where there were three more people who would hear the shots, come running, and find the murder weapon with your fingerprints? Isn't it more likely you would, let us say, invite your lover for a walk in the woods, take him to some remote place, put on your gloves—which, incidentally, would negate the paraffin test—shoot him, hide the pistol and the gloves, and run back to the lodge screaming that someone had shot your lover? Doesn't that make more sense?

"Ladies and gentlemen of the jury, if you accept Mr. Simpson's scenario, you have to suppose that Miss Rheinlander *wanted* to be caught, or didn't care, and so committed the murders in a way most likely to assure that she *would* be caught, arrested, and prosecuted."

Not a bad point, I thought. My impression was that the jury thought so, too. They stared hard at Kimball while he was making this argument, and one or two of them nodded.

"We need not, I believe, dwell long on the fact that Miss Rheinlander drove away from the lodge. In panic and terror, realizing she would very likely be charged with the murders, she fled. Might not any one of us have done the same?

"We need not dwell on her statement to Margaret Vogt that she had 'fucked up.' That was no confession. It was an acknowledgment that she had made huge mistakes in picking up and firing the gun, then in driving away. If she hadn't done those things, she might never have become a suspect.

"So far as her statement to Bess Whittlig is concerned—well, ladies and gentlemen, you have heard Miss Rheinlander speak, giving her testimony. Do you really believe she would say, 'I done it.'? Remember that Mrs. Whittlig was not paraphrasing. Mr. Simpson asked her for the exact words she heard from Miss Rheinlander. I

asked her to repeat the specific words, and she told us Miss Rheinlander said, 'I done it, you know. I done somethin' awful.' I cannot
guess, you cannot guess, what motivated Mrs. Whittlig to make the
statement, but its very words demonstrate that it is not true."

In the jury box, Grace Siegfried smiled. I wonder if she didn't
remember trying to teach Bess Whittlig not to say "I done it."

"In any event," Kimball went on, "can any of us think of a reason
why Miss Marietta Rheinlander, indicted for murder and already
advised by counsel, would confess to her jailer?"

That was a good point. Three of the jurors nodded.

Now Kimball addressed the one instance where his client had
damaged herself as a witness. "Mr. Simpson makes much of the fact
that Miss Rheinlander first testified that she had engaged in oral sex
with Congressman Bailey only once, then later admitted she had
done it many times. Why? Why the inconsistency? I haven't even
asked her. I am sure we understand why. She found it extremely
painful to talk about that subject. She was not just embarrassed to
have to make a public admission of it, not just before this courtroom
but before television cameras broadcasting this trial to the whole
world. She was not just embarrassed but was humiliated. So she
denied she did it habitually. But she had admitted it to her friend in
Pittsburgh and so was compelled to admit it here."

Lloyd George Kimball went to the rail of the jury box, and I
guessed he was about to finish.

"Ladies and gentlemen of the jury, I return to the fundamental
principle of law with which I began. 'Every person accused of an
offense is presumed innocent until proven guilty beyond a reasonable doubt.' Beyond . . . a reasonable . . . doubt.

"Section 2901.05 also says, '. . . the burden of proof for all elements
of the offense is upon the prosecution.'

"Why is that so fundamental a principle? Because we as Ameri-
cans, like the English people with whom the principle originated,
can hardly think of anything more horrible than being locked away
in a prison for a crime we did not commit. For that reason we have
built safeguards into the law, one of which is trial by jury, and we

require unanimous verdicts, supported by proof beyond reasonable doubt.

"The crime was horrible. Heaven cries for retribution. But it does not cry for the conviction of a person who is not guilty. The horror of the crime would only be compounded if we were to send off to life in prison a person who did not commit these three murders.

"And I submit to you, ladies and gentlemen, that no crime has been proved against the defendant Marietta Rheinlander. Circumstances have been proved, circumstances in which she *might* have committed these murders. But there has been no proof that she did.

"Beyond reasonable doubt?" He threw out his arms and shook his head. "The case has not been proved *at all,* much less beyond reasonable doubt. We ask for justice, ladies and gentlemen of the jury. We ask for application of the law. We ask that your verdict be not guilty."

Ken Simpson was entitled to the last word. He rose and spoke quietly.

"Mr. Kimball has argued that when I suggested to you that the defendant caught two of her victims in an act of homosexual intimacy I was only guessing, that there was no evidence of any such thing. It is true that I can't prove that's what happened, but it is more than just a guess. Dr. Chandra testified that both Congressman Bailey and Donald Finch had experienced sexual orgasms within a short time before they died. He testified further that Miss Erb had not experienced sexual intercourse within the hours just before *her* death. Miss Rheinlander testified that the congressman did not have a sexual emission while he was with her. Those two men may have had sexual emissions alone, or they may have had them together. It is reasonable to suspect they had them together.

"Mr. Kimball argues that Miss Rheinlander lied to you about how often she engaged in oral sex with Congressman Bailey because she was embarrassed to talk about it, was humiliated. If she is so embarrassed by it, why did she mention it? She testified that she 'offered to do something' to give the congressman sexual satisfaction. I didn't ask her about that; she volunteered it. Even when I asked her what she had meant, she didn't have to tell me. It was something that had happened between those two people when they were alone, and he wasn't alive to contradict anything she said. I don't think she was so embarrassed about it. I think she was indignant about it. I think it was one reason why she was furiously, drunkenly angry on the night of May 5.

"The State of Ohio does not ask you to send to prison a woman who is innocent of crime. The state asks you to send to prison a woman who is guilty, as the evidence has shown."

All that remained was for me to charge the jury. Neither lawyer had taken the two hours I had allowed, and there was time for my charge before we broke for lunch.

The charge to a jury is a dry business. In Ohio, almost all of it is in rules handed down by the Supreme Court. We judges don't make up our charges. For the most part we just read standard charges prescribed for us. What is more, we hand them to the jury in writing—print, of course—so they can refer to them during their deliberations.

I won't set it all out here. Just one or two points.

I instructed the jurors on the meaning of the terms "purposeful" and "prior calculation and design."

"A person acts purposefully when he performs an act from which certain consequences must be anticipated, and a person is presumed to intend the natural consequences of his acts. If a person discharges a firearm at another and that other person is injured or killed, it will be presumed that the actor intended to cause injury or death. In such instance, the person acted purposefully."

"To act with 'prior calculation and design' does not require protracted plotting and scheming. All that is required is that the actor have sufficient time to form an understanding of what he is doing, time to consider or reconsider, as contrasted to doing something as

245

an instantaneous reaction or in a moment of passion, and courts have ruled that in some cases not so much as a minute is required for premeditation. How much time is required is for you the jury to decide.

"If you find that the defendant killed one or more of the victims purposefully but without prior calculation and design, you will find the defendant guilty of simple murder and not of aggravated murder."

Since much of the evidence was circumstantial, I charged on circumstantial evidence:

"Circumstantial evidence is as good as direct evidence. It is not unusual for crimes to be committed in secret, and often circumstantial evidence is the only evidence that may be adduced. However, when circumstantial evidence is relied on, that evidence must not only be consistent with the guilt of the defendant but inconsistent with any other rational conclusion. If your neighbor has a big dog that runs loose at night and you have a small cat, the fact that you find your cat chewed up and dead one morning is circumstantial evidence that your neighbor's dog killed your cat. But it does not prove the case because another dog or some other animal may have killed your cat. That the dog runs loose at night and that your cat is dead is circumstantial evidence consistent with the guilt of the dog, but it is not inconsistent with another rational conclusion: that another dog or animal killed your cat. If the circumstantial evidence may be explained in any other rational way, it does not prove the guilt of an accused."

I then explained to the jurors that they would take into the jury room nine verdict forms, for the three possible verdicts in each of the three cases. The three possible verdicts in each case were: guilty of aggravated murder, guilty of murder, and not guilty.

"When you retire, you should first elect one of your number foreman or forewoman of the jury. Your verdict in each case, whatever it may be, must be unanimous. When you have reached a verdict in each case, the foreman or forewoman will sign the verdict.

"Now, ladies and gentlemen, it is almost noon. The bailiff will accompany you to the jury room and can be present for only one element of your deliberations. Please advise him as to whether you want to go out for lunch or begin deliberating, with lunch brought in."

The jury retired at 11:48 and sent out word that it wanted lunch brought in.

15

Is anything worse than waiting out a jury?

I went to the Alexandria House and joined the usual crowd for lunch, since Linda had decided to go home and make some telephone calls she needed to make. She said the jury would not come back that afternoon, and she did not mean to sit around the courthouse waiting. Ken Simpson and his wife went to his office and had lunch there. He had business waiting for his attention.

Marietta Rheinlander went back to jail. She would wait out the jury in her cell.

Lloyd George Kimball went to the jail and talked with her for a few minutes, and after that he came into the Alexandria House dining room, with Megan O'Reilly and Bob Mitchell, Miss Rheinlander's local lawyer, who had sat throughout the trial without saying anything, his only function being to advise Kimball on Ohio law. Bob led the group to our table.

"Gentlemen," he said, "let me introduce Lloyd Kimball and Megan O'Reilly." Speaking to them, he said, "Judge McIntyre you know. Dick Winter is our most experienced trial lawyer. And this is Pete Varner, another member of our bar. And Glen Myers, also a lawyer. Woody Schramm there, who is an insurance agent, is the only one of this notorious clan who's not a lawyer."

Kimball smiled warmly. "I've noticed you in the courtroom, gentlemen. Mr. Myers, you've been a great comfort to my client. I appreciate that. And, Your Honor, since I'm sure you won't quote it against me if I have to appeal, I want to tell you I appreciate the fair and skillful way you've conducted this trial."

"You had a worthy opponent, didn't you?" said Dick Winter.

Kimball grinned and nodded. "Damned if I didn't. I never underestimated him, but he's a fine young lawyer. Win or lose in this case, he'll do well."

"We expect that," I said.

"Well, it's been good to meet you, gentlemen. I assume we have a long afternoon ahead."

They went to their table. Reporters around the dining room had witnessed this meeting and would have given their eyeteeth to know what we'd said.

"Explain something to me," said Woody Schramm. "I hear you ruled the death penalty out of the case this morning. How come?"

"The basic law is that aggravated murder is murder with prior calculation and design, what we used to call premeditation," I said.

"Malice aforethought," said Dick Winter.

"Right," I went on. "That is punishable by life imprisonment, with eligibility for parole after twenty years."

"Twenty years doesn't seem much for committing murder," said Woody.

"I said *eligibility* for parole. A person who makes a good prison record and so on *might* get out after twenty years. Not many do. Twenty-five years is more likely, thirty in many cases. And some are never paroled."

"But what happened to the death penalty?"

"The law lists eight aggravating circumstances. If the jury finds one of those aggravating circumstances existed, then the death penalty can be imposed. They include killing for hire, killing while in a jail or prison, killing a peace officer, killing to make escape possible, or killing in the course of a rape, robbery, burglary, and so on. The aggravating circumstance in this indictment was killing to silence a witness. There was no evidence she had killed for that reason, so we had to drop that."

"So the death penalty is out of the case, then," said Woody, indicating by his tone that he was not satisfied with the result.

"Even if an aggravating circumstance had been found," I said, "the law also lists certain *mitigating* circumstances. They include things like strong provocation, duress, or stress; youth; insanity; no significant prior criminal record; and so on. If the aggravating circumstance had been left in the indictment, and if the jury had found she *had* killed Elizabeth Erb to silence her as a witness, then we would have had to call the jury back for a punishment phase of the trial, in which the jury would have been asked to weigh the aggravating circumstance and the mitigating circumstances and make me a recommendation. If they had recommended death, I would have had to make an independent finding that the aggravating circumstance outweighed the mitigating circumstances, before I could have sentenced her to death. All of which would have been reviewable on appeal."

"It sounds to me like we have abolished the death penalty," Woody grumped.

"Hear, hear," said Glen.

When I returned to the courthouse, I found a representative of Court TV waiting for me. Her name was Pamela Rogers—an attractive young woman—and she said she needed to speak with me in confidence. I took her in my office.

"Your Honor," she said. "Something has come up that we don't quite know how to handle. We've broadcast it, knowing of course that the jury here could not see it. We don't know if it has an impact on what the jury is considering, but we thought we should show it to you."

This sounded ominous. I had given the Court TV people a room in the courthouse—a storage room in the basement—for their equipment, and Miss Rogers asked me to go down there and view a tape.

The tape was mounted in their VCR, and they had a monitor for me to view.

"I have to explain just a little," she told me. "Last Wednesday Mrs. DeFelice mentioned in her testimony the serial number of the Smith & Wesson revolver. That went out live. On Sunday we rebroadcast a lot of the trial, for people who have to work weekdays and can't watch the proceedings live. That's nothing unusual. We do it all the time. Sunday afternoon we got a call. A man in Virginia said he recognized the serial number of the murder weapon: 94225. We sent a camera crew to take his statement. We broadcast it this morning, during the break. Your Honor ... it may have some impact."

"Well, let's see it," I said.

She ran the tape. I have a transcript, and it goes like this—

DAN MURPHY: Ladies and gentlemen, we are in Fairfax County, Virginia, and specifically at a gun club near Lake Barcroft. This is an indoor gun club, where pistols are fired at targets. I am speaking with Mr. Vernon Carter, the owner of Carter Gun Club. Mr. Carter, tell us about the Smith & Wesson revolver you heard about on Court TV this morning.

VERNON CARTER: Well, I seen some stuff about the Rheinlander trial in Ohio. I think it's an interesting case, and I'd watch more of it if I was at home more. Anyway, when I heard the woman from the Ohio Crime Lab talk about the Smith & Wesson pistol used in those murders, I heard her use the number 94225, and right off I knew it was a gun that was stole here at the gun club.

DAN MURPHY: Tell us about that.

VERNON CARTER: It's a six-shot .38. I bought it off a member of the club about 1976. His job took him to New York, where he couldn't have a pistol, so I give him fifty dollars for it. I kept it around here all those years. A lot of fellows liked to shoot it. It wasn't what you'd call accurate, but it was more like shooting western style than shooting a target pistol was, and a lot of fellows liked it. Members'd ask for it and fire a box of shells through it.

DAN MURPHY: What else can you tell us about it?

VERNON CARTER: Fer me it was a bad-luck gun. I spent the money to put a new barrel on it and right after that found out the cylinder had a little crack in it. So I couldn't let nobody shoot it no more.

DAN MURPHY: And you say it was stolen?

VERNON CARTER: I hung it up on a nail behind the counter. One day I come in and noticed it was gone.

DAN MURPHY: When was that?

VERNON CARTER: Oh, I'd say about eight, ten months ago.

DAN MURPHY: Do you have any idea who stole it?

VERNON CARTER: I'd hate to have to say. Nobody much comes in here but members of the club.

Whatever this new information meant, it meant nothing for the moment. The jury was out. I summoned Ken Simpson and Lloyd George Kimball to view the tape. There was nothing any of us could do about it now. Whatever significance it had—if any—this jury was deliberating without knowing of it.

Nothing is so formidable or mysterious as the closed door of a jury room when a jury is deliberating inside. Gene Hockenberry, my bailiff, sat in the jury box, waiting for a rap on the door. They might come to the door with an announcement, or they might come with a question or a request for a rereading of testimony. This jury did neither.

In legal theory we entertain the supposition that jurors were born yesterday and know nothing about a case. The theory is that the minds of jurors are *tabulae rasae*, blank slates, as were their minds at birth, so that the information they receive during the trial will be all the information they have. On the other hand, we also assume they match what a witness says to what their lifetimes of experience tell them can and cannot be true. They are supposed to be naive and shrewd at one and the same time.

In this trial we assumed the jurors knew that a car driven too fast around a curve on a gravel road is apt to slide off. We didn't need testimony to that effect. In a trial before a Manhattan jury, we might well need such testimony. Jurors bring into the jury room the common experience of mankind, as it differs from one place to another, one decade to another. We know they do and in one sense expect they do, while in another sense we suppose they don't.

It has been said that trial by jury is a cop-out. We don't really know what the truth is, so we send twelve innocents into a room and keep them there until they find out. They go in carrying the same baggage of deficiencies as we would carry: ignorance, prejudice, emotion, confusion, contradiction; and we think they'll put all that aside and reach a decision which we will declare is justice, by definition.

Sure it's a cop-out, and I'll join you in a campaign to abolish it— so soon as you suggest a better way of handling it. Trial by jury is the glory of our system of law and its shame, all at the same time.

Linda was right. The Marietta Rheinlander jury did not report on Monday afternoon.

About six o'clock they sent out word that they wanted to go to dinner and to their motel for the night.

Linda and I had dinner at the hotel that night. Reporters were bolder about approaching me now. A young man from *Newsday* came to us in the bar and asked if he could buy us a drink. I said no but we would buy him one. As it happened, he did in fact nip the bar tab before I could grab it.

"Do you, sir, attach any significance to the length of time a jury is out? I mean, there is a theory that the longer they are out the more likely they are to convict."

"And," said I, "there is a theory that the longer they are out the more likely they are to acquit. I doubt there is any significance in how long they are out."

"Do you have a guess as to how long they will take?"

"I expect a verdict tomorrow," I told him.

What I didn't tell him was that I would be decidedly unhappy if the jury did not come back tomorrow. The evidence before it was not all that complicated. If they didn't decide tomorrow, I would have to think they were deadlocked.

I dislike juries who deliberate for a week or more. I have to wonder what they are doing, and I have to suspect they are constituting

253

themselves little committees on public safety. In very few trials is the evidence so complex that a decision cannot be reached in a few hours. Of course, I haven't tried big antitrust cases and the like, where a trial may last months and the evidence load a truck. I do think that in the ordinary criminal case, the jury should decide within a day or so at most.

"I assume you would not want to comment on any element of the evidence," said the reporter.

"You assume correctly. I can't do that."

"If Miss Rheinlander is convicted, how soon will she be transferred to the reformatory?"

"Immediately," I said. "That is, within forty-eight hours."

"You will sentence immediately?"

"There is no probation after a murder conviction, and the sentence is mandatory."

"What sort of place is the reformatory?"

I took a sip from my martini. "Judges are taken on a tour of the chief state penal institutions, to see what kind of places we are sending people to. They're all grim. The women's reformatory impressed me as clean and well run. When I saw it, each woman still had her own individual room; there were no dormitory-style rooms. They—"

"'Rooms'? Not cells?"

"They're locked in, so what's the difference? Heavy wooden doors with little windows. A cot, a little table and a chair, toilet and basin, a sort of closet for hanging clothes—hanging uniforms, which is what they wear. Not too terribly bad, but not the kind of place you'd want your sister or daughter to live in."

The young man grinned. "No off-the-record guess as to how it's going to come out?"

I grinned back and shook my head. "If I had a guess, I wouldn't tell you, off the record or otherwise; but I honestly don't have a guess."

And that was the truth.

* * *

If that night was long for me—and it was long; I had difficulty sleeping—think what it must have been for Marietta Rheinlander. I got up in the middle of the night and took a snort: a shot of Scotch and a little water to help me sleep, which is better than taking a sleeping pill. (This is something I do no more than twice a year, incidentally.) It was an option not available to Miss Rheinlander in her cell. I can't imagine how she endured it.

The jury was brought back to the courthouse and resumed deliberations at nine o'clock. Once more we faced that formidable closed door.

I had work to do in my office, but from time to time I went into the courtroom and stared at the jury-room door. Lloyd George Kimball sat at the defense table, with Megan O'Reilly and Bob Mitchell. I knew how *they* felt, too. I have defended in my life, and I know how powerless you feel when you know you have done all you can and yet wonder if in some way you could have done more.

Ken Simpson came to my office about ten o'clock. He'd had time to get back to some of his regular practice, and he had two documents he wanted me to sign. I reviewed them and signed them.

The courtroom was still half full, of reporters mostly. Mr. and Mrs. Rheinlander were not there, and I wondered if Kimball had made arrangements to call them when the jury indicated it had a verdict. The reporters stood around talking. The TV lights were off. The cameramen stood protectively by their equipment, but they looked tired and bored.

In fact, my whole courtroom looked tired, a little dingy, and burdened with tension.

The jury did not return before noon. They sent out word that they wanted coffee and tea and sandwiches.

Linda and I took lunch in my office.

"What are you going to do about the man in Virginia identifying the pistol?" she asked.

"I'm not going to do anything about it," I said. "All I am here is the judge. I can't go looking for evidence. And Ken's not going to do anything about it. If she's acquitted, that's that; he can't try her again. If she's convicted, maybe Kimball will find enough in the identification to ask for a new trial. I spent plenty of time thinking about it during the night."

"Do you mean what that man said is meaningless?"

"That's not what I said. They've arranged to fax the membership list of the Carter Gun Club to the sheriff. Be a curious development if Marietta Rheinlander was a member, wouldn't it?"

Linda tossed her head toward the door—toward something beyond actually: the door of the jury room. "Dammit!" she said. "What could they be doing in there?"

A little before three o'clock we found out.

At 2:16 someone rapped on the jury-room door. Gene Hockenberry opened the door and learned who the jury had elected forewoman. Grace Siegfried told him the jury had reached a verdict.

Gene came immediately to my office and told me. I picked up the telephone and called Ken Simpson's office. Kimball and his associates were in the courtroom and knew what was happening.

We had to wait for Marietta Rheinlander to be brought from the jail.

I could not put on my robe in the jury room this time. The jury was there. I put it on in the clerk's office. When I saw Margaret Vogt leading Miss Rheinlander in, I entered the courtroom. The lights were glaring again. Every seat was taken, and some people stood around the edges of the room.

The defendant entered the courtroom still wearing handcuffs. They were taken off only as she stood at the defense table. For the first time, she appeared in court not wearing the pink cashmere suit or the white linen dress. She had not taken time to change or to apply makeup, so was wearing a gray sweatshirt, faded blue jeans, and flat shoes. Her face was wan and gaunt. She sat down. Sitting between Lloyd George Kimball and Megan O'Reilly, she looked like an inflated rubber doll that has leaked air.

Kimball, normally ruddy of complexion, was colorless too. He put a hand on his client's hand and sat slumped.

Margaret Vogt took up a station standing directly behind Miss Rheinlander. Deputy Bob Johnson came in and stood beside Margaret.

I rapped the gavel. "Let something be understood," I said sternly. "No one will leave this courtroom until the court is recessed. Deputies and other officers are instructed to enforce that order. There will be no demonstration of any kind when the verdict is announced. I mean that absolutely. This is a courtroom, and anyone who violates order and dignity, as happened last week, will be held in contempt, jailed, and fined. The jury will now return to the courtroom."

Ken Simpson sat back from his table, within reach of his wife's hand. Stephanie Simpson's hand rested supportively on his shoulder.

The jury came in and took their seats in the box.

The old story is that you can get a hint of what a jury has decided by watching its demeanor as it returns with a verdict. So . . . so, try it. This jury was somber. Some looked at the defendant, which it is said that jurors who have voted to convict won't do, and some didn't.

"Members of the jury," I said, "have you reached a verdict?"

Grace Siegfried stood, erect and stately. "We have, Your Honor," she said.

"Please hand your signed verdicts to the clerk."

Harold McCluskey walked to the jury box and received the verdicts from the hand of Mrs. Siegfried. He brought them to me. I glanced them over, and I knew.

"The defendant will rise and face the court."

Lloyd George Kimball and Megan O'Reilly had to help Marietta Rheinlander to her feet and support her from both sides. She shuddered visibly.

"The clerk will read the verdicts," I said.

This was Harold's moment on Court TV, and he adjusted his gold-rimmed spectacles and read:

"The State of Ohio versus Marietta Rose Rheinlander, case number 92 dash 54—"

This was the principal charge, that she had murdered Charles Bailey.

"We the jury, being duly impaneled and sworn, find the defendant Marietta Rose Rheinlander . . . *not guilty.*"

She slapped her hands to her face and began to sob. Her lawyers could not hold her up, and she sank into her chair.

Her father seemed to faint. Mrs. Rheinlander held him up, with the help of strangers sitting around them, and patted his face.

Ken Simpson stared at the table before him, and Stephanie gripped his shoulders with both hands.

"The State of Ohio versus Marietta Rose Rheinlander, case number 92 dash 55. We the jury, being duly impaneled and sworn, find the defendant Marietta Rose Rheinlander not guilty.

"The State of Ohio versus Marietta Rose Rheinlander, case number 92 dash 56. We the jury, being duly impaneled and sworn, find the defendant Marietta Rose Rheinlander not guilty."

I used the gavel for a minute and a half to settle that courtroom. At last I could say, "Members of the jury, you have heard the reading of the verdicts. Are these your verdicts?"

They all nodded.

Miss Rheinlander had collapsed. Her head was on the table, and her wrenching sobs overcame the mutter of the crowd in the court-room. Kimball put his arm around her and spoke to her. Megan O'Reilly clasped her hands.

I turned to the jury to thank them for their service.

16

I fear I have mentioned the Alexandria House, its bar and dining room, so many times it suggests we have no other good bar or restaurant in the county. That is not true. I have mentioned that our Rotary Club meets in the Bon Ton Restaurant. Many people enjoy the dining rooms at the Marriott Inn and the Holiday Inn. If you like to listen to a band and dance, you can have dinner at the Castle Club, only three miles out of town. You can also eat nicely in the dining room at the country club. I could mention other places. It is true, though, that the lawyers and doctors, the insurance and real estate agents, and so on, all like to go to the hotel dining room for dinner. As I've said, we usually sit down in the bar for a drink or two, then go to our tables for dinner.

What else would we do on the evening after the jury returned with its verdicts in the Marietta Rheinlander trial? Our moment of fame was apparently over. We supposed we were about to slip back into the obscurity to which we were happily accustomed—in the self-congratulatory mood of people who think they've faced a hard challenge and coped with it well. I mean myself, of course. The national news media said I was a good judge. They would not say otherwise in the accounts of the trial that would still fill pages and pages in news magazines. They spoke well of Ken Simpson. They even spoke well of our town.

No wonder that we assembled in a warm, satisfied mood in the Alexandria House bar that evening: Linda and I, Stephanie and Ken Simpson, Glen Myers, and Dick Winter, in our little group that would share a table. Margaret Vogt and her husband came in with Bob Johnson and his wife. They were not regulars in the Alexandria House and did not enter the bar but took a table and ordered beer.

News people—a great many of them were still in town—sat in the bar and at tables.

One of the tables set for six was a magnet for attention. A rumor had it that Lloyd George Kimball had reserved that table—which was true; the hotel told *me* if it wouldn't tell anyone else—and that Miss Marietta Rheinlander would probably appear for dinner.

I've described the hotel dining room. It would not appeal to city people maybe, but its warmth and homey style appeals to me. The maple tables are covered with red and white checkered tablecloths, and a candle burns in a hurricane lamp on every table. The only electric lights burning at dinner time are the lamps that illuminate the oil paintings of scenes from early Ohio history. Above the table where the Vogts and Johnsons sat hung a big painting of Indian chiefs signing some treaty or other. Their loincloths were modest enough for those who faced out of the picture, but the bare buns of the two with their backs to the room had caused a few people to suggest that someone ought to paint over them a little. I wondered what Miss Rheinlander would think of that idea.

We could have asked her if we'd been enough interested, for she soon entered the hotel and led her party along the hallway between the lobby and the dining room. The bar is to the right. She looked in, spotted our group, and walked into the bar. She said something to the others—her parents and her lawyers—apparently telling them to go on and take their table; and she came into the bar alone.

She wore a form-fitting black knit dress with a gold necklace set with emeralds, a gold bracelet, and the ring the congressman had given her.

"I want to thank you," she said to me. "You promised me a fair trial, and you saw to it that I had one. Is this Mrs. McIntyre?"

I introduced her to Linda.

"You are married to a wonderful man, Mrs. McIntyre," she said.

"Mr. Simpson," she said, nodding at Ken. "And is this Mrs. Simpson? You did your damndest. But you didn't do anything more than your duty required." She reached for Ken's hand and shook it.

She bent forward and kissed Glen Myers on the cheek. She said something in his ear. None of the rest of us heard it.

She glittered, I thought. I don't know exactly how to define that. Maybe it was something in her eyes, which seemed to reflect a little too much light, as though something had dilated them; and I wondered if she'd used something. She was patently savoring a moment of triumph. I didn't see her moment as a triumph for her, but that was how *she* saw it, and that was how she was enjoying it.

As she walked into the dining room, a few people applauded. It was inappropriate, but that was how *they* saw it.

Before she sat down at her table, she stepped past it and shook hands with Margaret Vogt and Bob Johnson. I couldn't help but think she was being patronizing, but I guess the Vogts and Johnsons didn't see it that way, for they smiled and exchanged pleasantries.

Her party consisted of her parents and her defense team: Lloyd George Kimball, Megan O'Reilly, and Bob Mitchell. Mr. and Mrs. Rheinlander were somber. The three lawyers were, as I saw them, brittle: alert to something. News people began to approach their table, and Kimball rose and gestured them away. "Tomorrow . . ." I heard him say. "Tomorrow morning."

We finished our drinks and moved from the bar to the dining room at about the same time that a round of drinks was brought to the Rheinlander table.

We were six, so we too had one of the big round tables. We were near the door. The round table with the Rheinlander party was in the center of the room. The Vogts and Johnsons were at a table beyond them, nearer to the wall, just under the big painting. Miss Rheinlander sat facing us. Kimball's back was to us.

Glen was fonder of martinis than Linda and I were, and two before dinner was not enough for him. He had ordered a third, and he turned toward the door to the bar to look for our waitress, hoping he would see her coming out with his drink.

"Jesus *Christ!*" he yelled.

Everyone turned to see what had made him yell and why he was scrambling up from his chair. We saw—

David Ogle. He came lurching down the hall, past the door of the bar. He held a pistol thrust forward in his right hand. His face was distorted with fury. In the door into the dining room he grabbed his right wrist with his left hand and took aim on Marietta Rheinlander.

"*Now, you bitch!*" he screamed.

Glen Myers threw himself at Ogle, like a football blocker. He hit him low, at the knees, and Ogle went down. Ogle snarled and shot Glen. He drew himself up on his knees and aimed again at Marietta Rheinlander. He fired just as Lloyd George Kimball threw himself against her and knocked her to the floor.

We saw blood and fabric fly from Kimball's shoulder. To our horror we also saw the bullet that had torn through Kimball's shoulder now strike Margaret Vogt square in the chest, knocking her back against her table, from which she crumpled to the floor. She had stood and drawn a pistol from her handbag, so putting herself directly in Ogle's line of fire. It was obvious that she was gravely wounded.

Ogle scrambled to his feet. Pistol thrust forward, he rushed toward Miss Rheinlander, who lay on the floor half under the table, half covered by the bleeding Lloyd George Kimball. Once again Ogle locked his left hand around his right wrist, to steady his aim.

Bob Johnson had drawn a snub-nosed revolver from a holster strapped to his ankle. (Like big-city policemen, our deputies are armed, on or off duty.) He took aim on Ogle and fired once. Ogle howled, clutched his belly, dropped his pistol, and fell facedown.

I've said nothing so far about how I reacted, or about how other people in the dining room reacted. I was too stunned to move—too stunned even to throw myself to the floor as Linda did, as Ken and Stephanie and Dick did. I was not the "calm judge, fully in command of himself as he had been throughout the trial, calmly watching the drama," who was described by one of the wire services. The truth is, I was scared out of my wits.

The comfy dining room in our small-town hotel was a scene of sheer pandemonium. The shrieking crowd had fallen to the floor and began to rise only after the last shot was fired and a full half minute of silence had passed. When people were on their feet—the news people in particular—they began to press forward to try to see and hear.

Bob Johnson knelt over Margaret Vogt. He looked up and shook his head. His judgment was right. She was dead, shot through the heart.

Lloyd George Kimball rose painfully, and Megan O'Neill helped him out of his jacket and began to press napkins to his bleeding wound.

I pushed my way over to Glen, who sat with both hands clutching his upper leg, blood oozing between his fingers. He was surrounded by solicitous people who had helped him sit up. "Where's my fuckin' martini?" he asked weakly.

Ogle rolled around on the floor, moaning. His shirt was blood-stained to the area of two spread hands. "Somebody . . . help . . . me," he muttered.

No one was in any hurry to help him. "He was the murderer all along!" somebody cried. "He killed all those people, and now—"

"No . . ." Ogle muttered.

What happened next was one of the strangest sights I have ever seen in my experience as a judge and lawyer.

Bob Johnson rose. He glanced down once at Margaret, then walked over to Ogle. He squatted beside him—squatted beside a man writhing in agony, with a spreading bloodstain on his shirt and now on his jacket—and arrested him for murder! He arrested him and read him his rights!

"I don't know who else you killed," the big deputy sobbed, "but you sure as hell killed Margaret. I arrest you for the murder of Margaret Vogt. You have a right to remain silent—" He went through all of it. He read Ogle his rights. And when he was finished, he said, "And I sure as hell hope you live to get what you got comin' to you."

Stranger still, Ogle wanted to talk. He shook his head. "I didn't kill Charles. Or Don. Or Liz. *She* did it." Lying flat on his back, he pointed in the direction of the defense table.

Marietta Rheinlander had been helped to her feet by now—and she had needed help; she had gone down hard and cut her head on the table or chair. She stood a little dazed, dabbing with someone's handkerchief at the blood running down her face from the ugly cut at the edge of her hair. She managed just the same to glare at Ogle with an expression of malice and hatred. I'm not absolutely sure she knew Margaret Vogt lay dead on the floor behind her. I am sure her entire attention was focused on David Ogle.

He pointed at her. "*You* did it," he said.

She said nothing. She turned to Kimball and said something I could not hear.

Ogle looked around. When he saw me, he spoke directly to me. "The only difference from what I swore to is that . . . the gun was mine. *I* brought the gun to the lodge."

Getting a little ahead of things, I will give you a fact. The list of members of the Carter Gun Club, which had already arrived in the sheriff's office by fax, included the name David Ogle.

"I'd brought it to Huntington months ago," Ogle said. "Then I brought it to the lodge. I was looking for a chance to kill *her*. Charles was mine . . . he loved *me*. Had for years. She was the problem. She wanted him. She tried to turn him against me. That night . . . she wasn't supposed to be at the lodge that weekend. It was supposed to be my weekend. But there she was, and she did the worst thing in the world. She went to his bedroom. I had to go to mine alone."

At least three and maybe more reporters had muscled their way close to Ogle and held little tape recorders out toward him, to record what he said.

"God, it hurts," Ogle said, and winced. "I want to tell what really happened. What . . . really happened."

"Go on," Ken Simpson said abruptly to David Ogle. He had moved from behind his table and was standing beside me, directly over Ogle.

"I wasn't asleep like I said. I was awake, hating that woman for what she was doing with Charles. I heard voices in the living room, voices that were low and . . . sort of intimate. I couldn't imagine what was going on. I got up, pulled on my pants, and went out there. Charles was there, on the couch. Don was with him. They were . . .

they were making love. Charles . . . and Don! I ran back into my room. I pulled on my gloves, rubber surgical gloves, and took the pistol from under my shirts in a drawer. I went back out. They hadn't even seen me. But they saw me now. I yelled at them. I told them I was going to kill them both."

He kept both hands clutched to his stomach, but it seemed to me the blood was only seeping out then, not gushing as it had done at first. He was weak, obviously, but he didn't seem to be growing weaker. I suppose he thought he was dying, which was why he was so anxious to make his statement.

"I pointed the pistol at them. Don jumped up, pulled his robe around him, and backed away, just shaking his head, not speaking. But Charles stood up and faced me. He smiled . . . he actually smiled. And he said, 'Could you really do it, Davey?' He was right. I really couldn't. I tossed the pistol on the couch, leaned back against the wall, and began to cry.

"Then *she* came out. She only took a second to guess what was going on. She was drunk. She was livid. She strode across the room and grabbed up the pistol. By then Liz had come in through the sliding glass doors. She'd heard me yelling, I suppose."

Ogle began to sob. The trembling corners of his mouth turned down. He pointed at Marietta Rheinlander. "She shot Charles. Then she shot Don. Liz didn't try to run. That wasn't the way it happened. She had her back to that woman because she was looking down at Charles. And *she* shot her in the back.

"I knew who was next. I ran through the sliding glass doors, that Liz had left open. I ran for the pool and then along the side of the pool, as fast as I could. She shot at me, but she missed me. Three shots.

"I ran around the house and back to my room. I got in through the door on the south side. I knew she'd fired all six shots and the pistol was empty. So I went back into the living room. She was standing there, with the pistol still in her hand.

"I was crying. I couldn't say anything. But she said something. She said, 'The only thing I'm sorry about is that I missed you.'"

All eyes turned to Marietta Rheinlander. She stared at David Ogle with unalloyed hatred. She nodded, and with a grotesque sneer she said, "Well, the deputy didn't."

David Ogle survived, much, I think, to his surprise. He spent two months in the hospital, then was transferred to the jail.

In the months before he came to trial a love affair lived and died between Marietta Rheinlander and Glen Myers. He was her hero. He had saved her life. He traveled back and forth to New York half a dozen times. He spent the week of Christmas and New Year's with her. He decided after a while that to her circle of friends he was a curiosity: a small-town lawyer who walked with a limp, spoke with what was to them an accent, and was intriguingly shrewd but insufficiently conversant with things they thought important. One Friday afternoon in February he got drunk and missed a flight to LaGuardia Airport. Actually, he didn't miss the flight; he didn't even go to the airport. She didn't invite him to come again. When she came here to be a witness in Ogle's trial, she didn't see Glen.

Ogle's case came to trial on April 12, 1993. Since I had witnessed the killing, I recused myself—that is, offered to step aside as the trial judge, in favor of a judge who had no personal knowledge of the case. Dick Winter, who defended Ogle, waived all objection to my trying the case. Since of course Ken Simpson did not object, I found myself in the news again.

The indictment charged Ogle with aggravated murder—that is murder by prior calculation and design.

The evidence was so complete that acquittal was hardly possible. The trial lasted a day and a half, and the jury deliberated less than an hour before returning a verdict of guilty.

Now the jury had to hear evidence and argument on the question of whether or not the death penalty should be imposed. That was not so simple. To make a murderer susceptible to the death penalty, one of several so-called aggravating circumstances must be proved.

One of those is that the victim was a peace officer engaged in the duties of a police officer.

Dick Winter argued that Margaret Vogt had been in the dining room for dinner and was not engaged in the duties of a peace officer. I ruled that when she rose and drew her gun in the hope of preventing Ogle from shooting Marietta Rheinlander, she was acting as a peace officer.

The jury recommended that David Ogle be put to death.

But there were mitigating factors. He had no prior criminal record. Also, the fact that he had not intended to kill a peace officer, while not a fact that could acquit him of the charge that he *had* killed a peace officer, was a mitigating factor as related to the question of whether or not he should die for his crime.

I pondered long and hard and sentenced David Ogle to life in prison with eligibility for parole only after thirty years. That he had murdered a deputy sheriff, and a woman at that, would not make prison life any easier for him. He shuffled out of our jail in chains and was taken to Ohio's prison reception center, from where a month later he was transferred to our maximum-security institution at Lucasville. It might have been merciful to electrocute him.

So far as I was concerned he was dead already, in a very real sense. So much of his intestines had been destroyed by Bob Johnson's bullet that he could not have a bowel movement but seeped all day into a plastic bag hung on a belt under his pants. He needed constant sedation to keep the pain within a bearable limit. He had lost forty pounds and was haggard, stooped, and beginning to turn gray.

My second episode of notoriety faded, thank God. Now I am besieged by would-be authors who want to write books about the Marietta Rheinlander case. I wrote my own as a defense.

The question they all want to address is this: Did Marietta Rheinlander kill Congressman Charles Bailey, Donald Finch, and Elizabeth Erb?

No, she didn't. By definition she didn't, because her jury, which had heard all the evidence, decided she didn't.

Or did it?

No. Let's be clear about that. The Rheinlander jury did not decide that Marietta Rheinlander did not murder three people. What it decided was that the prosecution had failed to prove she did—beyond a reasonable doubt.

The William Kennedy Smith jury did not decide he had not raped the woman he was accused of raping. It decided the State of Florida had not proved he did.

That's the way our system of criminal justice works. In no sense at all do I disagree with the verdicts in the cases I have just mentioned. But let's not misunderstand what those verdicts mean.

David Ogle lay on his back on the dining room floor, bleeding and giving what he may well have thought was a dying declaration. That he didn't die makes it no less a dying declaration if he *thought* he was dying. Many commentators and editorialists have chosen to believe him. Many believe his statement was the final, definitive, and true story of what happened on the night of May 5, 1992.

Other authors mean to write books about Marietta Rheinlander and David Ogle. They will know with some degree of certainty who really killed Congressman Bailey and his two staffers. I envy them their certainty. I have not been able to achieve it.